ROADS OF DOUBT

Center Point
Large Print

Also by William MacLeod Raine
and available from Center Point Large Print:

Clattering Hoofs
The Black Tolts
Long Texan
The Trail of Danger
Square-Shooter
This Nettle Danger
Saddlebum
Robber's Roost

**This Large Print Book carries the
Seal of Approval of N.A.V.H.**

ROADS OF DOUBT

William MacLeod Raine

CENTER POINT LARGE PRINT
THORNDIKE, MAINE

This Center Point Large Print edition
is published in the year 2019 by arrangement with
Golden West Literary Agency.

Originally published in the US by Doubleday
Originally published in the UK by Hodder & Stoughton

The text of this Large Print edition is unabridged.
In other aspects, this book may vary
from the original edition.
Printed in the United States of America
on permanent paper.
Set in 16-point Times New Roman type.

ISBN: 978-1-64358-237-5 (hardcover)
ISBN: 978-1-64358-241-2 (paperback)

Library of Congress Cataloging-in-Publication Data

Names: Raine, William MacLeod, 1871-1954, author.
Title: Roads of doubt / William MacLeod Raine.
Description: Large Print edition. | Thorndike, Maine :
    Center Point Large Print, 2019.
Identifiers: LCCN 2019013350| ISBN 9781643582375 (hardcover :
    alk. paper) | ISBN 9781643582412 (pbk. : alk. paper)
Subjects: LCSH: Large type books. | GSAFD: Western stories.
Classification: LCC PS3535.A385 R6 2019 | DDC 813/.54—dc23
LC record available at https://lccn.loc.gov/2019013350

TO BOB

CONTENTS

CHAPTER I

THIN ICE

BENEATH a starlit sky the car followed a winding road among the hilltops. The night was chill, as May nights are likely to be in the front range of the Rockies. Snow crunched under the wheels, and the crisp of frost was in the air. It stung the face of the girl snuggled down beside the driver in spite of the protection of the wind shield and of the upturned fur collar which wrapped her to the gleaming eyes.

By Joy's wrist watch it was two-thirty when the mountain cliffs drew near and the brown ribbon along which they were speeding plunged into Box Elder Cañon. Almost instantly the darkness pressed in on them. Except for a narrow strip of the milky heavens that canopied the gorge it seemed to fill the world with a tangible presence that was almost a threat.

The road wound tortuously along the face of the cliff. It was filled with unexpected turns. The headlights flung, nearly every minute, fan-shaped shafts of light into gulfs of space over the edge of which they seemed about to dive.

The driver handled the wheel expertly and surely. The least deviation to the right, and they would go crashing hundreds of feet to the creek below. Too narrow a swing at the sharp curves would send the machine into the rock wall; too wide a one would throw it headlong at the abyss.

Winthrop Ordway knew the road and his car. He had throttled down a little, but one unused to mountain travel would have thought the pace dangerously fast. For every inch of the way that black obscure chasm hugged the road like some monster of diablerie. In the darkness it had become a titanic living demon, and the murmur of the creek far below a voice out of the pit whispering a mesmeric invitation to leap into its depths.

But for an occasional word neither of them spoke. The girl was thrilling to the excitement of this wild night ride. She had no right here. The place was for her at this hour inhibited. The man was taboo. In accepting his invitation she had flung away the reins of discretion, had yielded to the spirit of adventure that sometimes set her reckless little feet on forbidden paths. Joyce Elliott was under the spell of the swift rush through perilous blackness, of her companion's dominant personality, of her own eager instinct for life abundant.

Ordway did not sound the horn as he swept around curves. Travel was light over the pass, and it was not likely any car would be coming up at this hour.

Again, as for the twentieth time they circled a high promontory, the headlights illumined the cañon enough to show green pine tips lifted out of blackness. The swinging car flung their flare on something else—a great boulder that had crashed down on the road.

The mental and physical reaction of the driver was instantaneous. Ordway cut off the power, jammed home brakes, and steered into the rock wall.

The car smashed to a halt and lurched sideways. Joyce was flung from the seat and momentarily stunned.

From a long distance Ordway's voice came to her faintly. "You hurt, Joy?"

A strong arm slid under her waist. She was lifted out of a litter of broken glass from the floor of a lopsided car. The girl was still a bit dazed, but she felt no pain. The heavy furs had protected her from the full shock of the impact.

"Don't think so, Win. How about you?"

"Right enough."

Set on her feet, Joyce found the ground still weaving dizzily. She caught at the astrakhan facing of Ordway's coat.

"Li'l' old world jazzing," she explained.

Again his arm slipped around her shoulders. Behind the firs across the abyss a full moon had come up. By its light she saw blood trickling down his cheek from a cut.

11

"You're hurt," she cried.

"It's nothing. I went through the wind shield. Sure *you're* all right?"

"Umpha!" She released herself with a short nervous laugh. Her glance took in the car. "Some smash. How bad is it?"

Ordway made an examination. "Wheel in splinters. Front axle badly twisted. Hood and fender junked. Fine business."

"Damn," she said tersely.

"Rotten luck," he agreed.

"I'll say so. What'll we do?"

"Have to wait here till someone picks us up."

"We can't do that. Maybe a car won't be along till morning. I've got to get to town." There was a note of excited protest in the girl's voice. "We'll have to do something."

He was a man of resource, but one cannot make adobe bricks without straw. They were fifty miles from the city, in a desolate gulch, no outside help within reach. The roadster was due for a week in a repair shop before it could travel.

Ordway shook his head. "No use starting to walk. It's ten or twelve miles to the mouth of the cañon. We'll have to stick it here."

Joyce Elliott was not of the panicky sort. All her life she had done as she pleased. Heiress of the ages, she had gone her gay and arrogant way as only an American girl of the Twentieth Century can. Conventions were made for others,

12

not for her, she held confidently. Therefore she had ignored them, trampled them down, laughed scornfully at them when they got in her road. Always she had despised the whispering tongues that found evil in high spirits and disregard of rules.

But there was a limit, and in this foolish escapade she had overstepped it. Even she, with all the prestige of her father's influence and standing, dared not come to town with the story of a broken car that had held her in the hills alone with Winthrop Ordway all night. If he had been another kind of man—one less notoriously ready to take all a woman would give—such a tale might pass muster. But it would not go in his case. He was too possessive. Why, it had been less than three months since rumours of a night ride of his with another woman had reached her.

She realized too that she had put herself out of court by her own lack of wisdom. The words with which she had scoffed at conventions, the freedom with which she had trod her careless path, would earn her a verdict of thumbs down now. If she was alone with Ordway till morning, no matter how high she held her head afterwards, it would be at best a scotched scandal. With pellucid clearness she saw this.

"I've *got* to get away, Win," she urged. "If I don't, there will be a lot of talk. You know that. They'll say all sorts of horrid things."

"Yes, they'll talk some," he admitted. "But it'll die down. Anybody's car is likely to get smashed."

With the astonishing candour of the modern *jeune fille*, eyes unembarrassed lifted to his frankly as those of a boy. "I happen to be just the one girl a scandal of this kind will hurt awf'ly. It doesn't have to be true—what they'll say about me. Some of the women that count most have rather got it in for me. I've never kow-towed to them—and I *have* hit the high spots, you know. If I'm trapped like this—with you of all men—they'll take it out of me."

"Why with me of all men?"

His question needed no answer. At any rate, she gave it none. Her mind was travelling to another phase of the situation. "And there's Dad. What am I going to tell him? How am I going to explain it?"

"Tell him the truth. He'll believe you."

She felt a flare of irritation at his failure to understand. Of course she would tell the truth to her father if it became necessary to tell him anything, and equally of course he would believe her. That was not the point she had in mind.

"You're wrong about this hurting you much, Bubbles," he went on to argue. "If you were another kind of girl, less frank and open in all you say and do—but people know you and won't believe harm of you. There'll be some joking, if

14

it happens to get out we had a smash—a little fun about joy riders and torch bearers. That's about all."

"You're 'way off," she snapped. Her nerves were a bit overwrought, but she was essentially fair-minded. After all, she was the victim of her own folly rather than his. The blame lay at home. "You'd better do something to that cut in your cheek, Win. It's still bleeding. I'll get the thermos bottle."

She stepped lightly toward the car, a slender exquisite creature with the lilt of youth in her tread.

On the light breezes of the night a sound was carried to them. They listened. It was the blare of a horn.

"A car coming," Joyce cried eagerly.

CHAPTER II

"NO GENTLEMAN"

ORDWAY ran to the horn of his car and began sounding it.

A shaft of light leaped across the gulf of evergreen foliage. There was a slither of locked wheels. An automobile came round the bend and slid to a halt.

It was a cheap touring car. On the front seat sat two men.

Into the rays of the spotlight Ordway stepped, a clean-cut well-groomed figure in the middle thirties. The close-shut mouth, hard resolute eyes, and salient cleft chin were hall marks of character. They announced him what he was—forceful, successful, and probably ruthless.

"I've had a smash. How about a lift to town?" he asked.

Arrow-swift came the answer from the driver. "No!"

"Down to the plains, then, if you're not going to the city. I can pick up a car at a ranch."

Again that explosive "No."

"What?" demanded the belated traveller sharply.

He was not easily disconcerted, but the rough-

16

ness of the refusal took him by surprise. There was a challenge in the voice, hostile, acrimonious.

"I'm not taking passengers to-night," the man behind the wheel said curtly.

"It's Mr. Ordway, Hallack," the man beside the driver murmured. The words were an explanation and a protest. They had back of them annoyance and bewilderment. Why should Bob talk like this to one who sat in the seats of the mighty and might some day be very useful to him?

"I see who it is," the driver answered brusquely.

The value of Winthrop Ordway to the interests with which he was affiliated lay largely in his versatility. He was a master of finesse, but he could use the direct attack with brutal efficiency. Not the least of the qualities which had carried him from the insecure position of a financial freebooter to a place in the inner councils of the leaders of Wall Street had been his audacity.

He walked quickly to the side of the car and looked up at the driver. "Oh, it's you!" There was something akin to contempt in the great man's voice.

The one to whom he spoke said nothing. He swung the spotlight round so that it fell full on the handsome florid face, so strong, so arrogant, and so complacent. What he found in it was a stark and pitiless selfishness, a sinister force that expressed itself insolently in success. He had battled with its potency and been beaten by it.

"I need your car. What are your terms?" Ordway asked crisply.

"I won't do business with you."

"I'll buy it. What's your price?"

"Not for sale."

That the human eye is a prince of deadly weapons is a true word. The steady regard with which each looked at the other was like the grinding of rapiers, harsh and steely.

Nervously the third man broke in. He was small, with a mind cut on the same pattern. If he had been a piece of merchandise the manufacturer would have labelled him a second. It was a deep-rooted instinct of his soul to bow down to wealth and power.

"There's room enough for them behind, Bob," he suggested, mentioning the obvious.

The eyes of Ordway pivoted to him instantly. "Do you own the car?"

"No, Mr. Ordway. It's Hallack's car, but of course—" The sentence died indefinitely. The thought behind it remained suspended in air, amounted in fact to no more than vague apology and exasperation.

At a glance Ordway sized up his value as a factor in the situation. He wiped him from the map and gave his attention wholly to the other.

When he spoke it was clear that his will was restraining an imperious temper. "I have a lady with me," he said in a low voice. "It is necessary that she get back to town. She's been out in the cold for hours."

In the darkness none could see the change that passed over Hallack's face at mention of the woman, the tightening behind closed teeth of ropelike muscles in the lean cheeks.

"You can't refuse to take her. You can't leave her here to suffer," Ordway continued. "Whether you want to take her or not you'll have to do it."

After a moment, Hallack: "Have I said I wouldn't take her?"

"You said you wouldn't carry passengers—"

"But nothing about a passenger."

"I'm not splitting words. What are you driving at? Will you take us?"

"No."

"What then?"

"I'll take her, not you."

A spark of anger flashed into the cold eyes of the financier. "You'll take her and leave her at the address I give?"

"When she's my guest I'll arrange details with her, Mr. Ordway," the younger man answered frigidly.

Ordway ripped out, his temper lost. "You're a damned uncivil brute, Hallack. I'd like to drag you down and thrash you till you can't stand."

The words had not died out of his mouth before the driver was beside him.

"Soon as you like," Hallack said with quiet

ferocity, a dangerous light blazing in the dark eyes.

The big man glared at him, battling back the lust of combat. He did not accept the invitation. An impasse blocked the desire that surged up in him. He owed something to the girl whom he had led into a compromising situation. Her reputation must be protected. That was the first obligation on him. It would be an idiotic thing to fight the man who had it in his power either to help clear or tarnish this. Hallack was trading on his necessities, but just now he had to put up with the affront.

"I've got to stand your insolence," he said in a low, thick voice. "You'll never know how much I'd give to lay hands on you, young fellow. But it's a luxury I can't afford. I accept your offer. Take the lady home and I'll stay here with the car."

Hands clenched in coat pockets drawn tightly forward over the hips, Hallack laughed with bitter irony. "It's *lèse-majesté* to oppose when your royal highness gives orders. I ought to jump at the crack of the whip as your slaves do. Too bad you can't have me strung up by the thumbs."

"Maybe I can some day. I'll live in hope," Ordway flung back angrily.

Taken with a proper allowance of salt, the indictment thrown out by Hallack was a true enough one. Ordway was in the habit of riding roughshod over opponents and of driving subordinates to the limit. Back of his restless energy was a flinty quality of moral fibre that expressed itself callously. Enemies said that he was colour-blind in points of rectitude, wholly unscrupulous in the weapons with which he fought. It was not necessary to show that he was masterful. The evidence of it rode in every word and gesture.

From the darkness of the wrecked car the young woman came into the light. If anybody had been watching him closely Hallack might have been seen to register surprise, as directors of the silent drama put it. This was not the person he had expected to discover with Ordway.

She went straight to her friend. "What is it, Win? Doesn't he want to take us?"

"He's a sulky devil and he's got a grudge at me," her companion answered, not troubling to lower his voice. "You'll have to go alone with them."

"And leave you here?"

"Yes. I'll get in somehow before morning."

A child of impulse, she spoke quickly now. "I'll not go."

Ordway drew her back toward his car to gain more privacy of speech. " 'Fraid you'll have to, Joy," he said. "You can't stay here. It won't do."

She knew it would not do, as well at least as he did. Facts and probabilities marshalled themselves as arguments. But there was in her a loyalty that rebelled against leaving in trouble the partner of her escapade.

"Make him take you too. What's the matter with him? It's all nonsense you staying here. I wouldn't do it."

The voice of Ordway fell to a murmur. He explained, without going into detail, that it was wiser not to anger the fellow. She contended with spirit. Stressed words flashed out of her sentences. It was easy to see that her slim body was a dynamo of energy and will.

The other two were at work rolling the boulder from the road. Hallack resented savagely the situation, its implications and obligations. He did not want to help Ordway or any of his friends out of trouble. He did not want to have anything to do with them. In his soul he carried scars burned deep into his life from contact with him and his kind.

As to the girl, he was moved to no reaction of chivalrous feeling at her plight any more than he was to gentleness at her young willful beauty. Clearly she was used to having her own way. Once she stamped her foot with a flapper's gusty temper. Yet, he judged, she was less crude than the average of her years and sex. The flowerlike head was gracefully poised. From the turban-bound coils of golden hair through which an amethyst-headed pin was stabbed, to the firm but finely modelled ankles she was wholly patrician, a product of a background of wealth and leisure where she had been carefully and carelessly nourished.

The boulder hung on the edge of the embankment a moment before it crashed down through the firs into the bed of the creek below. The echoes of its descent reverberated from cliff to cliff.

As Hallack returned to the machine the girl moved quickly to meet him.

"Why won't you take Mr. Ordway? You've got to let him go. He's been hurt. You can't leave him here." The words rang out, urgent and imperious.

He smiled, cynically, with no warmth. "If Mr. Ordway will put it that way—ask me to take him in because he's hurt and afraid to be left alone—I'll rush him to a hospital. I wouldn't leave a yellow dog if it needed help."

Ordway, coming forward into the light, told him bluntly where he might go. He did not want any favours for himself. In the back of his mind was another thought. It had occurred to him that perhaps it would be better for the sake of appearances to send Joyce in and stay with the damaged automobile.

"No—no!" she insisted. "I'll not go without you."

Ordway's gloved hand caressed lightly her fur-clad shoulder. "Oh, yes, Joy. It'll be all right. I'd as soon stay as not."

"I'm not going." She flung her decision like a challenge at Hallack.

"Please yourself about that," was his instant cold retort.

The man travelling with him spoke up, peevishly. "That's foolish."

"But it goes, Randall," the younger man snapped.

"But why—why?" she demanded. "It's outrageous. It's hateful."

"Yes?" he mocked.

"Nobody with any right feeling would do it. And Mr. Ordway hurt, too."

"So dangerously wounded," he jeered.

"Come, Joyce. Forget that part. I'm not hurt. It's a scratch," her friend assured.

The girl's attention was wholly concentrated on this stranger who stood like a rock in the way of what she wished. She had not gone very far in life yet. The inexorable force of it had been warded from her by wealth and love. Always she had been able to get what she wanted when she set her strong will to it. An opposition so senseless and so obdurate irritated her.

Beside Ordway's well-packed bulk the man looked slender. But with the quick sure judgment of the outdoor girl she guessed him a trained athlete. He had flung off his coat to work at the boulder, and as he stood under the spotlight he showed brown and tough. There was in his leanness no looseness of frame, no stringiness, no ill-nourished muscles. Probably supple cords of steel moved lightly at command beneath the firm flesh.

Her sense of baffled annoyance flashed into hot words. "If you claim to be a gentleman—and I suppose you do—"

"I'm making no claims whatever, except that I own this car and mean to decide who rides in it."

"Well, will you let Mr. Ordway go with me?"

"I will not," he answered stonily.

Her eyes were wells of glowing anger. "I never was treated so in my life—never. Even though you're not on good terms with Mr. Ordway— since that's what's the matter with you, I suppose—if you have any generosity, any—"

"I haven't," Hallack cut in with sardonic bitterness. "You'll get along faster if you just assume I'm no gentleman and let it go at that. Are you going down with me or not?"

"No," she flamed.

"Yes," said Ordway.

She turned on her friend with the little touch of feminine petulance not unbecoming in one of her age. "What do you think I am, Win? I'll not go and leave you here. I'll not do it."

"We've been all over that," Ordway reminded her patiently, a friendly smile on his bloodstained

25

face. "I'm not hurt, I keep telling you. And you've got to go. It's best all round."

He did not rehearse again the arguments to support his case. They raced through her mind as she stood torn by doubt. He was right. She had to go. For her father's sake she must go, even if she herself had been willing to face a scandal. And she was not. It was all very well to laugh at the clacking tongues of the jealous when one had the upper hand and was riding the top wave. But these tongues were whips of scorn to the defenceless. She had once seen a woman at the Rocky Mountain Club under the lash of a social condemnation that ignored her. She could see her now, smiling resolutely to hide an aching heart, while former acquaintances contrived to miss meeting her pathetically wistful glances. Even a tenth part of such humiliation Joyce had no mind to endure.

"I'll go," she said sulkily.

CHAPTER III

SWEET NINETEEN
WRINKLES A FOREHEAD

HALLACK stood back while Ordway brought a wrap from his own car. About to take the seat beside that of the driver, Joyce hesitated an instant. It was in her mind to reject the place and join Randall in the tonneau. But her training had given her a touch of the hard worldly finish of the modern debutante. She was not going to let this detestable man who had declared himself no gentleman think that she was daunted by his rudeness. Moreover, she was cold and it would be warmer in front.

"Call me up in the afternoon, Win. Auction at the Stantons, you know." Ordway had finished tucking the rug about her. Their eyes were locked together and sending wordless messages.

"Yes," he said significantly. "Don't worry. Get your sleep out, Joy. You need rest."

Under the hood the starter was giving forth jerky protests. The driver had taken his seat and was plainly anxious to be off.

"I won't," she promised. "Good luck. And tie up your cheek."

The engine purred. The wheels turned. Joyce

looked back and saw Ordway swallowed in the black void they left in their rear.

The car flew down the mountain road, its driver intent on the immediate business before him. The automobile was light, inclined to skid and jump the track. There were places where the road had been blasted into the quartz. This was ice-coated and very slippery. If Hallack carried chains he did not stop to adjust them.

Always close beside them ran the gorge, a misty pit of bottomless depth throwing out a sinister threat of disaster. Joyce sat on the side next the chasm. When they swept around curves and the lights flung a glare of white brightness into the upper voids of the cañon a tingle of excitement ran through her. A driver herself, she knew the peril of mountain travel with reckless hands at the wheel. This man was an expert. She could feel it in his touch, in the certainty with which he took the dangerous spots. But he drove fast, and as the car lunged into the black emptiness ahead she had the feeling that each instant they were coming to the edge of the world and were about to leap off.

She sat tight, offered no protest, let no small cry of alarm escape her during the ten-mile plunge down to the plains. Indeed she responded to its thrills, nerves stimulated to high tension. There were moments when the excitation of the senses keyed her to a psychosis bordering on apprehension. The rush of the night air, the darkness ahead, the close risk, all contributed to give zest to the ride.

For a mountain road the Box Elder one was good. It had been surfaced with disintegrated sandstone taken from the immediate vicinity. But even while Joyce was congratulating herself on this they struck an ice glaze and the back wheels skidded out.

It was touch and go, but Hallack apparently never had an instant of doubt. He knew exactly what his car could be depended on to do, and with sure skill he swung it time and again back to the road.

The passenger counted herself a good sport. It was her pride that she played the game. She rode and swam well, turned in a rather low golf score, and was the best tennis player among the women of her set at the Country Club. From these athletic pursuits she had taken on an outdoor point of view on the surface at least essentially masculine. Native courage and a certain downright candour contributed to make her what she was, one of more independent cast of mind than most of those with whom she associated.

All night she had felt herself lifted on the wave of an adventure. It had been with her through the dinner and dance at Mountain Crest, and it had swept her into the mad prank of a joy ride with Winthrop Ordway. The smash had brought her back to earth, but she found herself rising to the swell of it again.

It was this quality of effervescence in her spirits that made the name Joy so appropriate, though with their accustomed perversity her flapper friends preferred to call her Bubbles. It expressed for them that state of mind which set her skipping sometimes on the mountain-tops of delight. At such hours emotions rode her, swept her into unwise decisions. She was now the victim of one of these impulses.

After Hallack guided the car through the gateway of the cañon to the plains her elation died and gave place to the inevitable reaction. She was in a pickle, or she would be if the story got out. What had possessed her, after leaving the lodge at Mountain Crest, to let Winthrop Ordway swing into the hills to cross Ramshorn Pass instead of making him take her home with the others through Red Cañon? The sensible thing would have been to run straight back to town.

Second thoughts were often wiser ones with her, but the trouble was that she seldom waited to take them. Before they had gone a hundred yards she felt she had made a mistake, but her pride made her reluctant to acknowledge it. She was afraid Winthrop and the people in the other cars might laugh at her for a quitter.

He had promised to get her home soon after the others. None the less it had been an error to go racing over the moonlit hills with him long after midnight for a fifty-mile detour. She had done it, she supposed, because the exhilaration of her spirits craved expression in the freedom of that rush through a world of dim and sleeping mountains. It did not occur to her that the primary motive might have been the fascination exerted over her by Ordway's splendid vitality.

Of course, some version of the story would get out. She was too conspicuous in her small world to escape. It would be discovered that she had not got home till morning, and all the tongues she despised would start clacking. Her cheeks burned at the thought of it. She would hold her head up and there would be no open scandal. It would all be discreet whispering. But her name would be smirched. There were plenty of people ready to believe the worst of her. It had not been the first of her indiscretions by many, but she was afraid it would turn out to be the most disastrous.

It was characteristic of Joyce that the thought of her father distressed her most. She could dismiss the others with an impatient "Oh, well, what's done is done; a joy ride's only a joy ride." But she could not do that with Jarvis Elliott.

He was never a man to scold or to give her many directions as to the ordering of her life. But he had distinctly gone out of his way to warn her about Winthrop Ordway. He had said nothing about the fact that Ordway was the most prominent of his business enemies and was leading the combination to defeat the construction of the railroad upon which he was engaged. That no doubt had been in the back of his mind. Perhaps he had thought her disloyal, but he had not implied it. The few curt sentences he had spoken had referred wholly to the reputation of the man in his relations with women. He knew nothing about the facts, he admitted, but no girl could afford to be seen much with one about whom such things were said. She had better give him up.

Joyce understood that his advice held the quality of a command. But it had caught her at an unfortunate time, while she was in the grip of one of her swift, eager enthusiasms. Ordway was different from the slangy slick-haired boys she had known. He was bigger, harder, altogether more forceful and vigorous. About him was a glamour of success, of a fighting and perhaps not altogether blameless past, of a future that might carry him to the top rung in the struggle for supremacy. He was so sure of himself that he made others sure. It flattered her that he had offered her comradeship and was, she guessed, going to ask her to be his wife. She liked him. How much, she did not know, but she was sure it was a lot. He had a way with women.

So she had let herself go with him. The fascination had grown, and she had been seen with him everywhere. This had been easier because her father had been called back to New York on financial matters connected with the funding of the cut-off. He had returned only two days before. Mrs. Antwerp, her chaperon, was a kindly old lady with no control whatever over the willful tempestuous girl.

Joyce wondered if her father would hear about this foolish frolic. She was afraid he would. He knew a good deal more than he mentioned as to what she was doing. And if he heard about it, how seriously would he regard it?

Not a word had been spoken since the car had started in the cañon. They were drawing near the city when Joyce took note of this. She glanced at the sombre young man beside her and her resentment stirred at his indifference. He was no negligible personality. The lean, clean-cut face, so dark and sardonic, belonged to one of at least potential mark. Why his insolence to her when she had asked a favour? Why his cool dismissal of her now as one with whom he did not care to talk? Heaven knew she did not want to talk with him, that if he gave her a chance she would snub him promptly. But that was no reason for ignoring her. She had always been the centre of her world. It was her heritage and the achievement of her individuality. She accepted attention as a matter of right. What was the matter with the stick?

If she had been able to read Hallack's thoughts

33

they would have surprised her. He had not the remotest idea who she was, but he would have hazarded a bet that she was a spoiled child of fortune unable to pay her way in the world by doing a single useful thing. She looked a hothouse plant, delicate and dainty and disturbing, an orchid of a rare variety developed at great cost. Such women moved him to exasperation, deeper for a recent bitter experience through which he had passed.

Yet curiously there ran through his disapproval an undercurrent of reluctant admiration. He did not look once at her. But he saw the lovely head set proudly above the small white throat. An impression renewed itself in his mind that nature had with soft caress modelled the light body lovingly, alive to all the infinite seductions of grace and charm.

They drew into the suburbs of the city and crossed a long viaduct.

"Where shall I leave you?" Hallack asked with businesslike curtness.

"About Third and Williams, if it won't take you too far out of your way."

He followed a boulevard along the bank of a stream for a mile until he came to the Country Club district. In the grey light of coming day he could see dimly a putting green to the right. Beyond this, he knew, was the polo field, hidden in pre-dawn mists.

"I'll get out here," the girl said abruptly.

"Thought you said Williams and Third."

"This suits me better."

When he had stopped the car she stepped out, said a formal and ironic "Thank you," and turned on her heel.

The engine was still running, but Hallack did not engage the clutch. His dissatisfied eyes followed her light-stepping progress to the sidewalk. He did not like to leave a woman, almost a girl, alone in the silent street at this time of night. But if he offered to see her home he knew she would turn on him and joyfully flay him.

"Hadn't you better go with her, Randall?" he suggested.

The older man—in point of fact the chief under whom he was working—negatived the proposal. "No. She had you put her off here so we wouldn't know who she is or where she's going. That young woman knows her way about. I expect she's been hitting it up lively with Ordway and has to cover her tracks. Did you notice that soulful look they gave each other just before we started? They've got their alibi all fixed up probably, but he'll call her up like he said to make sure it's getting across and they're not getting their wires short-circuited. It won't look any too good if it gets out she reached town after five in the morning from an all-night joy ride with him. I don't know much about society folks but I guess even they have to draw the line somewhere," the little man surmised.

Hallack listened gloomily without comment.

"Where'd she been with him anyhow?" went on Randall. "What business has a girl of her age being out with a fellow like Ordway at three o'clock in the morning—joy riding alone with him away up in the hills? What are her folks thinking about? Haven't they got any sense? Don't they look after her at all?"

The man at the wheel had no answer. He had asked himself the same questions. Were these audacious flappers of the new age innocent in spite of their shrewd, hard wordliness, their incessant hunt for pleasure? Or had civilization really slipped a cog and abolished all the old standards of virtue and decency?

Swiftly the car rolled along the silent street into another flanked by expensive houses set spaciously in ample grounds. After a time it struck a section of smaller homes packed closer together and from this ran into a crosstown thoroughfare which brought them to their hotel.

They entered and registered, leaving the car at the curb.

Ten minutes later Hallack was asleep.

CHAPTER IV

"WHERE THE BROOK AND RIVER MEET"

JOYCE crossed the boulevard and moved up a side street. The day was still very young, if it could be said to be day at all. Over the street and the houses bordering it the impalpable atmosphere of night hung heavy. The grey sifting into the sky was scarcely more than a promise of light.

A milk wagon, with a lantern hanging close to the hand of the driver, rattled across the street and into an alley just before she reached it. Halfway up the second block she cut across a lawn, skirted the corner of a big house, and stopped directly under a second-story window.

She hesitated. It had seemed at long range a simple thing to come here and rouse her friend, so much wiser than to face the curious blank-faced servants at home, but now that the moment had come she grew panicky. Suppose the butler should hear her instead of Louise, or suppose it should be Mr. Durand, or even Mrs. Durand. What explanation could she give that would suffice? She could see incredulous suspicion freeze the face of her chum's father when she told him that Ordway's car had broken down in the hills. Her acquired reputation for recklessness, for disdain of conventions, would serve her ill now.

She wished she had not come, but wishing it, could think of no alternative that would be better. In any case, she had to go through with it now. She could not stay here till daylight or go wandering through the streets.

From the drive, after an ineffective little shout or two, she gathered a handful of gravel and threw it at the window above.

"Wese! Wese!" she called in a sibilant whisper.

No answer. Apparently all the world and his neighbour were sunk fathoms deep in sleep. Again her voice sounded, and again, at intervals, for several minutes.

She flung more gravel at the unresponsive window. Her voice was no longer a whisper. It held a note of anxious shrillness. Was she going to spend the rest of her life trying to waken Louise?

In despair she gave up, then more resolutely tried again.

From a third-story window a head appeared.

"What is it?" a sleepy voice wanted to know.

Joyce recognized it as belonging to a house-maid. "Will you come down and let me in, Katie?" she asked.

"Who is it?"

"Joyce Elliott. I'm locked out. Hurry, please."

The head was withdrawn. It seemed many hours before the door opened, all of them compressed within five minutes.

Miss Elliott thought it well to give a careless sketchy explanation of the cause for her being here. "Thanks, Katie. I'll go to Louise's room. You needn't come with me. Car broke down and kept us all for hours. Awf'ly cold."

"Yes, miss." The maid's voice was deferential, but for an instant in her eyes was a fugitive flicker of sly mockery. She had the downstairs suspicion of those whom she was paid to serve. The story would, Joyce knew, be all over the servants quarters before breakfast.

"Thought we never would get away. Dreadful nuisance." Joyce yawned elaborately, to suggest a stupid time among a group of stranded people.

"Yes, miss." Katie smoothed her tousled hair and gathered the dressing gown closer to her. "You never can tell with them automobiles."

They separated at the stairs, the maid to take the back way. Joyce had a sinking sensation in the neighbourhood of the heart. She had scored her first failure. Katie was too demure, too decorous. She believed what she believed, and it was not the version that had been given her.

"Good of you to let me in. I'll remember it," Joyce said with a little smiling nod of dismissal.

She took the treads softly and moved gingerly along the dark hall, keeping contact with the wall by the touch of an outstretched hand. Louise had the third room on the right. Finding the door knob, she turned it slowly and noiselessly. She stepped into the room and closed the door behind her.

A girl lay asleep on the bed, her slim body resting on one side, an arm outflung over the coverlid which was moulded to the shape of her slender limbs.

Joyce moved forward quickly, took the hand in hers, gave it a little pressure, and whispered "Wese."

Brown eyes, dewy and filmed with sleep, struggled open and fastened themselves, startled, on Joyce.

"Why, Bubbles! You here? I thought—"

"I've had rotten luck, Wese. The car broke down in Box Elder Cañon. Thought it better to come here than to go home. Just got to town."

Louise glanced at the radium-faced clock on the dressing table. That look brought her wide awake with the information it gave. "Hot dog! It's past five." She sat up, one side of the small face flushed where the pillow had pressed it. "Where-ever have you been? Why, it's been *ages* and *ages* since I got home."

Her friend nodded. "Yes. First it was tire trouble. Then we had a smash in Box Elder

Cañon, as I said. Just wrecked the car." A ghost of a smile twitched at the sweet mouth whimsically. "I expect Winthrop's still there blessing the man who left him."

"Didn't he come back with you?" Louise laced her fingers round two small knees. The filmy nightdress, clinging to the lines of the form, brought out the immature contours of throat and bosom.

"Did you hop off and *fly* back?"

Italicized words had a way of leaping out of her sentences impetuously. She was a piquant and colourful young person, usually very much alive from the small dancing feet to the small dancing eyes.

"Two men came along in a flivver—civil engineer kind of men, or something of that kind, though one of 'em wasn't a bit civil. He had a grudge at Win and wouldn't bring him in. I told Mr. Man a few things about himself."

"I'll bet you did," the girl in the bed agreed promptly.

Joyce was in process of undressing. Her fingers were busy as she talked. "But I didn't get very far. He put me out of court by saying he wasn't a gentleman anyhow and it didn't matter what I said."

"The plot thickens," declaimed Louise, and she flashed a quick sidelong look at her friend. "What *time* was it when this grouch with the tin Lizzie

41

rescued you? Pajamas in that lower drawer there, kiddie."

Joyce took her time to answer. She was rummaging in the chiffonier. "It was a scandalacious hour, Wese. I'm trying to forget it—Where's the coat that goes with this pink suit? Oh, here it is—Of all the fool things I ever did, that was the craziest, to go scooting over the hills with Win Ordway at that time of night."

"I'll say it was," agreed Louise cheerfully. "I've been on petting parties of my own. I claim to be some speed, but Winthrop Ordway, in the wee a.m.'s—going some, if you ask Wese. It's not as if you didn't know his line. Everybody does."

"Oh, his line!"

"'S all right," Louise defended, nodding her wise little head. "All the samey, you know it. How long is it since Tessie Barnes—?"

Indignantly Joyce remonstrated. "If you're going to class me with Tessie Barnes—"

"I'm not, but you have enemies, my che-ild. You ought to have seen Esther Dare lift her eyebrows and smile when you two started up the hill road. She made a *scandal* out of it without a word said."

"Oh, well, you know Esther! A thimbleful of brains and no judgment."

"Yes," admitted Louise, and added in the slang of her set: "A necker too. But don't forget she can talk a mile a minute."

Joyce laughed ruefully, buttoning the coat of the pajamas round her slender supple body. "Hope she doesn't find out when I got in."

"Oh, she will. Make your mind uneasy about that." The brown eyes of the girl in bed rested on her friend thoughtfully. Joyce was and had been for some weeks carrying on a desperate flirtation with Ordway. How much was back of it? Did she know exactly how far she meant to go? Louise had a good deal of the gamin in her and something of the faun. She was in for a good time and knew how to look after herself. It was in character for her to be a hard and wary young nymph. But Joyce—well, she had a way of letting her emotions and enthusiasms run riot. She was perhaps too generous in friendship, not out for herself enough.

"You're a Job's comforter, whatever that is."

Louise hugged her knees with her arms and rested an impudent little chin on them. "I like speed myself, and nobody can say I'm a gloom. But you're such a *fast* worker, Bubbles, so full of the devil when you get started. You're keen." A little laugh welled out of her, a blend of admiration and expostulation. "You step on the gas *hard,* I'll say."

Slipping on a negligee, Joyce sat down before the glass, shook out her hair, and began to comb it. "I do let myself get carried away sometimes," she admitted judicially. "But if you think Winthrop Ordway's trying his line on me you've got another guess coming. Far as that goes, you don't like to miss anything yourself, Wese."

"Ye-es, but I don't let my temperature run up. I pop a thermometer into my mouth whenever I suspect myself of it."

"I pull up too once in a blue moon, you know."

"It's not what you do, Bubbles. It's the way you do it," Louise explained. "You're such a whirlwind, and you never stop to think how a thing will *look*. I'm crazy enough, goodness knows, and I go petting lots more than you do, but you get so kinda *carried away* when you're having a good time. Everybody thinks you're a whiz, and of course people talk."

"I can't keep stupid people from talking, can I?" Joyce asked impatiently. "Is it my fault if they think horrid things?"

"It is, and it isn't," the wise little flapper decided. She let the question uppermost in her mind flash out. "Did you go to his chalet on Ramshorn?"

Joyce answered, without equivocation. "Yes."

Her friend wagged a small head sagely. "That's you, Bubbles. You go and do a crazy thing; then when someone asks you about it you tell the truth instead of fibbing."

"Why should I fib? We only stopped to get a rifle Win wanted."

"Do you expect anybody's going to believe that?" Louise asked bluntly. She added an exclamation of meaningless flapper slang: "Sweet mamma, take my hat and shoes!"

"Wese Durand, you pig-minded little snip, if you think—"

"I don't, and you know I don't," interrupted the philosopher on the bed. "I *know* you. But you can't get away with that story—not with folks who *want* to think the worst. Forget it. You never went near that Swiss chalet."

"I didn't mean to scatter the information broadcast," Joyce explained.

"Don't. It'll only get you into trouble. I'm a clam. Lucky you didn't tell someone else."

Joyce protested indignantly. "It'd be pretty rotten of any one to think I can't go driving with a man without harm."

Momentarily Louise changed the subject. "Who let you in?"

"Katie. I suppose she'll talk."

"Will she? Like a house afire."

"Oh, well!"

"It was kinda foolish of you," Louise ruminated aloud. "Honest Injun, Bubbles, has Winthrop Ordway got you going?"

"Not so you'd notice it," Joyce answered quietly.

"Course you'd *say* that. But *has* he?"

"I wonder."

"Don't blame you a bit. I'm *crazy* about him too. If it was a bit of use I'd vamp him. Let him crook a finger and I'd come running." Louise always spoke in superlatives. Her friend understood that she meant only to indicate an interest in Ordway. "But what's the use? I hang around—and *look*—and *look*—and he doesn't know I'm on earth."

"Shall I tell him?" Joyce asked, an edge of satiric humour in her voice.

"Absolutively no use."

"He may wake up some day and discover you. Winthrop doesn't miss many bets of that kind. He's a big man—the biggest I know except Dad—and he'll go a long way before he gets through. But—"

"Are *you* going with him on that long journey, dearie?" Louise asked in the interests of information.

"I was saying, when you interrupted with your impertinence, my dear, that he does like to be admired by attractive and attracted young women. He purrs like a sleek cat when you feed it cream."

"I'm an attracted young woman all rightie, but am I an attractive one?" Louise wanted to know, a smile twitching at the sweet spoiled mouth that expressed her careless and audacious personality.

"You'll do in a crowd."

The girl in bed watched the comb passing

through long, heavy ripples of wavy gold. She yawned sleepily.

"You do have the *loveliest* hair, Bubbles. I don't see how you take care of so much the easy way you do. Mine's a mop." Her mind had strayed from that most interesting theme of the young girl's thoughts, *He* and *She,* but it switched back promptly. "You're the funniest *ever.* If a man was rushing me off my feet the way Winthrop Ordway is you, such a whiz as he is—and if I went around with him everywhere like you do—and got myself talked about for him, I couldn't any more sit back and pick him to pieces—"

From her father Joyce had inherited a mind that faced facts, an imperative to look at people and things clear-eyed and straight. She would be swept into an instant friendship, but she could, given time, detach herself and watch her friends as part of the passing show. For one of her ardent temperament it was a rare and saving gift. More than once it had made her pull up one of her impulses with a tight rein while in full tilt.

She stifled a yawn. "Is it so funny that I use my eyes and my brains, Wese? That's what they're supposed to be for, you know."

Joyce put out the light and crept into bed beside her chum.

"You're cold, you poor kid," Louise said, her soft warm body cuddling close. "I don't wonder—up all night in that *horrible* gulch." Her velvet-smooth arms tightened around the neck of her friend in a tender little hug. "Don't you worry, Bubbles. I'll swear on a stack of hymn books you got in soon after I did."

"You're a dear," murmured Joyce drowsily.

The arms of Louise relaxed and fell away. The two snuggled into comfortable positions and began to breathe regularly and deeply. They fell asleep, these charming young creatures not so many years emergent from the chrysalis of childhood.

Types of that amazing complex, the American girl of good family, they were paradoxes full of contradiction. Least of all did they understand themselves. It was impossible for them to realize why they were such a problem to the older generation. Innocent yet full of shrewd worldly wisdom; flippant and audacious, and cherishing in their heart's sanctuary an unconquerable belief in romance; soft and sensuous, but hard as nails; tricky as fauns, yet responsive to a rigid though peculiar code of their own; pampered and spoiled, still holding within them an unsuspected capacity for sacrifice that is the inheritance of their sex: they were Twentieth-century variants of all the daughters of Eve, modern to their fingertips, sophisticated to the nth power—and primitive as those who walked in the forgotten childhood of the race.

A strange complex, surely! The standards

of their sex and class that had been building for generations they tossed carelessly away. Experience began with them, in their own persons. It ended with them. Were they products of their environment—of relaxation due to war weariness, of the moving picture and jazz and the automobile, of a slow loosening of moral fibre going on for generations? Were they merely the extreme expression of world-wide pathological conditions? Or is the swing of the pendulum about to carry back to types of earlier days?

Who knows?

CHAPTER V

WESE HAS AN ATTACK OF POETRY

THE clock on the dressing table was striking twelve when Louise stirred, turned, flung out her lean arms in a yawn, and opened drowsy eyes.

Joyce, sitting at an end table, hung up the telephone receiver. She wore a pair of her friend's mules and over the pajamas a negligee. There was a look of comical dismay on her mobile face.

"I'm in for it, Wese. Called up the house to let 'em know where I am. Been talking with Aunt Ant." Thus she designated with affectionate disrespect her chaperon, Mrs. Antwerp. "She says Dad's hot on my trail. He 'phoned everywhere this morning and found I'm here. Soon as I wake I'm to call him up at the office."

"What'll he do?" asked Louise. She was a loyal little soul, but she was human. If her friend was in a pickle she naturally wanted to get all the enjoyment out of it she could.

"Good gracious! How do I know? Paddle me. Put me on bread and water. Stand me in a corner. Shut me in a dark closet."

"I'd hate to have him get after me. He's so—

so rod-of-ironish. What is it they called those old Roman fellows who put out their kidlets to freeze to death so's they'd grow up strong—Spartans?"

"I won't exactly enjoy my little talk with him," Joyce admitted ruefully. "But I've got to buck up and go through with it."

She reached for the telephone again.

"Main 222, please . . . Oh, is this Mr. Smithers? I want to speak with Dad . . . Yes, Joyce Elliott . . . If you please . . . Joyce talking, Dad . . . Yes . . . Yes . . . I'll be there . . ."

"What'd he say?" demanded Louise as soon as her friend had hung up.

"Not much, but, my! the way he said it. I'm to meet him at his office this afternoon at three."

"But we're going to the Stantons."

The face of Joyce bubbled to a smile that momentarily filled it. She had a way of doing things thoroughly, with all her might, of throwing herself wholly into the emotion of the hour.

"You're going to the Stanton's, my dear. A subsequent engagement for me. I'd like to catch myself telling Dad I couldn't come when he calls me up on the carpet and giving as a reason a bridge drive at the Stanton's."

"Maybe you can come when he's through with you—if there's enough of you left. . . . Wonder if Winthrop Ordway is back yet."

"He's to call me up."

"To find out whether you got safely home with

the ice man or the garage helper or whoever he is," Louise added, twisting her small-featured face to a grimace. "Did you try to vamp him on the way, by the way?"

"He was horrid. I didn't say a word to him."

"But that *would* be a good line," her friend persisted, struck by its possibilities. "If you didn't go too far with it. Think I'll try a crush on that Viking at the filling station. I might get a whang out of that. Isn't he a *splendiferous* thing? And probably *heaps* more interesting than Jimmie. I'm fed up with *him*. There's not a surprise left in him for me. I know him from A to Z. Two minutes before he means to kiss me I'm reading his signals."

"Tableau of Wese Durand giving Jimmie Stanton the bounce. Tableau of Wese snaring another poor man," prophesied Joyce. "Let's dress, baby vamp. I've a million things to do to-day."

She passed lightly to the bathroom, her slender athletic body perfectly poised. From it she emerged, glowing, radiant, tingling with life.

Joyce had perhaps overstated the case when she had spoken of a million things to do that day, but the remark was essentially true. The tired business man does not work half as hard as the American girl of leisure. She begins her day late, but to make up for that she ends it early. About midnight she blithely says, "It's a peach of a night. Where'll we go now?"

As all the world knows, she has been travelling fast since the War; but not even the wisest can answer, except in an immediate sense, her own question as to where she is going. She is blasé, but her sophistication is skin deep. She cannot help letting a gay enthusiasm sparkle out of her when she forgets her pose. It is born of her enduring faith in romance waiting for her just around the corner. To-morrow is always for her a new day. Meanwhile, she is wholly occupied with the present one.

They reached the luncheon table late, for breakfast. Louise was full of chatter. She hardly gave her mother a chance to get in an occasional word. It was the easiest way of parrying inconvenient questions. Like many of our present-day mothers, Mrs. Durand had a very vague understanding of her daughter. The glimpses she had into the soul of that eager, vivid, restless bundle of contradictions perplexed and disturbed her. She shrank from learning too much about the girl's activities and her reactions to them, even though from a sense of duty she tried to keep herself informed.

"What time did you get home, Wese?" Mrs. Durand managed to interject in a pause.

"The clock does not strike for the happy, Mother. See Schiller, third-term German, Scrafford teacher. 'Member how she used to take off her glasses and say, *'Young ladies,'* Bubbles?" Louise, with a grapefruit spoon to represent the pince-nez, gave an elaborate and finished imitation.

Presently Mrs. Durand returned to the attack. "Katie says she let you in this morning, Joyce. Didn't you all come home together?"

"Oh, cars get separated, Mother." Louise shrugged this away as of small importance. "Mr. Ordway had tire trouble."

"What time did you say you got in, Joyce?"

"Oh, Mother darling!" protested her daughter, and plunged into another lead of poetry that providentially jumped to her mind:

" 'We live in deeds, not years, in
        thoughts, not breaths;
    In feelings, not in figures on a dial.
    We should count time by heart throbs.'

English Three, Senior year, Miss Reynolds. Aren't you glad I didn't waste all that money you and Dad spent to make a perfect lady out of me, Muzzy?"

"You're talking nonsense, Wese. I've asked two questions, and you haven't answered either of them."

"We got home early, Mother. That is, kinda late. You know how crazy a crowd gets about sticking around, and the moon was *scrumptious*." Louise rather fancied the poetic inspiration as a distraction. She declaimed once more.

54

" ' 'Tis the witching hour of night,
    Orbed is the moon and bright,
    And the stars they glisten, glisten,
    Seeming with bright eyes to listen—
      For what listen they?'

Keats. English Three. Again Reynolds."

Joyce read in Mrs. Durand's manner a quiet determination to find out the facts. She decided it was better to face the situation rather than to try to dodge it.

"Wese got in about two o'clock," she explained. "We had an accident—ran into the wall of the cañon—and we didn't get a lift for a long time. I got in after five."

"So Katie said. Anybody hurt?"

"Mr. Ordway was cut a little—not seriously."

"How many were in the car?"

"Just the two of us."

"Oh!" The monosyllable was eloquent of meaning. "Where did you say the accident took place?"

"Mother strikes a trail and follows it to a funeral," Louise said with a giggle meant to decentralize attention.

"In the gorge," Joyce answered the matron. "It was awf'ly dark. We swung round a curve and there was a boulder in the road. Mr. Ordway had to run into the side of the road to miss it. He smashed a wheel."

"Did the boulder fall after the other cars had passed?"

"We came home another way—down Box Elder."

"Across Ramshorn Pass and through the cañon?"

"Yes."

Mrs. Durand fell silent, and in that silence Joyce felt that judgment was being passed. She wished her friend's mother would scold her for what she had done, would fuss in a motherly way over her folly. Instead she let the fact stand frigidly.

Louise rushed into small talk to cover the embarrassment, but Joyce was wretchedly aware that Mrs. Durand was busy with thoughts.

The girl carried to the interview with her father a sense of being already under condemnation.

This did not show in her manner. She parked the car and walked, a glowing picture of arrogant youth, into the outer office of the Mile High Investment Company. Her little heels clicked firmly on the tiled floor. She held high the small golden head. A delicate colour glowed through the creamy silk sheen of the cheeks.

"I have an appointment with Dad, you know," she told her father's secretary.

Smithers was middle-aged and subdued. He

had a militant wife and two up-and-coming daughters. "He's busy just now, Miss Elliott, but he said you were to wait."

The door of the inner office opened. Joyce rose and moved forward. A man came out, the one who had driven her down from Box Elder Cañon a few hours earlier. On his face was the look of one who has just come into a fortune.

The girl and the man stared at each other as they passed without a word. It would be difficult to say which was the more surprised at the meeting. Joyce did not give him another glance as she stepped toward the desk behind which her father was standing.

They faced each other for a long moment in a steady silence, Jarvis Elliott and his daughter. At first sight the relationship between them was not apparent. The contrast between the grim railroad builder and this pampered child of his wealth was striking. The slender grace of the girl, her lovely golden charm, seemed to hold little in common with his rugged strength. What freak of nature was responsible for so alien an offspring to this man of iron?

In the grizzled sixties though Elliott was, he stood foursquare as a grey mediaeval castle. In frame he was heavy but not tall. Long arms hung from very broad deep shoulders. The head, magnificent in the impression of poised power it gave, was leonine. Keen eyes gleamed from under shaggy overhanging brows. One glance told that he was a man's man.

Yet, oddly enough, a close observer would have found in Joyce some part of her inheritance from Jarvis Elliott. She had his steady eyes, though the colouring was different. There was something of his force, of his courage, in the upstanding way she faced him even though he was the one person in the world she feared. It was plain she did not intend to resort to any feminine plea for mercy, to the weakness of tears. And that was characteristic of Joyce, always had been since the days of her childhood.

"You wanted to see me, Father?" she said at last.

He walked to the door and closed it.

"Sit down," he said brusquely.

CHAPTER VI

"WILL YOU STAND THE GAFF?"

HALLACK had put in a call with the night clerk for eight-fifteen. It seemed to him that he had not been asleep a minute before the room telephone began to buzz. Just three hours earlier he had tumbled into bed.

He took his bath, shaved, dressed, and was in an adjoining restaurant within twenty-five minutes. Here Randall joined him. The older man was still heavy-eyed with sleep, and he brought with him an early-morning grouch. He was past the age—if there ever had been such a time for him—when he could work all day and drive all night without impairing his vitality.

The glance he flung at the clear-eyed brown-faced man opposite him reflected an irritation born of fatigue and envy. Beneath the tan a warm colour glowed in Hallack's cheeks. He was wearing laced boots, corduroy suit, and flannel shirt, all of them the worse for service. But he was one of those men who can come out of a manhole looking clean and fresh.

"Don't you ever get tired, dammit?" Randall growled as he picked up the bill of fare.

59

His assistant laughed at this characteristic greeting. Still hardly thirty, he had an iron constitution and an inordinate capacity for work. He could go till he was ready to drop, snatch two or three hours sleep, and buckle to the job again with zest for another grilling stretch.

"You'd think Elliott would have more consideration than to drag us down here in the night," continued the smaller man testily. "That's always the way with big guns like him. They're slave drivers—don't care how much trouble they put other people to. You had it right when you told Ordway that, though it was a fool thing to do." He snapped at the waitress, "Coffee—oatmeal and cream—hot cakes."

"Elliott's looking at the job, not at us," Hallack suggested. "You've got to say for him that he never spares himself either. In a way he's paying us a compliment by assuming we're not giving him an eight-hour day."

"Hmp!" snapped the other. "If he wants to pay me a compliment I'd rather he would raise my salary."

"Jarvis Elliott is the kind of man I like to work for," the younger engineer went on. "He thinks big and plans big. Take this road. It gets a grip of you. When you're working on it you feel some of his great vision. To throw a railroad across the Rockies where the best engineers of the country say it can't be done, to cut two hundred miles from the transcontinental route, to open up a vast virgin region to settlement and make it tributary to this city—that's a marvellous dream."

"You've said it—a dream," grumbled Randall. "Can't be done."

"It can. I'll put my faith in Jarvis Elliott. He dreams, and translates his dreams into reality. That's the difference between him and a fellow like Ordway, say. Ordway keeps his cold fishy eyes on the dollar. He's thinking all the time about himself. Not Elliott, though. He could make far more money if he didn't take chances. But he's gambling—gambling big for the state and city he loves."

"That's the way you interpret him." Randall smiled with cynical amusement. There were not many visions left in life for him.

"That's the way I interpret him," Hallack agreed. "He's not the richest man in the state, but he's by all odds its first citizen. If he were playing his own hand he'd divert his money into the usual financial channels—play safe. But that wouldn't be Elliott. He's an empire builder."

"He's got you buffaloed, anyhow, Bob. I'm not knocking him, you understand. He's all right, and I'm not telling everyone I think he's bit off more than he can chew," Randall explained with returning good nature. "Why should I worry, anyhow, so long as he pays my salary?"

"I know you, Fred," his subordinate grinned.

"You like to kick a bit, but you're sold on Elliott just as much as I am. You know he's a sane strong fighting leader, and you'll follow him to a fighting finish just as I shall."

"Not so sure about that," Randall grunted. He looked at his watch. "Say, we'll have to hustle."

The clock was striking nine when they reached the offices of the Mile High Investment Company. This was one of Elliott's subsidiary concerns, the one with which he had started business thirty-five years ago. It dealt in the production of coal. For most of his financial life he had been in this building and in these rooms. Though his interests had developed and ramified he still clung to his old quarters as he did to old friends.

Four or five men, evidently miners, were waiting in the room. They talked together in undertones, but with a note of excitement in their voices.

Smithers drew Randall and Hallack to one side. "Mr. Elliott wants you to come back at two o'clock. There's trouble at one of his mines. He's got to settle that now."

Hallack put in the intervening hours attending to some affairs of his own in town. From an early afternoon paper he gathered that the trouble at the Invincible mine was a local one. It had to do with conditions of labour, an unpopular super-intendent, his rules, and the manner in which he enforced them.

Promptly at two the engineers were back at the offices of their chief.

Elliott sat in frowning thought at his desk when they entered. He seemed visibly to push out of his mind the matter that was troubling him. "What's the news from the front?" he asked.

"Hallack has been out in the hills all week," Randall reported. "He thinks he's found a feasible route to the summit of the Pass."

Elliott turned upon the younger engineer eyes that drilled into him. "How?"

"You know the hogback above Virgin Creek Park?"

"Yes."

"We can run the grade along the south slope, creeping up the flank as we go."

"You think so?" challenged the empire builder.

"I know it," answered Hallack quietly, meeting him eye to eye.

"Good. But how do you reach the hogback?"

"A spur runs out from the park through the timber. I'll show you on the map."

The map was brought and unrolled. Elliott had been over the ground several times. His eyes followed intelligently the point of the pencil as it indicated the proposed line for the grade.

"It'll take a bit of engineering to get over the rim, but we can do it," Hallack explained; "once out we swing to the left here across the hills and make a sharp horseshoe curve."

63

His chief asked a crisp question or two, then, chin in hand, gazed in a long silence at the map.

Again his hawk eyes focussed on the young man. "Sure of this? No guessing?"

"I'm sure we can make the hogback when we reach it, and I'm certain we can get out of the park by the spur. I haven't had time to make the surveys to determine the best way over the hills from the park to the hogback, but I'll stake my reputation it can be done. I've ridden across a dozen times."

Into the heart of the grim railroad builder there came a glow of gratification. He was putting this line through against tremendous natural barriers, every foot of the way in opposition to the transcontinental system which dominated the transportation of the city and state. The burden was being carried on his own shoulders. In different capacities he had tried a dozen men and found them wanting. On the fingers of one hand he could count those to be depended upon to take large responsibilities and meet them. For months he had been watching this youngster. He believed he had discovered the man to take Randall's place.

For Randall would not do. He had technical knowledge, could work out details accurately, and had a comprehensive experience that should have given him initiative to cope with emergencies. In an ordinary job he would have succeeded. But this required faith, audacity, a fighting edge, and grim determination. Randall was not cast in that mould.

He showed this now. "I haven't been over the ground carefully myself. It's possible Bob may be mistaken."

"Yes," assented Elliott. Then, like a flash, "Why haven't you been over it yourself?" he demanded.

"I've been over it of course. I mean I haven't checked up the surveys—haven't satisfied myself the route is a workable one."

"Don't quibble, Randall," his chief ordered. "Why haven't you satisfied yourself? What have you been doing that's more important than this?"

The face of the older engineer flushed. "I had blue-prints to get out and the camp to move. I had to verify the surveys along Thunder Mountain."

Elliott made no comment. He plunged into some details of organization he had planned. Clearly, concisely, in the simplest and most direct fashion, he made plain what was in his mind. The vital force of the man broke through verbiage, so that he expressed himself without the waste of a word.

His firm fingers rolled the map up swiftly. The engineers understood that the conference was at an end. They rose to go.

"Randall, I'll see you here at five this afternoon," the railroad builder said. "Hallack, wait a minute."

The younger man remained.

Keen eyes, steady as the rock of Gibraltar, gleamed from under grizzled brows at the engineer. They searched him through and through. Like a shot out of a gun came Elliott's first words.

"Ever meet Winthrop Ordway?"

Hallack stiffened. Into his eyes came an expression harsh and steely, a flash of feral savagery. "Yes."

"Know him well?"

"No and yes. I've met him only a few times, but—I know him."

"You're going to know him better. Ordway is in charge of the Midwestern & Pacific campaign against us."

"I'd heard so," the engineer replied.

"He's the best man in the country for the job—daring, resourceful, wholly unscrupulous. He'll go the limit—stick at nothing."

"That's how I size him up," the younger man agreed.

"If I build the Gateway Pass cut-off the M. & P. becomes a bad second in the race to the coast instead of a good first. Ordway means to see I don't build it. Back of him are financial interests and influence far stronger than mine. There's only one way to beat him. We've got to outgeneral him and outfight him."

Hallack nodded appreciation of the point. He

66

wondered why the chief was telling him this. It was not Elliott's custom to confide in subordinates, rather to listen to opinions and give decisive orders.

"Outfight him, outgame him, outguess him," the old railroad builder continued, and in his grim voice was a sound like the far challenging roar of a lion. "The cut-off is going through—if I live."

"Yes," said the field man, and he had not the least doubt in the world.

"What about you? Will you stand the gaff? Can you fight on after you're beaten? Can you do things other men say are impossible?"

Bob Hallack declined this chance of telling how good a man he was. "All I can say is that I'll give you the best that's in me."

"Not enough—unless the best that's in you is A 1. Is it?"

"There's only one way to find that out, Mr. Elliott. Try me."

"That's what I'm going to do. From to-day you're chief engineer of construction on the cut-off."

Hallack showed none of the elation that swept in waves through his blood. "What about Randall?" he asked quietly.

"Not big enough for the job."

"He's a good engineer, with a list of successes back of him and no failures."

"Too conservative, too tied to precedent, far

and away too cautious. I've got to have on the cut-off someone not afraid to take chances."

"Is he leaving you?"

"Not unless he insists. You and he change places."

"Does he know?"

"He'll know later. I want to go over this thing with you to-day when I have more time. Meet me here at six-thirty. We'll go to dinner at the club."

The subject was for the moment closed. Hallack knew himself dismissed.

As he walked out he met a young woman going in. She was the girl he had brought down from Box Elder Cañon a few hours earlier.

CHAPTER VII

"I'LL JUMP
AT THE CHANCE"

JOYCE would rather have taken it standing, but her father's words left no option. She sat down.

Elliott walked back of the desk, drew up the swivel chair, and rested his forearms on the blotting pad. The steel-grey eyes fastened to those of the girl and held them locked.

"Where were you last night?"

"We went to a kinda dinner-dance at Mountain Crest Lodge. Didn't Mrs. Antwerp tell you?"

"She understood you were coming home after the dance. Why didn't you come?"

"I got in so late I thought it better to stay with Wese."

"How late?"

"After five. We had an accident and smashed the car." Joyce recognized how damaging an admission this was. Her eyes met the stern ones of her father steadily. She was facing a judge, not an indulgent parent.

"Was it a drinking party?"

"No," she answered.

"No liquor there?"

"A cocktail or two. That was all."

"You drank?"

"Oh, yes. Like the others."

"But nobody was under the influence?"

"Not that I noticed." Then, with a flash of the truth that was fundamentally a part of her nature: "Not very much, anyhow."

"This accident. Was anybody hurt?"

"Mr. Ordway was cut by the glass of the wind shield—not seriously."

"He took you to the dinner?"

"Yes."

"And was driving you home when the accident occurred?"

"Yes, he was driving."

"How many in the car?"

"Just he and I. It was a roadster." A faint flush of angry colour began to beat into the cheeks of the girl. What had she done to deserve a manner so coldly inflexible?

"When was this?"

"About half-past two—maybe three," she added recklessly.

"Where?"

"In Box Elder Cañon."

"I thought you said you were on the way home from Mountain Crest Lodge."

"We came home over the hills—on account of the moonlight."

"All the party?"

"Just our car." Her voice had taken on a perceptible edge of defiance.

"Let's get this clear, Joyce. After the dance broke up you went for a run over the hills alone with Ordway. Did you stop anywhere before the accident?"

"At his Swiss chalet on Ramshorn Mountain. He wanted to get a gun."

"How long did you stop?"

"Not more than a few minutes."

"Was anybody else there?"

"No."

"How did you get to town after the accident?"

"Two men came along in a car and picked me up. The driver was the man I met as I came in."

"You mean Hallack?"

"That's what Mr. Ordway called him."

"Ordway knew him?"

"Yes. There had been some trouble between them. He wouldn't bring Mr. Ordway to town. I had to come with them alone."

Elliott mentally filed away for future reference this information as to the relation between the two men. Just now he stuck to the subject of the hour. In one sense he had a single-track mind. No tempting bypaths could lead him from the issue. There was a matter to be settled with Joyce. He meant to determine it now.

That was Jarvis Elliott's way. He might find out that which would wound him greatly. He might precipitate a breach that would make his heart bleed. For this golden girl was the secret joy and pride of his life. Always the rush of her sweet and eager enthusiasms had charmed him. Always he had delighted in the vigorous independence that differentiated her. He wanted the best for her, a full life culminating in love and happiness. But he desired too that her soul should not grow fat and slothful, that it should not compromise with Fate and accept second bests. He craved for her that she might . . .

". . . wear with every scar
Honour at eventide."

Love is usually dumb. He could not put his feeling into words. He could not break through the barrier of age and circumstances that separated them. All he could do was to deal with the facts, even though he knew that facts are often lies unless correctly interpreted.

Many men, to save their own feelings, would have accepted the explanation of the broken car, scolded the girl, and passed over the matter. Elliott would not do this. He had to know the truth, as nearly as he could find it out. Joyce was of those to whom life may bring utter shipwreck. She was ready to give herself too generously to those in whom she had faith. He must protect her if he could.

"What's between you and Ordway?" he asked bluntly.

The girl shrank from this attack and resented it. She did not know herself how much was between her and her father's business foe, nor did she want to know yet. He had become the most important figure in her life. That was enough to know till time should tell her more.

"What do you mean—between us?" she asked.

"I mean his love-making. How far has it gone? Where do you stand with each other?" His searching eyes were like surgeons' probes.

Joyce flushed angrily. There was no parrying a crude direct thrust like this. It had to be met, but she protested hotly within herself that it was not fair. Her father had a right to call her on the carpet for things done. He had no right to go behind them.

"There hasn't been any love-making," she flung back at him.

"You've been with him all his spare time, I understand. Every day you've spent hours with him—riding, golfing, dinners, dances. I warned you to have nothing to do with him because he's a dangerous man. You chose to override my advice and be with him so much that people have talked. Finally you carry your infatuation to the point of scandal." He checked with a lift of his hand her flaming protest. "Do you expect people to believe that he is not making love to you?"

"I don't care what evil-minded people believe," she cried.

"I do, about my daughter," he disagreed. "I care a great deal. But I care more about seeing her plunge into an affair which may bring her great sorrow."

"Can't a girl be friends with a man without everybody talking about it?" Joyce flared.

"No—not that kind of a man, not the way you're going at it. You say there's been no love-making. Where are you headed for, then? What's he driving at?"

Joyce had not been entirely candid. There had been some tentative love-making in the early days of their friendship, and she had put an end to it peremptorily after some skirmishing experiments. Ordway's respect for her and his interest in her had increased. Out of the first phase of their affair had emerged another. She was fighting the attraction that drew them together, yet she was eagerly submitting herself to its influence. Their meetings became, under the surface, battlegrounds. She got flashes at him that showed her a stranger hard, unmoral, and without principle; and again other moments of insight that seemed to give the denial to what she had discovered. He fascinated her, yet stirred deep within her the maiden that stretched out hands and pushed him back.

"I don't know. I suppose he likes me. He's good fun."

"It's time you found out, then," Elliott answered, and to her his voice sounded harsh. "You may be sure he knows exactly what he wants of you."

"Isn't it conceivable he just enjoys being with me? He's not an ogre, even though he is your business opponent. I like him." She said it with a flash of challenging eyes.

"I don't. He's a wolf. I intend to see he doesn't devour you."

"I'm not Little Red Riding Hood."

"You're the girl that has let herself be compromised by his attentions."

"That's not true," she flamed out.

"Isn't it? Look at the facts. He takes you to a drinking party up in the hills."

"It wasn't a drinking party. I told you it wasn't," she interrupted.

"The men had liquor with them and you were drinking. I'm not claiming it was a wild orgy. After the dance is over he doesn't bring you straight home as the other men did their partners. He spends half the night with you alone in the mountains, he takes you to his summer lodge, and finally he smashes his car so that he can't get you back at all. You get in at daybreak after being out all night with him alone. He has compromised your reputation definitely and completely."

"Because we had an accident?" she asked stormily. "Don't other people have trouble with their cars?"

"Not at a time so unfortunate for them as that. If they do, they pay the penalty, as you'll have to pay it."

"I won't. People aren't so narrow-minded any more. You're busy all the time with your railroad and everything. You don't see that times have changed." She wanted to stamp her foot at his clear-sighted recognition of her dilemma.

His eyes flashed out under the shaggy brows. "Have they changed so that a girl of nineteen can spend a night alone with a man—and such a man as Ordway?"

"If you think that of me—"

He cut into her angry wail. "I believe exactly what you've told me. But the crowd you go with won't believe it . . . If I've been too busy to look after you—well, we'll change that. You can make your plans to go with Mrs. Antwerp on a trip to Japan next week."

She flew out at him. "You're treating me like a child."

"I treat you like a child when you act like one. If you don't know how to behave properly, if you cheapen yourself as you did last night, even in

76

the eyes of the man you were with, then it's time for me to take charge of you."

The golden head lifted proudly. "I didn't cheapen myself with him. He's big enough to understand." Then, under swift impulse, she fired a broadside full at him. "He intends to ask me to marry him."

They looked at each other, steadily, in a full-charged silence. He did not question the fact. He did not ask her how she knew. His mind and soul leaped to the essence of the situation.

"And you—what will you tell him?"

The irresistible impulse pressed upon her to tear his heart in return for the shame he had driven home to her, to salve her wounded pride by hurting him.

"Why, of course, I'll jump at the chance, as any woman would."

Man of iron though he was, he flinched at the shock of it. His face hardened to a grey expressionless mask.

"I'd rather see you marry a man with a pick and shovel in a sewer. I'd rather see you live and die unmarried."

Deliberately, she misinterpreted his feeling. "Of course you don't like him because he's against you in business. Mr. Ordway doesn't feel that way. He admires you tremendously. He says business ought not to be carried into personal relationships. And he's willing to be friendly if you are."

"I'm not."

"He thinks one ought to be large-minded about such things—"

"Joyce, if you marry him he'll ruin your life."

"I don't think so. You're prejudiced, you know. Anyhow, I'm a good sport. I'll take a chance," she said airily, quite conscious that she was acting like a minx.

"He's a destructive force, like a submarine— no morals, no conscience, no principles to hold him on a straight course. The man's entirely selfish. That genial friendly way of his is all camouflage. As sure as you marry him your life is shipwrecked."

He spoke with finality, without the least doubt, and his words had weight with her, the more because he was so quiet, so self-contained and free from bluster. But the instinct was still strong in her to punish him for interfering. She had an advantage, one with which she could stab him to the heart, and the perverse desire to use it.

"Isn't that what stern parents always tell willful girls when they don't choose a man they like?" she asked saucily. "That they are older and more experienced and know best and little girls should do as they're told?" She finished on a high note of forced laughter.

He felt more than a sense of baffled impotence. Within him was the cold of despair creeping toward his heart. In opposition to the girl's folly his strength might break itself in vain. He might argue, but arguments would be futile. Vanity or caprice or self-will might wreck her life in spite of him. Against her own desire it would be impossible to save her. It came to him sadly that he was out of touch with her. His deep brooding love was of no avail. She must go her own way, to her own destiny.

"Am I a stern parent, Joyce?" he asked, and deep in his eyes was something that called to her.

She steeled herself not to respond to the message that was so much tenderer than his words. Her pride had been wounded, the glory of her young wings clipped. The very fact that she was in the wrong held her from him.

"Thought you mentioned a trip to Japan," she flung out flippantly. "As if that would do any good while telegraph lines and cables are open."

"No," he admitted, and his hand lifted in the least little gesture of despair, "it wouldn't do any good if you're determined to ruin your life. I withdraw Japan."

"It's my life," the girl cried wildly. "I've a right to live it as I please."

"You've a right to live it as you ought," he corrected. "It isn't yours to throw away."

"I'm not talking about throwing it away, but about marrying a great man—or, anyhow, one who's going to be."

"No man is great unless he's good."

"He's good enough for me."

"No, Joyce. None but the best is good enough for you." He yearned to express the flood of feeling in his heart, but the habit of restraint was too strong for him. "You're on the wrong track, girl. I've been to blame. I've seen where you were drifting, but I thought your eyes would be opened presently. You've been living for yourself only—for excitement and sensation and pleasure. Nobody can find happiness in that."

"I live the way the other girls do," she retorted, still clinging to her thought of a grievance. "I'm not ninety, I'm nineteen. I've a right to a good time."

"Yes, as a diversion, not as an end to live for. I didn't know how much this fever had grown on you. It's hard for me to believe that you're my little Joyce, the healthy-souled girl who went fishing with me at Trappers Lake two years ago." He pulled himself up abruptly. "Will you promise me one thing—to do nothing secretly, to be open and aboveboard with me in any move you make?"

He did not know that she had to summon her pride to crush back an imperative impulse to fly round the desk and fling herself into his arms.

"Yes," she said, and to the word added the pledge of frank honest eyes.

"That's a bargain, Joyce."

She left him, her heart heavy with woe for him.

80

She knew she had hurt him cruelly. A hard icy lump in her bosom had driven her to it.

Joyce drove home, went to her room, threw herself on the bed, and broke down.

CHAPTER VIII

AN INVITATION DECLINED

WHEN he thought about it afterward Hallack was glad he had not yielded to the temptation to set forth his merits to Elliott. The railroad builder guessed at them or he would never have promoted him. He was glad, too, that he had not mumbled any embarrassed thanks. He was not being chosen for personal reasons, but because his work stood up and he was the best man for the place.

Of that last Hallack had no doubt whatever. His confidence was scarcely egotism. It was more impersonal, was born of technical skill, of energy, of knowledge of the job, of the enthusiasm he was giving to it. If any one could put the cut-off through he felt he was the man. He had ridden and tramped over every hill and hollow up in the deep-snow country the road must traverse. In the dead of winter he had shuffled across the pass on webs and spent weeks making observations as to watersheds, depth of drifts, and periods of precipitation. Talks with old-timers, small cattlemen in the mountain parks, who knew from shrewd observation and long experience the hiemal meteorology of the region, confirmed the conclusions he drew. Men in the Forest Service had given him valuable information. Under the direction of Jarvis Elliott and the inspiration of contact with him he was prepared to do the impossible.

Brain and nerves keyed to a high tension, he strode down the busy street, a god from Olympus. Not since the fingers of fate had reached out and crushed his faith and hope like an empty eggshell had the sense of power so flooded him.

At last his big chance had come. If he put it over, if he solved the problem of building a roadbed across the great divide in this country of high peaks, he would be hailed as a leader in his profession. For A. C. Truesdale, after a thorough investigation in behalf of the M. & P. a dozen years ago, had reported that no workable grade could be found down from Gateway Pass. Manders, too, had later turned in an adverse decision. And both of them were top-notchers.

But he had one tremendous advantage over them. He had roosted up there in the land of blizzards and avalanches when it was thirty below zero. From every angle he had approached the problem. As yet he had not solved it. But he understood the conditions, just as a careful mother does the constitution of her child.

The cut-off was such a big thing. It meant so much more than a personal triumph. Its success would put the city and the state in an impregnable traffic position. He had a strong sense of kinship with Jarvis Elliott. That rugged old pioneer was his ideal of a leader. He belonged to that fine class of industrial captains who work for the common good as well as for their own profit. There were many of these, he felt, though not as many as there should be, not as many as there were going to be now that the social consciousness of the country was better developed.

But Elliott was an especially good example of the type. He had that combination of imagination and daring essential to the breaker of new trails, the audacity that sent lines of shining rails tortuously into highlands where settlers had not ventured. He reversed the law of nature which decrees that railroads shall follow and not precede civilization, and in doing this he flung into the scales of chance the fortune built up by a lifetime of struggle. To Hallack's ardent fancy, grim grey Jarvis Elliott was a knight of the new régime, one who kept his glaive and armour always bright.

The engineer's footsteps had brought him fortuitously to a street of banks and office buildings. From the entrance of one of these a young woman stepped lightly. She was a long-lined brunette, luxuriously furred. The dress, the delicate disdainful poise, the perfection of detail, announced her one of those expensive orchids produced by our modern social system.

A new tan-coloured limousine and a liveried chauffeur were waiting at the curb. As the young woman sank into the soft cushioned seat the slant of her oval dusky eyes picked up Hallack. Instantly her gloved hand gestured to the chauffeur not to start the engine.

In the eye of Tessie Barnes sparked a gleam of expectant adventure. Her blood glowed. She had been a tremendously disturbing force in the life of Bob Hallack, and what was of much more importance he had been one in hers. There had been a time, to use her own phrase, when she had been crazy about him. This passionate emotion had worn itself out, as such thrilling episodes always did with her, but he could still set her pulse beats strumming. Months ago he had wrenched himself definitely out of her life. Now that luck had thrown him her way she did not mean to let him escape easily.

The dark liquid eyes that met those of Hallack were soft with a tender wistful appeal. They asked for mercy and not justice; at the same time offered paradoxically forgiveness because his less finely attuned soul had failed to understand her.

"It's been ages since I saw you, Bob, and I've wanted you *so* much," their owner murmured reproachfully.

All the life was frozen out of the engineer's set face. Inside of him a knife blade twisted in a wound not yet healed.

"What for?" he asked bitterly.

"I've needed you. And I wanted to explain—lots of things." The dark long-lashed eyes were misty with vague hectic messages.

His voice fell, to exclude the chauffeur, but it held the note of chill finality. "Quite unnecessary. Why take the trouble?"

"You never gave me a chance to tell you—how it happened." A faint wave of natural colour beat into the cheeks beneath the make-up. "I don't think you were very generous. Do you?"

"You wouldn't," he agreed.

She guessed he was holding himself tight-reined.

"Oh, I have wanted you, Bob." A voice of moving cadence was included among the weapons she had at command. "If you'll get in and ride with me a little way—out to one of the parks—where we can talk." She moved aside and drew in her skirt to make room for him.

"No," he said flintily.

"Yes, Bob." She made no least motion toward him, yet impalpably she seemed to stretch out hands that drew him to her. "Don't be horrid. I've got to—tell you."

He did not want to hear her apologia. The very presence of her—the quick and flashing beauty, the throbbing voice with its unexpected runs, the well-remembered expressions of the dark and vivid face—all stabbed him like dagger thrusts.

The boyish impulse was strong in him to run away and hide his hurts.

For she had meant so much to him in those dear dead days when he had moved in a haze of illusion created by his own imagination. He had wanted her, longed for her till he ached. Every fibre of his being had seemed to respond to the witchery of her charm. The memory of those hours still had power to lash his shrinking soul even though he now knew that the woman of his dreams was not and never had been Tessie Barnes.

All he asked of her was a chance to forget. He did not tell her so. His refusal was more blunt and crude.

"I don't care to hear it."

A quiver of the small bewitching mouth that he had kissed so often reproached his cruelty. "You're so hard, Bob. You never make allowances. I have to be what I am, don't I?"

In a flash of illumination he saw that this was true. Why should he blame her? Was it her fault that all the pretty ways, all the gift of expression that had been so enchanting, had no soul back of them to give enduring life? He looked at her clearly for the first time, all the lights of his mind turned on her, and saw her for what she was. The anger against her died down for lack of fuel to feed upon. If she had betrayed his love, it was only because faithlessness was an intrinsic part of her nature.

"You never understood me," she went on, and the full-throated voice throbbed with the pathos of the martyr. "I really truly loved you, Bob. But it wouldn't have done. You ought to see that. If you weren't selfish—"

She interrupted herself at his ironic smile, to say with a flash of irritation: "Well, aren't you—trying to hold me when you're poor as a church mouse and you know I have to have things?"

"I'm not trying to hold you."

"No, but you were. And you won't listen to what I have to tell you." Into her throat came a choke of emotion genuine even though not deep. "You believe—horrid things about me. You won't let me explain."

"There's nothing to explain—nothing that isn't quite clear to me."

"There is, too." Again a faint wave of colour stained the soft cheeks. "I want to tell you about—how Mr. Ordway—"

"I'd rather not listen." His face was grim as that of a hanging judge.

She dropped her eyes, and the subject. "Oh, Bob, you don't understand. Don't you see how it was about you and me? It was—dear. I *wanted* it to go on. And I didn't care whether you had money or not. But I couldn't marry you. I saw that when I quit being so crazy about you. I'm not made to be any poor man's squaw. Why, I can't even do my own hair. I have to be waited

88

on by a woman. Can't you see it wouldn't have done?"

"Yes, I see," he answered.

"Well, then, what's the use of being mad at me?"

"I'm not mad at you."

"Why do you act so hateful then—and spoil everything—setting yourself up on a—a stupid pedestal of ice—and judging me?" she cried.

"I can't help my judgment, Mrs. Barnes," he said stiffly.

"You can too." A film of angry tears made a haze of him to her. She knew she had failed, and the sense of it hurt her vanity. "It's just that you're such a prig. I suppose you couldn't possibly be wrong—or do wrong."

She waited for Hallack's apology. It did not come.

Swiftly she turned from him and gave the chauffeur the signal to start.

Hallack, bleak-eyed, watched her go. The exaltation with which he had walked the streets had gone out like a blown candle.

CHAPTER IX

THE HOUR AND THE MAN

A T six-thirty Smithers showed Hallack into the office of the president of the Mile High Investment Company.

Elliott closed his desk and rose.

"We'll walk," he said when they reached the entrance to the building.

With a deep breath he fell into his stride, the easy reaching gait of one who has been a natural athlete and is still endowed with great energy. It seemed to his guest that he looked absorbed and harassed.

Presently he referred indirectly to this himself. "It's been a hard day. Thought we never would get the difficulty with the miners adjusted. I don't understand it yet. There's something about it . . . A week ago everything was all right—the best of feeling. I know because I visited the mine and talked with the men. Then this came up out of a clear sky. Why? Graves may be overbearing, but—Pshaw! The whole thing was cooked up. Could Ordway be back of it?"

"It would be like him."

"Yes. Anything just now to embarrass me, to tie my hands. Through all the conferences I had the feeling that two of the men's representatives didn't want to come to an agreement. They kept throwing up objections. Only half an hour ago they gave way, when I threatened to go over their heads to the men themselves."

Elliott fell silent. The younger man did not disturb his reflections with talk. He had a capacity for letting conversational lacunas take care of themselves.

At the City Club Elliott arranged for a small table in a corner of the large dining room. When they were seated he began to talk, trenchantly, incisively, in a low voice that carried only to Hallack.

"I've been watching your work. You take hold with both hands. I think you'll do . . . I'm going to tell you what we're up against. Your end you know—fighting nature in the hills, finding and building grades where the best engineers say it can't be done. I'll be down here at grips with Ordway and the M. & P. crowd working out a way to finance the road and to hold my right of way after we've got it. I'll have to play politics and business against them all the time. It's like a game of chess with me on the defensive throughout. The least slip—the first false move— and I'm gone. Understand?"

"In a general way, yes."

From the hall outside came the sound of voices and laughter. A jovial group trooped into the room, Winthrop Ordway at their head. His smiling confidence, his debonair good-fellowship, the glow of his exuberant vitality and well-being, seemed to fill the place. To one and another of those dining he called friendly greetings.

Catching sight of Elliott, he moved toward him and flashed a gay white-toothed smile. "How are you, Mr. Elliott?"

"Well, thank you."

"Good. Saw by to-day's papers that you're having trouble at one of your mines. Hope it's nothing serious."

"No." The railroad builder's deep-set eyes held no answering warmth.

"Then you'll get it settled without a strike. Congratulate you. They're always annoying things."

Ordway rejoined the group he had left. He had given no sign whatever of recognizing Hallack.

Elliott went on, talking to his engineer, at the point where he had been interrupted. "The fight between them and me goes on not only here, but at Washington and New York. They attack my credit and my financial standing in Wall Street. Just now the fight at Washington is centering on Arapahoe Cañon. Strong interests are at work with the Department of the Interior to have it reserved for reservoir purposes. The claim is that it's an outlet for a natural storage basin needed for a reclamation project. The real purpose is of course to bar us from going through, to put a cork in the neck of the bottle so that we can't get out of the hills."

"Yes." Hallack raised a point. "Are you sure about Arapahoe Cañon, even if you win the legal fight? I've been working only up at the Pass, you know. Didn't Truesdale and Manders both say Arapahoe Cañon was impossible?"

Elliott smiled, enigmatically. "Neither of them is infallible. I had a partial survey made by Maclure on my own account."

"I didn't know that. Maclure was a good man. He said it could be done, did he?"

"I'll tell you what he said—some day. You'll not mention Maclure's name in this connection to any one?"

"No."

"I had him work under cover while he was doing some engineering on an irrigation project."

They had reached the demi-tasse when an attendant brought word to Elliott of a man named Smithers who wanted to see him on important business.

"Show him up."

Smithers came in with an air of nervousness. He was never quite sure of himself.

"There's been an explosion at the Invincible mine, sir," he said. "Word from Mr. Graves just reached me over the 'phone. I came at once."

"Anybody hurt?"

"He doesn't know. There's a shift imprisoned in the mine. Mr. Graves is clearing the way for rescue work."

"I'll talk with Graves. Have my car brought round at once. I'll take you with me, Smithers. You too, Hallack."

Elliott moved swiftly out of the room to a telephone booth.

Within ten minutes a chauffeur and the three passengers were racing for the suburbs of the city.

There was no conversation. Each of the men was busy with his own thoughts. An hour passed.

The road wound close to mine dumps and the small houses of workingmen.

"Coalville," Smithers told the engineer.

The chauffeur throttled down. Near the shaft house of the Invincible he stopped the car.

A man moved forward to meet Elliott. He was the assistant superintendent of the mine.

"How bad is it, Dawson?" the owner asked.

"Don't know, sir. Pretty bad, I'm afraid. There's been an explosion. A tunnel caved and trapped six men."

"Fire damp?"

Dawson shook his head. "Don't think so. The fans were going."

"Graves below?"

"Yes, sir. He went right down with a rescue party. A cross-cut is on fire."

Hallack's eyes picked up the drama of the scene—crying children clinging to the hands of excited women, the sullen suspicious glances of coal-blackened workmen focussed on the mine-owner, the shadows of the night pressing upon the arc-lit tragic circle of which the central and dominant figure was Jarvis Elliott.

Watching now that strong quiet face, so sure, so interwritten with the lines of leadership, Bob Hallack vowed fealty afresh. If Elliott read the threats of the passion-tossed countenances surrounding him, he gave no sign of disturbance. For no reason except that their minds had recently been inflamed against him, they held him responsible for what had taken place. He knew he was blameless. The accident—if it turned out to be one—had come to pass through no fault of his. All the safeguards recommended by the state mining inspector had been adopted by the Invincible management. Every hazard that could be eliminated had been removed.

The injustice of these grown children did not disturb their chief now. He was wholly concerned with the imperative of saving their comrades below.

"I'll go down myself and look the ground over, Dawson," he said decisively. The grizzled brows moved with short swift sweeps of the stabbing eyes. "I'll take you, Hallack—and you—and you."

The men indicated moved forward at once to the cage. They recognized by instinct the man of the hour.

The mine engineer moved a lever and the bucket dropped into darkness. A flash of light every few seconds showed that the cage was passing a station. At the fifth level it stopped.

This tunnel was the entrance to the tomb in which six miners two hours earlier had found living graves.

CHAPTER X

A DISENGAGEMENT IS ANNOUNCED

JOYCE felt better after her tears were spent. The storm had cleared the atmosphere. At any rate, she and her father had crossed swords and come to an understanding of a sort. They were at least honourable enemies in the matter of Ordway. He knew she did not intend to give him up.

She felt a very great tenderness and respect for her father. His sternness had been that of love. When she had brought defeat to him by the simple announcement that she would accept Ordway as soon as he offered himself Elliott had taken the blow like a thoroughbred. He had not stormed at her or raved or threatened. He had not wasted energy impotently. She liked that in him. It went without saying that this did not mean he was ready to surrender her to his foe. He would fight for her to the last ditch.

Ordway was giving a little dinner at the Rocky Mountain Club that evening and Joyce dressed for it with particular care. She had a feeling that she might be going out to battle and would need all the feminine weapons she could summon.

Louise and she were alone together for a minute in the dressing room at the Club.

"Heard anything about last night?" she asked, lightly.

"Oh, Esther Dare was at the Stantons' lifting her eyebrows and *wondering* where you and Winthrop Ordway went and *when* you got in, and wasn't it *romantic* of you to be so free and untrammelled. She'd start something if she could."

"Why does that girl hate me?" Joyce mused aloud.

Louise continued to dab deftly at her make-up as she answered. "That's easy. Because you're in and she's on the edges. Because you're genuine and she's not. Because you don't think much of her and haven't taken the trouble to hide it. She's green-eyed, old dear, and r-r-revenge is sweet." In a burst of confidence she deflected to the subject uppermost in her mind. "Say, Bubbles, I'm going to tie a can to Jimmie Stanton to-night."

"Poor Jimmie!"

"Poor nothing! Once it's over he'll be as glad as I'll be. Enough's enough." She wheeled round. "Do I look all right?"

Joyce made the proper answer and they went arm in arm to meet Ordway and the others.

The dinner went very well. Joyce was the gayest of the party, but her high spirits were a little forced. She thought she detected curious glances turned her way by two or three women at another table who had been at the Stantons' that afternoon. It might be only fancy that the manner of several older women was chilly when she spoke to them.

Under cover of a general burst of animated talk and laughter Ordway lowered his voice.

"Is it all right, Joy?"

"Ye-es. Right enough. Dad and I had a round-up."

"He heard you got in late, then?"

"Yes."

"Was he hard on you?"

"He wanted me to cut out a few things— including Winthrop Ordway."

"Interesting. Am I going to be cut out?"

"We'll see how you behave," she answered, smiling at him.

"I'm afraid if I behaved like an angel I wouldn't satisfy your father."

"No," she admitted judicially. "He's rather got a down on you. I daresay you deserve it."

"But if I could satisfy your father's daughter—"

"Yes, yes," she encouraged.

"Think I'll finish that sentence later in the evening, Joy."

"Oh, if it's as serious as that I don't think I want you to," she murmured with a flash of eyes that had stolen the glow of soft pansies.

After dinner the party adjourned to the home of one of the girls for an informal dance.

Here Louise Durand carried through her program as to Jimmie Stanton. After a fox-trot they disappeared into a small den off the library that by some lucky chance was not occupied by a petting couple.

Jimmie sat down on the couch beside the girl, caught her hand with a quick pressure, looked ardently into her eyes, and began his "line."

"You wonderful girl!"

Louise laughed, with perfect good-nature. She had heard it before. "Yes, I know. I'm different from all the others. So much *soul* in my eyes. And I remind you of that angel in what-d'ye-call-him's picture. Before you knew me you were just a wild careless boy with dark secrets in your past. But now—"

"What's the matter with you?" remonstrated Jimmie indignantly.

"Nothing, except that I've got a fierce hunger. Nell never does start the eats soon enough."

"Say, what's that stuff you're pulling to-night?" demanded the outraged Jimmie. "You kinda make me tired, if you wantta know, kid."

She flashed to dimples. "Jimmie, you're a wiz. We both make each other the teentiest wee bit tired. Isn't it lucky we've found it out?"

"Ditching me, are you?" he asked, vanity in arms.

"No, Jimmie dear, we're ditching each other."

"Who's the fellow?" asked young Mr. Stanton,

with the bitter laugh of the strong man disillusioned for life. Jimmie was going-on-twenty.

Louise removed a long golden hair from his sleeve. "I haven't picked him yet," she explained calmly and cheerfully. "Whom would you suggest? I want a nice live one, you know, so you won't be ashamed of him as your successor."

"Of course, if you're heartless—"

"Oh, don't be tragic, Jimmie," she breezed on. "You know well enough we've worn each other out. You'll have lots more fun with another girl. There's Margaret Van Loan, for instance, you always liked her and—"

"Thank you very much," interrupted Mr. Stanton with dignity. "I'm quite capable of choosing my own friends."

" 'S all right. I'm not buttin' in." Her smile coaxed him to good humour. "But, say, Jimmie, wouldn't it be a *good line* if we just quit, without quarrelling or anything—said nothing but nice things about each other? I'd like that. It'd be *scrumptious*—and anyhow I *do* want to stay friends with you."

She was sitting very close to him, playing with one of his coat buttons. Now she lifted a glance designed to melt the hardest heart.

He grinned, with no great zest. The situation was, however, piquant. He rather liked that line Louise had proposed. Jimmie was, technically speaking, a nice kid, and he knew very well that it was time he and Louise ended their little affair.

"What's the use of vamping me now?" he wanted to know. "Save that for the other fellow. And about knocking you, Wese. Well, you know I've moments when I like to think I'm a pretty decent chap."

"Oh, you are, Jimmie. The best *ever*," she burst out.

"If you'd like me to write you a letter of recommendation for my successor—"

"What could you say for me?" Louise asked, eyes bubbling with fun.

"Heaps. I could say you're a square little sport and the best pal ever a chap had. I could tell him he'd never be dull a minute with you and when you chucked him after you were through you'd make him like it."

"Now, Jimmie, that's no fair. I'm not chucking you. We're chucking each other. No, we're not doing that either, 'cause we're always going to be pals. But I'm *for* that letter, *strong*. Will you honest to goodness write it?"

"Surest thing you know." He hesitated, before adding with friendly malice: "You gotta give me my cue, Wese. How do we put over this good-bye-but-Heaven-bless-you stunt? Do we stage it before a select circle of admiring friends? With a referee to tell us when to break away from the farewell clinch? Or do I merely wear crape and look mournful?"

"There's a *vulgar* streak in you, Jimmie."

"Yes, thank you," he agreed.

"But all the samey you're a nice boy."

She rose and held out a hand.

Jimmie put both of his in his pockets. "Come off. You can't pull *that* on me. We haven't just been introduced at a pink tea."

"Oh, well!" The dimples flashed again. Louise turned up to him poinsettia-blossom lips.

He kissed them.

Both swung simultaneously to the threshold of the den. A man and a girl were coming in.

"Caught!" announced Ordway with a smile.

"Glad it's you, Bubbles," Louise sighed.

"Is this your way of announcing that you're reengaged to Jimmie?" asked Joyce.

"It's our way of announcing that we're *disengaged*. It's Jimmie's birthday, and he's putting away childish things," explained Louise.

"Including debs?" Ordway inquired.

"Including this deb," the girl replied with a curtsey. "Let's go, Jimmie. There's a fox-trot starting."

She caught him by the hand and they ran out of the room.

CHAPTER XI

JOYCE JUMPS

"EXIT the flapper," Ordway said, leading the way to the lounge.

He was riding the high wave, had been on the crest of it all evening. It showed in his colour, his animation, the confidence of his stride. To-night he could move mountains. He was ready to rewrite a certain Biblical prophecy to make it read, The strong shall inherit the earth.

Joyce did not care to sit down. She was restless and excited, her eyes brilliant, her pulses throbbing. Deflecting, she stopped at a small table, picked up a book incuriously to look at the title, and dropped it.

"What *is* a flapper?" she asked, not for information but to escape if possible an atmosphere that was becoming electric.

Ever since Winthrop Ordway had begun to monopolize her earlier in the evening she had been on a rising tide. Partly it was the reaction from the strain of the day, partly the fillip given her by his great physical vitality, and partly too the knowledge that he had brought her here to finish the sentence he had interrupted at dinner. It would not do to be carried from her feet.

"A flapper is an infant a thousand years old, a sweet and charming little devil without manners, modesty, or reverence," he told her.

"Thank you," she replied meekly, imps of mischief flinging up their heels in her eyes. "Tell me more nice things about myself—after you've given me a cigarette."

"No cigarettes now. I want to talk. You're no flapper—never were and never could be—but I'm ready to tell you about yourself. That's why we're here."

"Oh, is it?" Her laugh was less nonchalant than she could have wished. She wondered if he could see the pulse throbbing in her throat. "Thought maybe you brought me in to tell me about *your*self. Isn't that why men usually sit out dances?"

It was a fair hit, so far as Ordway was concerned. He was shot through with egoism. The discussion of his past, present, and future always interested him.

"Partly about myself too," he admitted, no whit disturbed. "I hope it's going to be the same thing, and that when I think about myself after this I'll be thinking about you too."

A slick-haired youth and a bob-haired maiden appeared in the offing of the library, showed visible disappointment at discovering this choice petting spot preëmpted, and vanished without a word.

"Better go slow, Win," Joyce suggested in a carefully careless voice. "You're on thin ice. Count twenty before you speak again. You never can tell what a woman will do, you know. That perfectly harmless remark of yours now—"

"I know what I hope she'll do," he answered gravely.

Their eyes met. She felt the lift of the crashing waves within her, the tumult of surging emotions. This was not in the least what she wanted, to be swept from the open seas of freedom to the harbour of matrimony. It had not at all been in her mind when she had yielded to the fascination of a desperate flirtation with him. Vanity had moved her, for he was one who bulked large; and the driving desire for excitement, increased by his reputation among women and his relation to her father; perhaps too the wish to win over a formidable adversary to the side of her father in the railroad fight impending. But she had been unable to control the mercurial currents that had galvanized her and lit fires in her she did not before know were a part of her nature.

In her other affairs with men and boys—and she had passed through her share of them—it had been a secret pride that she had remained mistress of the situation and herself. Now she was abashed at her helplessness to hold an even pulse.

Her eyes fell. The point of a small slipper

picked at the rug upon which they stood. Automatically she noted that it was a Sarouk.

His strong hands closed on hers.

She spoke, tremulously. "Wait, Win. I've got to think."

"Yes," he agreed, willing to prolong the pleasant suspense that scarcely reached doubt. "It's a surprise, of course."

"Not exactly." She laughed, trying to escape lightly to a plane of reason undisturbed by fluttering nerves. "You've been telegraphing it, you know."

"Have I? Oh, you women! What don't you know!" he said, laughing softly, triumphantly.

"I don't know what I'm going to answer you," she went on hurriedly, observing in him incipient signs that he was about to overwhelm her hesitation man-fashion. "Listen, Win. I want to talk—to tell you how I feel, well as I can."

"Fifty years to do that—after we've settled the important fact. Joy—Joy!"

"No—now. Let go my hands. We'll sit down."

They moved to the lounge. Joyce did not look at him but she was intensely aware of him. He was vitally masculine, a masterful man born for leadership. Six feet to a hair, straight and strong, he carried just enough bulk to temper his restless energy without impairing its power. The girl felt a vague but powerful tug drawing her toward him.

"Talk, my dear," he told her with smiling confidence. "Tell me what you want to say—then make me the happiest man alive."

"Would it make you that—if I said yes?"

"Don't you know that, Joyce?" His hands went out to her again.

She shook her head, both to the invitation and the question. "No. That's just it. I don't. When I get to thinking about it I find I don't know you at all—the *real* you. I don't know what you're like. You're big, of course. So's Dad. I can understand him because he's simple. But you're not. I'm never sure of what you think or feel."

"Do you want to be too sure?" he asked. "I'm willing to have you stay a mystery to me for a while. If you weren't that—if I knew all you were going to say and think and do—if you were quite obvious to me—no delightful little surprises and inconsistencies—I'm afraid I wouldn't be so keen for you."

"Ye-es," she admitted. "But that isn't quite it." She crossed her slim silk-clad ankles and looked down at them. "Of course I'd want my husband not to be an old story to me, but I'd want to be sure of him too—to know that we felt the same about some things."

"What things, dear girl?" He took a flier at answering his own question with another. "Books and plays and bridge and sports?"

"No. And it isn't just that I'd want him to agree

with me. He'd have to be right, even when I was wrong, about the things I mean."

Her air of perplexed earnestness amused him. He had not the slightest idea what she was talking about. It probably was of no importance, but he was willing to humour her fancy.

"I'll promise always to be right about those vexing problems, whatever they are," he said lightly.

Joyce did not accept the offered lead as an escape from her doubt. She wanted him to understand the difficulty, but she had a reluctance almost boyish about putting it into words. A code of honour was individual and personal, not to be talked over and dragged out for inspection. Yet it involved one's whole attitude and reaction toward life.

Winthrop Ordway's strength, his dynamic personality, the ease and certainty with which he became the dominating figure in every group, were aspects of the man that fascinated Joyce. Comparisons with her father were inevitable. Both had the controlled and intelligent energy that compelled success. But in the case of the younger what was the animating principle of that force?

The daughter of Jarvis Elliott recognized in him a hidden idealism that had by inheritance become her own. The brusquerie of his manner never deceived her, though secretly she stood in awe of his judgments. To her he was Chaucer's "verray parfit gentil knight."

But Ordway—What was the spur to his power? Was her father right when he called him a destructive force? Was his creed of success divorced from ethical and moral considerations? Someone had sent her recently a marked newspaper editorial that described him as a Goth and a Vandal, a modern buccaneer of business who destroyed more often than he built. The figures were mixed, but the meaning was plain. It might be true. In spite of his surface geniality he might at bottom be wholly selfish and unscrupulous.

"I'm still on the anxious seat, Bubbles," he reminded her.

Her little worried frown, fixed on him, still persisted. He was awfully likable when he pleased, she admitted. It was a subtle flattery to her that he always took the trouble to put his best foot forward in her company.

Then there was that queer something that at times drew her to him so strongly, that just now was welling up in her again. Was it love?

"I don't want to marry you. It would hurt Dad awf'ly, and I'm not going to do it if I can help it. Besides, I don't know you well enough. And I won't be rushed into it. Of course, I like you lots, or I wouldn't be thinking of it."

"You're going to like me more," he prophesied. "I improve on acquaintance."

"Oh, you're Winthrop Ordway." She flung a little smile at him, as though the mere statement covered a good deal of ground. "Not many women could help liking you—if you wanted them to care. I make your vanity a present of that. And there aren't any who wouldn't be flattered at being chosen by you. I'm all puffed up about it. You're a great man, you know."

"Not as great as I mean to be."

"No. That's a consideration too. Besides, you're such a magnificent specimen to parade as the captive of my bow and spear. I ought to jump at you. It's the chance of a lifetime."

His smile met hers. He knew she was not half as cool and calculating as she pretended. If she married him—or rather when she married him—it would not be because of any adventitious aid of wealth or fame. It would be because she found in him something strong and vital that called to her irresistibly. The soul in Joyce Elliott's flamelike personality was a fine and sensitive flower. He wanted her because she was the best. It was to be noted of him that he always got what he wanted.

He rose and looked down at her, flashing a message that set going again in her the clamorous beat of many tiny drums. She was ardent of nature, quick of response. In her was youth blest with superabundant vitality and health.

"Jump!" he urged, almost in a whisper, and his hands gripped hers tightly.

111

She rose, unconsenting eyes held fast. "No—no!" she cried softly.

He swept her unresistant into his arms. It was characteristic of Joyce that even while he held her close and kissed her lips and eyes and the little depression at the base of the bare throat she did not deceive herself with a lie. She wanted to be kissed by him. If she had not she would have found a way to sidestep the crisis she had seen coming.

With both hands Joyce pushed him from her. "You—barbarian!" she gasped, with a little laugh tremulously doubtful of itself.

Her glance swept him shyly, curiously. To Joyce this was an unusual experience. For though she was modern to the fingertips she held to individual reservations. Her fastidious sense found "petting" repugnant and she possessed dignity enough to protect herself. It was in its way something of an achievement that she had travelled at the pace of her set and generation, passed through the various phases of flapper and debutante, and yet had not allowed the slick-haired youth of her acquaintance to hold cheap the charm of her sweet and vigorous person.

A magazine writer had once described Ordway's eyes as fishy and very, very cold, like deep water just before it freezes. He would have used different phrasing if he could have seen them now. They were lit up, as though from inner fires, from the glow of a volcanic crater boiling to the rim.

"The man you are going to marry," he amended.

"Don't be too sure of that."

"I never quit, Bubbles. It's in my horoscope to win."

"You're boasting of it—already," she challenged.

He laughed, in a jubilant glow of satisfaction with himself and life. "No, I'm telling you."

"You always take what you want, I suppose? You never by any chance ask for it."

"In this world, dear girl, you never get by asking. You have to seize good things with both hands and hang on."

Her answer flashed at him. "I'll tell you this, Winthrop Ordway. You can't take me by the throat and carry me away. I'm no cave girl."

His desirous eyes absorbed her, so straight and slender, exquisite as a bit of choice porcelain, vivid in her momentary resentment as a crimson poppy. The filmy lingerie she wore and the little old-rose georgette he could have crushed into one hand. The up-to-date maiden of to-day has reverted to the scantiness of attire that characterized her cave dwelling ancestress, but Ordway could find nothing else in this little aristocrat to remind him of the childhood of the race. She was the product of ten thousand remote streams of influence that had poured both before and after birth into the channel of her being. In a sea of environment and heredity she was tugged at by innumerable cross currents of which she never dreamed. The sum of them made her what she was, that unknown quantity, the American girl.

Louise and Jimmie Stanton swept into the small room in a gale of animation.

"It's a camel walk, Bubbles. My dance, you know. Let's toddle," the boy cried.

"Ours too, Mr. Ordway," Louise shrieked, above the music. "If you didn't ask me, you *meant* to. Now didn't you?"

"Of course he did, Wese. I heard him mean to." Joyce turned to young Stanton, twitting him gaily. "Old remorse on the job, eh? You know this isn't ours. You shamefully deserted me. I've been sitting here a wallflower while you did the trot you promised me with a prettier girl. Oh, Jimmie, I didn't think it of you."

He snatched her hand, swept her into the dance step, and out of the room. The barbaric jazz took them through the library into the great open hall.

A middle-aged man in an overcoat with a turned-up collar was being admitted at the front door. Joyce heard her name. Her swift eye took in and recognized the man as her father's secretary Smithers. He looked pale and harassed.

The girl's arms dropped from her dancing partner and she ran to the door. "What is it, Mr. Smithers? Is Father—Does he want me?"

"He's been hurt, Miss Elliott—out at the Invincible mine. I came to get you. There's a car at the door."

All the lights jazzed before her eyes. She fought down the dizziness by sheer will power.

"Get my coat, Jimmie," she said in a low tense voice.

CHAPTER XII

THE FIRE FIGHTERS

WISPS of smoke, drawn by the suction of the shaft, drifted through the upper air strata in the tunnel. As they moved forward a wave of heat rolled out to the party Elliott was leading.

A man emerged from the darkness. He was naked from the waist up, blackened and grimy and sweat-stained.

"How goes it, Nick?" someone asked.

"We're gettin' closer. It's that damned stope burnin' above us that's gonna beat us."

"Do you know whether the men back of the cave-in are alive?" asked Elliott.

"Some of them, anyhow. We can hear them tapping."

"Then we'll get them out." The mine owner spoke quietly, confidently. He was taking off his coat and waistcoat. Already all of the party were perspiring from the heat.

Graves had divided his group of rescuers. Some of the men were working with picks and shovels at the mass of fallen rock and coal which filled the drift while others kept a stream of water playing on the fire above from the nozzle of a hose that had been dragged in.

The air was foul from steam and marsh-gas released by the explosion and the breaking of the coal. So hot were the walls of the drift that the hand could not touch them. Swirls of smoke swept down and drove the workmen back or forced them to crouch and breathe the purer air near the floor.

A man pushing away a tram-car of excavated rock stumbled and went down. Hallack dragged him back to the shaft and left him there to recover. When he reached the battle-ground again Elliott was organizing the rescuers into relays.

"Take your men out and send down fresh ones," he ordered Graves. "We'll take this turn and turn about. Let Dawson come down with the new gang."

The superintendent and his force staggered out from the tunnel. They were ready to drop with exhaustion on account of the fierce and grilling heat they had endured.

Elliott took charge of the water nozzle, Hallack of those working at the cave-in. They timbered as they went, wedging their sets against the rock walls and the roof.

It was a horrible nerve-torturing task. Smoke rolled at them and inflamed their eyes and throats. The terrific heat was scarcely endurable. It drove one and another of them back to get a breath of cooler air for a few seconds before they plunged anew into the inferno. Eyebrows crisped and lips cracked. The cloth of their trousers and shirts charred.

From the other side of the wall they were removing came the sound of picks. The imprisoned miners were working for their own freedom.

Steadily, hour after hour, the sappers stuck to the job. Every man there knew the danger. The fire above might cut them off from the shaft. It might release gases any moment that would produce a fearful explosion. There might be a second cave-in behind them. But the rescue work went on without a moment's relaxation. At intervals of thirty minutes the men relieved each other, dogged, grim, haggard. Their indomitable grey-haired leader held them to it as he held himself. It was almost more than human nature could endure. Every few minutes someone collapsed.

"How much farther?" asked Elliott hoarsely, speaking into Hallack's ear.

The engineer, with the skin peeling from his body, had borne the burden of the work at the face of the excavation. "Not far—a few feet now. Hope we get a hole picked in the sustaining wall without another cave-in," he answered.

"Let me know when you're ready to break through. I'll get the men back out of danger."

"Yes," agreed Hallack in the small parched voice that was left him.

A quarter of an hour later he gave the signal. Elliott ordered the rescuers out of the drift. He did not go himself, but stuck to the hose nozzle to keep back the roaring fire a few moments longer. The brass was so hot that he could not hold it in his hands without a cloth to protect the flesh.

Hallack swung the pick lightly and carefully as he dislodged a great lump of coal. From the first there had been rumblings of small slides in the tunnel, an irregular increasing trickle of dust and gravel from the burning stope. It was possible that the least disturbance would release a hundred tons of shale and slack upon them.

"Careful. Don't hurry. Better let me make the opening," the engineer called to the imprisoned men.

With his bare hands he scooped out rock and coal dust. A gleam of light showed through the wall. Someone within, unable to restrain his impatience, was tearing at the barrier with the edge of a shovel.

"Let be," Hallack ordered. "You'll bring the whole thing down on us."

A small slide filled the opening. Again Hallack patiently removed the rubbish. This time a large flat piece of slate had wedged itself above and held the rubble from sliding.

The air of the cave in which the miners had

been caught was cool compared with that out-side. The hot furnace blasts had been shut off from the trapped men by the mass of waste that held them prisoners. Bob Hallack, clawing at the enlarging hole, knew that he was close to the limit of endurance. He knew too that the grizzled old fighter at the hose nozzle, standing up to his job while the leaping flames shrivelled him, held on only by sheer nerve.

A man crawled through the gap.

"Any of you hurt?" Elliott's dry throaty voice croaked.

"No."

Five others followed the first.

A small avalanche poured into the drift and half-filled the passageway between them and the shaft.

"Hurry! Hurry!" urged Elliott, the hose still in his hands. The deep-set eyes were red and swollen, his shirt in crisp and blackened shreds.

The men crept over the new-fallen mass of debris.

The mine owner dropped the useless hose. With a gesture he ordered the engineer to precede him. Hallack obeyed.

Another roar of falling refuse, a thick cloud of dust, filled the chamber.

Hallack turned. His chief lay pinned beneath the attle. The engineer called to the men. Two of them came running back. One snatched up a crowbar and with the end of it pried away a large rock jammed against Elliott's thigh. At the same time Hallack dragged out the body.

The engineer picked up the unconscious man and half carried, half dragged him to the shaft. Here he collapsed.

When the cage reached the surface two of its occupants had to be lifted out. In the fresh air Hallack came to almost at once.

He tried to speak. From his parched throat the words came after two or three efforts in a whisper. Graves had to bend down to catch them.

"Better build a bulkhead in the drift and starve the fire," he suggested.

"I'll do that," the superintendent promised.

CHAPTER XIII

AN INFANT CRYING
IN THE NIGHT

THE bright lights of the car bisected the night as it roared into the darkness. Joyce sat between Jimmie Stanton and Smithers. She asked questions that crowded to her brain.

How badly was her father hurt? Where had they taken him? How had it happened? Was Smithers sure Doctor Albert and Doctor Van de Vanter had started? Had a local doctor been called at once? What had he said? Was her father conscious? Had he asked for her?

Satisfied that aid was being rushed to him as fast as possible words died from the lips of Jarvis Elliott's daughter. She was intensely, dreadfully anxious. Apprehension had stricken the vivid life from her. To Jimmie she seemed to shrink into herself, a pathetic and childish little figure of woe. Wrapped in furs, with only the profile of the white harrowed face showing, she looked small and forlorn.

His hand went out, found hers, and gripped it. She smiled, wanly, and let her fingers lie in his. If it helped Jimmie to think that his sympathy comforted her, she would not withdraw from him.

The boy's friendliness could not lift her fears, but it melted the hard lump in her throat. Presently her face began to work. She cried, softly, noiselessly as she could. What Jimmie did not know about women would fill a library shelf, but some instinct told him that his friend would find relief in tears. He let the overflow of distress spend itself.

The car swept into the country through the suburbs of the city. It passed into a section of irrigated vegetable truck farms and out of this to one of larger ranches. Fields of oats, wheat, and alfalfa bordered the road. Shadowy cattle grazed inside of barb-wire fences. Out of the darkness twinkled lights of farmhouses, suggesting peace and cozy warmth within. The stars showed, an innumerable array of them. Across the heavens a broad milky ribbon slashed.

Through villages the car plunged. It gathered speed whenever it struck again the open road. An easy grade was leading to the edge of the plains where the foothills were rooted.

Joyce was feverishly impatient. Would this journey never end? Her mind was filled with her father and his condition to the exclusion of all the interests that had seemed so important until half an hour ago. From her soul welled up a cry of despair. She loved him so—and she had been such a selfish daughter, so negligent of his wishes, so indifferent to his anxieties about her.

Only a few hours before she had deliberately struck at his heart because he had wounded her pride and self-love. Motherless from childhood, she had gone her own willful way even when she knew it worried him. The gentle lady whom her father had selected as her duenna had not the firmness, even in the days of her bobbed-haired and slim-legged early teens, to resist her imperious will.

Joyce wished now, as all of us have done when death has struck at someone dearly loved, that she could live over again the years and show her father how she cared for him. She prayed, with a child's self-centred directness, for another chance; flung the appeal up from a tortured heart, and offered terms to the Almighty if He would grant her supplication.

"O God don't let him die . . . don't let him die. I'll be good. I'll show him how I love him. And if You give him back to me I'll not go on as I have. I'll be different. O, I can't lose him . . . I can't . . . He's all I've got. I can't live without Dad. If You'll give him back to me, if You'll grant my prayer just this once . . ."

She stared up into the millions of miles of space in which the earth whirls, a frightened tremulous child just awakened to her helplessness. She could only repeat her heart-wrung formula over and over again to that half-malign, half-beneficent force her imagination conceived as

God. No infant's cry could have been more naïve. She wanted, with passionate earnestness, to placate any resentment He might feel toward that sinner Joyce Elliott and to win the boon she craved.

For the second time that night the chauffeur slackened speed as he passed down the main street of the coal camp. He drew up at a frame bungalow which had a lawn in front and what in the moonlight seemed to be a rose garden in the rear.

A woman came down the porch steps to meet Joyce, a buxom matron with a kind and winning face.

"I'm Mrs. Graves," she explained.

"My father!" Joyce cried.

"The doctors have finished setting his leg. It was broken and crushed. We don't know yet, my dear—"

"Take me to him, please."

A man was sitting on the top step. He rose to make way for Joyce. Absorbed though the girl was in her father, filled with dread of what the next few moments might reveal to her, the automatic action of her mind registered recognition. This haggard sunken-eyed man, in whose peeled and swollen face she read a story of agony endured, was the one who had brought her down in his machine from Box Elder Cañon this morning so long, long ago.

She passed into the house and into the room

where her father lay. He was coming out from under the anesthetic painfully, the reaction of what he had endured expressing itself subconsciously in moans and sighs. The battle underground, the operation, the hurts he had suffered, had written on the indomitable face ten years of age. All her life he had stood to her for Greatheart puissant and invincible. To see him now, stricken and broken and helpless, was a thing to clutch the heart.

From Joyce's throat there came a little wailing sob. She moved forward, dropped on her knees beside the bed, and with an ineffably tender caress encircled the maimed body, her arm above the coverlet.

A hand touched her shoulder. Joyce looked up. She had known there were others in the room but she had not seen them. Straight as a plummet her whole being had concentrated on the one she loved.

At her side was Doctor Van de Vanter, a surgeon known all over the state. "Careful, young woman," he said, and his smile was warm.

"Is he . . . will he . . . ?"

Van de Vanter was a broad-shouldered raw-boned man with the uncultured face of one who has risen from the ranks. One might have guessed him a contractor if it had not been for the long delicate fingers that did wonders daily in the operating room.

"His leg is broken in two places and his nervous system has been greatly shocked. There may be internal injuries. We don't know yet." The words were not reassuring, but in the rugged face was something that comforted. It was that look of abiding strength which comes to doctors who make their profession mean to them what it should.

"You won't let him . . . will you?" she pleaded.

He understood the hiatus. There are thoughts one dare not put into words.

"We're going to do our best—Doctor Albert and I and the nurse and you. Don't despair, my dear. Your father's a fighter. I would judge he has a strong constitution."

"What can I do?" the wan, big-eyed girl begged.

"Just this. You can be cheerful and happy when you're near him. If you're going to have nerves I can't let you stay here."

"Oh, I'm not. I won't," she promised. "I'll do whatever you say. Please let me stay. I've got to be with Dad."

"That'll depend on you."

The spirit of Jarvis Elliott came back into the world, smiled on his daughter faintly, and wandered into space again. As she listened to his delirious snatches, Joyce's mind went back to a hundred memories that revealed the strength, the tenderness, the poise that flowed deep and strong in him like the current of an unhurried river. He was a great man—the only really great one she had known intimately—and he was simple as a child. There had been in his love for her a quality of understanding that was fine and noble. He had trusted her, even while he guarded and watched over her.

Why had she been so intractable and self-willed? Why had she been so perversely eager for pleasure and excitement? In the bottom of her heart she had always wanted to know him better, to be the kind of daughter who is a comfort and an aid. But he had been so strong, so absorbed in big things. The sand stings of life did not disturb him. He did not have to be protected from them. There was so little she could do for him. So she had made her own interests, gone her own way; and a barrier had grown between them over which their love had not been able to leap without frustration.

She blamed herself for it, as the generous soul always does. For back of that impasse which always stands between youth and age she had warmly felt her father's brooding tenderness. To the limited perspective of her short life this was immutable and eternal, just as was the granitic fineness of his rugged character. What she did not realize—what indeed the new generation often fails to fathom—was that her own emotion and deep feeling, repressed and often belied by the selfishness of her ego, jumped the chasm of years and "got across" to him whose blood flowed in her veins. Her soul ached for a chance to show him her devotion. If he could only understand once—once before the waters of the deep river closed over him—how much she cared, how wholly she admired—

And he had always known it.

It touched her nearly now that his snatches of delirious talk referred so largely to her. His wandering mind had cast back to the days of her childhood, to the years that followed the death of her mother. She could read in what he said his pride in her pluck, her tart tongue, the essential honesty of her.

Why was it, then, she wondered, with that strong tug of love and kinship always drawing them, that they had drifted into habits of life so totally at variance? There had been weeks when they scarcely had seen each other, when she had known only vaguely where he was. It had been a joke once between her and Louise that she had thought her father up in the hills and he was in New York on financial business. She had discovered this when the local papers mentioned his name as a guest at the Commodore Hotel.

A queer thing, life, she reflected, and never guessed that a million other perplexed souls had been over the same ground many times. It took hold of you, and warped you, and deflected you, and tossed you about like a chip on a swollen current. All the time you thought yourself—how was it Henley put it?—Captain of your Soul?—until Fate malignantly put its foot on your plans and crushed them like an empty eggshell. She had been used to having her own way. A part of the pride of her youth had been in the knowledge that she *could* get what she wanted if she played her hand astutely and willfully, or with the gay charm of sex in case that line was indicated. What could a woman not do, given good looks and buoyant health and the proper background? It was this sense of growing power that had made life so intriguing.

And there before her on the bed lay the answer Fate had given—her father broken and crushed, struck down at the height of his activities. Her strength had become weakness. She was an infant crying in the night.

CHAPTER XIV

STORM-TOSSED

ALL through the night the note of young despair persisted. Joyce's sublime confidence in her power to get what she wanted was rudely shattered. She knew very little of sickness. To her inexperienced eyes the change in her father was appalling. The shadow of death was creeping over him, she believed. It might be a few hours, a few days, but . . .

When the first grey streaks of dawn were lightening the sky Doctor Van de Vanter came into the room, talked in a low voice with the nurse, and examined the patient. He gave directions about treatment after consulting with his colleague.

Joyce followed them out and closed the door. "What do you think?" she asked, imploring eyes clinging to the surgeon's as though in them lay life and death.

Van de Vanter said it was too soon to know anything decisively, that the expected reactions were taking place. "One patient at a time is enough. Mrs. Graves is making you some breakfast, Miss Elliott. You're to eat it. Then you're to lie down and sleep for a few hours."

"Oh, I couldn't sleep," she protested.

"Doctor's orders, young woman," he told her with assumed gruffness.

"Will you wake me if . . . ?"

"If there's any change, yes. But we don't expect any at present."

The breakfast that Mrs. Graves had prepared was a tempting one. The superintendent's wife sat opposite her guest and talked while Joyce ate. Hers was a cheerful and sympathetic soul. The flow of talk she kept up was more nourishing than the food, and that the girl found unexpectedly appetizing.

"The men have been coming here all night to find out how your father is. You know there was some trouble—outsiders came in and stirred the men up. Well, it had just been fixed up, but the word hadn't reached all the miners. Mr. Graves thinks one of them, an ignorant foreigner likely, must have set off a big charge of dynamite and started the fire and the cave-in. Anyway, they were angry at Mr. Elliott, the men were, some of them at least. But that's all gone. You should hear them talk of him, my dear, because he went down into the mine and risked his life to save them. He was the last man to leave the tunnel—wouldn't go till all of them were out. That's how he got hurt, at the very last. You've a grand man for a father."

"Oh, don't I know it?" Joyce cried, and bit her lower lip to keep back a breakdown.

"I said to my Jim an hour ago that Mr. Elliott was going to get well. He's a big strong man—and what's a broken leg and some body bruises. I don't believe he has any internal injuries at all. The men all say, 'Tell the docs not to let him die,' and I tell 'em he's not that kind of a man. We need him, all of us, and, please God, he'll be with us many a year yet."

"You really think so, Mrs. Graves?" begged the girl, the eager longing of her soul pouring through the soft wistful eyes.

"I do that. I've seen many a poor fellow hurt in my time. You will if you live around the mines, you know. Your father has a good strong pulse. His heart'll stand up and carry him through . . . You look like a rag, with that tired white face of yours. So I'll just tuck you up in bed and you'll have a nice little sleep. It'll do you a world of good."

Joyce wanted to lie down in her clothes, but her hostess would not have it. She found the girl a nightgown and made her undress, after which she arranged windows and blinds, patted the soft white cheek, gave it a motherly kiss, and vanished from the room.

Though sure that she would not sleep, Joyce was lost to the world within a few minutes. Completely exhausted, she fell into the sound deep recuperative sleep of youth.

When she awoke the wrist watch on the table

beside the bed told her it was past noon. She dressed. Mrs. Graves must have heard her moving about the room, for presently she tapped at the door.

Joyce was doing up her hair. She turned in the chair swiftly. "How's Dad?"

"He's asleep, and that's the best thing for him. The doctor doesn't want him disturbed. Soon as he wakes the nurse'll let you know."

"The doctors don't think he's worse, do they?"

"I'm sure they don't," the older woman assured her cheerfully. "Doctor Van de Vanter has gone to the city—an operation at one of the hospitals there. He wouldn't have left your father if he had thought there was any immediate danger. There have been a lot of 'phone calls for you. I took the numbers. And here are two telegrams. And there's a gentleman waiting to see you. He said not to wake you—as if I'd a-done that anyway."

Joyce ripped open the yellow envelopes. They contained inquiries from friends about her father. "Did he mention his name?" she asked.

"The man waiting? Yes. Mr. Ordway."

The girl finished doing up her hair. Her hostess chatted volubly, so that it was only necessary to murmur an occasional "Yes" or "No." Joyce did not want to see Ordway yet. She had given him scarcely a thought since the news of the accident to her father had come. The reactions of her mind now were born rather of instinct than of ordered

134

reason, but it was quite clear to her that she did not intend to divide herself at present. Nobody had any claims on her but the man lying on the bed in the next room. She was not going to spend any time or any emotion upon anybody else. The matter of her relation to Winthrop Ordway would have to wait.

She considered sending him a note asking him to go away for the present. Her father regarded him almost as a personal enemy. It had been through him that she had wounded the man now lying mangled and broken in the next room. She felt that it would be akin to disloyalty to see him.

But Ordway had not been to blame. He was the same man with whom she had passed through an emotional scene only a few hours since. Of course she must see him. It would be both weak and unkind to refuse.

She respected, however, an obscure feeling that led her to meet him outside rather than under the roof where her father lay. From the porch Joyce saw him forty or fifty yards down the road. He was amusing himself by tossing nickels to a scrambling group of miners' children.

Ordway caught sight of her, flung up a hand-greeting easily and negligently, and strode swiftly toward her. She watched him coming, a man strong and dominant, born for conquest. It was written in his salient chin, in his confident stride, that he was of those who claim and take the spoils of the victor.

For the first time in her life she resented this certainty. Wasn't he a little too well-groomed, too successful, too overflushed with health and well-being? The careless, almost arrogant, gesture of his personality—the intimation that he rode of right life's topmost wave—had been her own until a few hours ago. What right had he to be so smug and so complacent while her father lay in the valley of the shadow?

This was not fair to him. She knew that. It was not his fault that Jarvis Elliott had been hurt. He had come at once to offer his services to help her. Why should she blame him?

It was perhaps in recoil from her instinctive criticism that she let him bury both her hands in his while his eyes fastened on her.

"You poor child! You've been worrying yourself sick," he accused.

There was a quiver at the corners of her mouth. "It's been—rather awful," she confessed.

"How is he?"

"He's—asleep," Joyce gulped. She dodged facing the facts of her father's condition in spoken words, for this brought a lump into her throat and a break into her voice.

"That's fine." He took up another phase of the subject almost irritably. "He shouldn't have gone down into the mine. They ought not to have let him. There are plenty of men to do that sort of thing. It was the superintendent's job."

"Was it? Father must have thought it was his too." She spoke quietly, but there was a flash in her eyes. She resented what he had said, none the less because there was a measure of truth in it. This quixotic capacity for self-forgetfulness was precisely the quality in her father's strength that made it winning. In a flash it came to her that Ordway had none of it. All he could find in its expression was foolish waste. "Mr. Graves told his wife that nobody but Father could have held the men at the rescue work."

"Even so, he had no business there. His life is worth more than that of a hundred labourers . . . Let's take a little walk. You need it."

"I want to be here when Dad awakes."

"Of course. We'll not go far—up that hill, say. It's your duty to him to keep in trim, you know."

"Ye-es." She hesitated. "I'll run in and see what the doctor says. I'd only go a very little way anyhow."

Doctor Albert told her that her father was resting comfortably. No unfavourable symptoms had developed. The signs were distinctly hopeful. Probably the patient would sleep for some time. He urged her by all means to take a walk.

Joyce rejoined Ordway.

They passed down the narrow crooked little

road flanked by small frame cottages. It was a squalid enough place in spite of the attempts Jarvis Elliott had made to render it habitable. There were a community hall and a clubhouse for the men on a hill at the bend of the street. Joyce pointed them out to her companion.

"That's the right idea," he agreed. "Keeps 'em more contented. Cheaper than strikes."

"That's not why Dad does it," she answered with a flash of indignation.

"No? Why does he do it?"

"Because it makes them happier. A coal camp is a horrible place at best. Those who live and work here are entitled to some pleasure after the risks they take."

"It's good business, no matter why he does it."

A man passed them on the road, a lean clean-built fellow of the outdoor engineer type. Joyce recognized him at once, though the tanned face was peeled and swollen from the effects of the fire fight underground. He and Ordway passed without sign of recognition.

"Who is he?" Joyce asked.

"Name's Hallack. An engineer. Expect he works for your father."

She remembered having seen him at her father's office. "I believe he does." She added, after a moment: "Why does he hate you?"

He shrugged broad well-packed shoulders. "Why do fifty men hate me?" he asked indifferently. "I suppose I pushed him out of my way some time."

Joyce repressed an impulse of curiosity to drive home an inquiry for more definite information. The engineer interested her.

"Perhaps he's connected with the mine," she suggested. "That's probably it. You noticed his face? How it's burnt from the fire?"

"Yes." Ordway knew of more interesting topics of conversation and he steered for one of them. "Have you thought about what I said last night, Bubbles?"

"No." Her eyes carried swift attack. "And I'm not going to as long as Dad's so ill."

He smiled, not at all disturbed by the sharpness of her answer. "Then I've a double reason to pull for him to get well in a hurry."

The girl's resentment disappeared in a whirl of anxiety. "Oh, Win, do you think he will?"

"Of course he will," he said with a reassuring pressure of his fingers upon the muscles of her forearm just above the wrist. "And meantime perhaps there's something I can do for him—business that I can carry on for him—about the cut-off, say—or anything else. I want you to feel that I'm entirely at his service."

She shook her head. "I don't think there is. Thanks, just the same. He talked about Arapahoe Cañon two or three times last night. It seemed to be on his mind."

Joyce did not see the quick leap of his eyes at her when she mentioned the cañon.

"Well, if there's anything I can do you'll let me know."

"Yes," she told him. Then, with a sigh, added: "I'd be the happiest girl alive if he'd hurry up and get well. Oh, I do hope—I do think he will. Don't you?"

Again he told her he had no doubt of it, and from his assurance she gathered hope.

CHAPTER XV

THE PHILOSOPHY OF "IF"

HALLACK consulted with Brokaw, the lawyer who represented the Gateway Pass Cut-off. They decided there was nothing to do but go ahead with the work in spite of the condition of their chief. Both of them felt hampered on account of lack of definite knowledge of his plans.

"Elliott has a way of playing his own hand," Brokaw said. "Even when he trusts a man he does not tell him more than necessary. It's annoying at times. For instance, take the Arapahoe Cañon business. I went to Washington and saw the Secretary of the Interior personally, after filing all our papers in the case. When I came home Elliott heard my report, made a comment or two, and passed the matter as though it were of slight importance. I had a feeling that he was holding in reserve something about which I was not informed."

The engineer nodded agreement. He too had met this some reticence in Elliott, and, oddly enough, when he had asked a question about Arapahoe Cañon. What was this mystery connected with the cañon? Hallack would have

141

given a good deal to see Maclure's report on it.

He went to Smithers, who rather reluctantly overhauled the chief's desk to see if the report was there. It was not.

"It's probably in his private safe-deposit box. I haven't access to that," the secretary explained.

Before Hallack returned to the hills he met Brokaw again.

"We'll play it out because we can't let go now," the lawyer said. "But if Elliott dies the cut-off is doomed. It doesn't matter a jackstraw whether you work out a feasible grade. Ordway and those back of him will see that the bonds don't move. Without Elliott's genius for finance and his tremendous energy the project is lost. I'll be frank. He never convinced me that it could be put through, but I was willing to take a gambler's chance because I knew him and because the road would be such a big thing for the city and state."

Hallack carried into the hills with him a sense of increased responsibility. Brokaw might be and probably was a good lawyer, but he would never do to lead an enterprise like this. The illness of Elliott was a heavy blow. He had told the engineer that a single false move on the chessboard at which he and the M. & P. made their moves might prove fatal. How would it be possible to avoid mistakes while the directing head lay delirious? Ordway would not chivalrously hold his hand until the recovery of his opponent. Big business campaigns of rival corporations against each other are war. They are fought out ruthlessly. If the situation had been reversed Elliott would have taken instant advantage of it.

The work of Hallack hitherto had been up near the divide, in the country of deep snows, among the steep and narrow gorges that cut like titanic swordclefts into the backbone of the continent. But now his mind focussed on Arapahoe Cañon. He decided to have a survey of it made at once.

He sent for his first assistant, vice Randall resigned, an engineer named Thomas Hill with whom he had been at college. Hill had just returned from the Andes where he had been building a short spur of a railroad to tap a newly discovered ore field.

"I'm putting McSweeney on the work near the summit," Hallack explained. "I want your help down at Arapahoe. You know what Truesdale and Manders said about it. If they're right—if there's no workable grade through the gorge for us—well, we can't know it too soon. Take a party down there and get the preliminary work done. I'll join you Monday and we'll satisfy ourselves once for all."

Hill was a big ruddy man with a voice that came out of his chest like the booming of a bass drum. "Aye, aye, Captain," he said, saluting.

Twenty-four hours later Hallack, far up in the Rockies, was poring over some blue-prints in his tent by the light of a lantern when Hill lifted the flap and stepped in.

Hallack's surprise showed in the first questioning look. His assistant should have been sixty miles away.

"Too late," Hill told him. "Ordway has a gang at both ends of the cañon and I couldn't get in. He's got it corked tight."

"You mean they wouldn't let you in?"

"Just that. The man in charge was very sorry and all that, but they were doing blasting for a power site and it wouldn't be safe. He had orders not to let anybody in."

"He has. We'll see about that." Hallack's jaw muscles tightened. "Were the men armed?"

"I didn't see any arms, but they've got guns. You may depend on that. They're a nice bunch of plug-uglies."

"Gunmen, of course," Hallack commented.

"I told the fellow he had no right to stop me, that the Department of the Interior hasn't given a decision against us. He said again he was obeying orders, but he wouldn't tell me whose."

"We know whose. I'll show Ordway he can't pull his strong-arm methods on me and get away with it. That irrigation reservoir and power site application is a camouflage. It's a move to stop us, but it won't work. If Arapahoe offers a satisfactory grade we're going through."

"I don't quite see how we're going to find out

144

whether it does or not, Bob, unless we dynamite one of Ordway's camps out. You don't want to go that far, do you?"

"We'll cross that bridge when we come to it." Hallack unrolled a map and pinned down the corners with bits of quartz. A pencil-point in his fingers traced the course of a stream shown on it. "This is a copy of Manders's map of the cañon survey. The difficulty is at this point where the gulch swings to the left with a sharp drop."

"Yes." Hill nodded understanding.

Hallack looked up, his narrowed eyes hard and shining. "I picked you because you're a fighter, Tom. I can get plenty of fellows who know their business as well as you do, but when I heard you could be got I jumped at you because of your football record. You never would quit."

"Oh, well, you were some sticker yourself, my captain," boomed Hill. "Wherefore the flowers?"

"I don't care anything about the mouth of the cañon. Here's the storm centre." The pencil-point rested on the blue-print at the bend of the stream. "If you and I can get down there for forty-eight hours we'll know whether we can put a line through or not."

"I'm told there are no side gulches leading in. How do we get down?"

"From above. At night."

"Down a fifteen-hundred-foot rock wall?"

"Exactly that."

The audacity of the adventure gripped Hill's imagination. It was certain that no living man had ever gone down either of those sheer walls, and Bob was proposing to do it in the darkness. He gave a deep bass boyish whoop.

"When do we pull off this Matterhorn stunt?"

"There's plenty of moonlight now. We'll have to haul supplies there. How would Monday night suit you?"

"I always had a fancy for breaking my neck on a Monday night. Lead me to this yawning chasm."

"I don't say we can get down," warned Hallack. "But we can try. I'll scout around the top and look the situation over. It stands to reason there must be a way down."

"There's a way down," admitted Hill, grinning.

"A safe way, then, since you're so particular."

"You're right I'm particular. Except three others I'm the only boy my mother has." Tom's eyes were sparkling. He was pleasantly exalted with the adventure of life. Quite without envy, he knew that he would never have thought of acquiring technical information in this mad way. Bob Hallack had imagination, and with it the quality that had made him so superb a leader on the football field, an instinct for the weak points of the opponents' line against which to hurl the attack.

"I'll saddle at once and start to-night," Hallack

announced. "Load up the flivver with rope, tackle, and provisions to-morrow evening and drive at night. Better bring your revolver. I'm taking mine. Don't let any one know where you're going. Ordway probably has a spy among us. You'll need a couple of men. Think I'd bring Anderson and Chapin."

"It's a long ride on horseback," Hill suggested.

"Yes, but safer. If they heard a car they might start looking for it. I'll reach the cañon by morning or soon after."

"Well, if you find that safe way down—and if we reach the bottom all right—and if Ordway's plug-uglies don't pot us while we're down there—and if we get back to the rim with whole skins—here's hoping Arapahoe Cañon appreciates all the trouble we're taking to pay it a visit and reciprocates by giving us the grade we want."

"The way you put it there's a good deal of *if* in the proposition, Tom," his friend said, smiling. He too was warming up to the adventure.

"It's a great little word. If a girl hadn't chucked me in the Eocene period and blasted my young existence I'd probably still be wrapping up candy in a drug store," Tom affirmed cheerfully. "It's the *ifs* that give life zip. When there aren't any left a fellow fossilizes."

"I'll guarantee you won't do that as long as we're working on the Gateway Pass proposition."

"Not a chance," agreed the big man promptly.

They arranged details, after which Hallack saddled and rode into the night. Not four men in the camp knew he had gone.

It was a star-splashed night. The mountains rose black and sheer to the sky, a jagged saw-toothed line without perspective. For hours he rode steadily, sometimes with the faint soughing of the pines murmuring in his ears, now far down in draws and gulches, again among the tops of the high hills.

The early morning light began to sift into the skies. He looked down into smoke-coloured lakes of mist that filled the hollows. He saw the sun come up out of a saddle in the ridge. The peaks took on the definite detail that comes when light floods them. It was midday before he reached the cañon.

A mile or more back from the rim he unsaddled and picketed his horse. On foot he undertook a reconnaissance. As he drew nearer he used the cover of a grove of pines. He did not regard this preliminary survey as at all dangerous, but he did not want to apprise the Ordway forces of his presence and make them more alert. The chances were that the leader of the parties which held the mouths of the gorge was paying no attention to the high line fifteen hundred feet above. He was not expecting madmen to drop down from the skies to the river bed. In that narrow winding ravine it was not possible for an airplane to find room to operate.

All day he crouched close to the rim of the great earth fissure, studying the contour of the walls as he moved slowly back and forth. The sheer descent was appalling. A pebble dropped from the hand would first strike six or seven hundred feet below.

The character of the chasm drove him closer to the upper entrance of the crevasse. Here the distance down was not so great and there was some slope to the walls. For hours he lay on a flat rock, examining the terrain through high-power field glasses. Without making the attempt it was impossible to be sure, but he found a place that seemed to offer a chance of a descent. Far below was a fault in the strata that formed a ledge angling down toward the river. How far the ledge went, what was below it, he could not see from where he lay. Tom and he would have to take a chance that the surface of the rocks nearer the bottom of the gorge was broken enough for foot and hand holds.

Voices drifted to him occasionally from far below. Once there were sounds of shots. He could see three men practising at a target. Smoke from an unseen camp fire, thin and wispy, floated up. He even sniffed, or imagined that he did, the faint odour of the resinous pitch pine.

The sun was again sliding into a crotch of

the range when he rose and walked back to the draw where he had left his horse. The western sky became a glory of crimson and gold, the hill crotch a cauldron of melted jewels, opal and topaz and amethyst and ruby. With the coming of dusk the more vivid tints faded. Below the upper reaches of the snow-ribbed mountains a violet haze blurred the sharp outline, and as the stars came out this deepened to purple and at last to a soft blue-black.

If he had been a tenderfoot Hallack would have found the camp in the draw a lonely spot, even beside his roaring fire. The wind in the pines made mournful soughing sounds. Once a mountain lion screamed and sent an involuntary shiver down his spine. But he was used to camping alone in the hills. Almost as soon as his head had found a comfortable spot on the saddle he was asleep.

When he wakened gulfs of blue stretched above in which floated islands of white clouds—shifting islands that changed shape as he watched them, growing tenuous and drifting into each other and parting again as though unseen hands pulled at them.

He dressed and prepared breakfast.

A voice from the upper edge of the draw startled him.

"Is my name in the coffee pot, Bob?"

Big Tom Hill was grinning down at him.

CHAPTER XVI

FLIES ON A WALL

AS Bob Hallack looked down into the black void of Arapahoe Cañon from the rim he felt an extreme reluctance to start the descent. It was one thing to plan the adventure with the cheerful sunshine warming the slope upon which he sat; it was quite another to attempt the hazard by the uncertain light of a moon which served to show the dangers without simplifying them by making each problem a definite one.

Hill slipped the loop over his friend's head and tightened it under the armpits. "We'll pay it out slowly," he said.

Hallack, on hands and knees, worked backward to the edge. There was a queer sinking of the stomach when the solid ground fell away from his feet. He clung, face down, to the mossy rock, and pushed himself inch by inch from its support. A moment more, and he dangled like a gasping fish in mid-air. Far above was the Milky Way of powdered stars. As far below, it seemed to him, was the bottom of this murky pit to which he was consigning life and limb.

"All right?" called Hill.

"All right," his chief answered cheerfully, and

151

from the bottom of a doubtful heart meant all wrong.

The men above began to let down the rope. Hallack spun round like a fowl on a roasting-jack. He skinned his face against the wall. His knees rasped against sharp projections. In his efforts to keep from being flayed he forgot about the perilous enterprise upon which he was engaged.

The face of the precipice sloped inward. He swung dizzily in space, not even a reaching toe touching anything solid. To his exaggerated fancy it seemed that he had been lowered hundreds of feet. Soon those above would come to the end of the rope, and he had not yet reached the outcropping of rock that was to mark the real starting point of the journey.

Even as this thought flashed through his mind his foot struck something solid. He was at rest on a sloping ledge of cliff wide enough to give standing room.

He freed himself from the loop and gave the signal to Hill. The rope jerked upward. To Hallack, crouched on that narrow incline with a gulf of space at his feet, hours seemed to drag past before he caught sight of Hill slowly descending. In reality the time could not have been more than ten or fifteen minutes.

He caught at Tom's leg and guided it to a foot hold.

"That's that, anyhow," the big man said as he

shook the loop from his body and stepped out of it.

Again Hallack jerked the rope three times as a signal to those on the edge of the precipice above. He and his companion hung on to it. A long twisting snake dived past them into the chasm. It was the rope, released by Anderson and Chapin.

The two on the ledge drew it up. Each of them looped himself to an end of the coil.

Hallack was the lighter of the two. He was also the leader. He went first, creeping for a few yards along the narrowing shelf.

"A kind of trough runs down from here, Tom," he called back. "Looks as though we could make it."

Hill joined him. They peered down into the shadows which swallowed the precipitous trench.

"Looks chancy," the big man suggested. "Wish we could see where we were going."

"You first, Tom," his friend told him.

Tom understood why he was to lead the way. It was the less dangerous position. The one in the rear could support him with a taut rope but would have to come down unassisted.

The big fellow manoeuvred himself, face to the wall, into the trough. Except for the grade, which was close to ninety per cent., the going was not bad. Rough projections of feldspar gave hand and foot holds. He lowered himself carefully, testing every place upon which he put his weight, while

Hallack, braced against the possibility of a fall, kept the rope tight.

"Near the end of your tether, Tom. Find a place where you can sit tight a while," Bob called down.

The climber came to a place where a boulder was jammed into the trough. "This'll do fine," he answered, and slipped the loop from his waist.

Hallack lowered to him both packs. They were awkward as well as heavy. In them were surveying instruments, blankets, and food. From the floor on which he stood Bob slid down into the wedge-shaped trough-fault, found a toe hold, and began to descend. A moment of squeamishness ran through him as he clung to a knob of quartz and groped with his foot for an outcropping rib on which to rest it. If he should make any mistake in the choice of a prop, if a muscle failed him at a pinch or his nerves went panicky, he would plunge to the rocks a thousand feet below. The dizziness passed almost instantly. He moved hands and feet from one anchor to another with the sureness of the expert mountaineer.

Presently he stood beside his companion on the boulder, cramped between the angling sides of the conduit.

Hill swung over the edge of the smooth stone and disappeared from view. Bob leaned back, bracing himself with toe and knee. He paid out the line foot by foot.

A cry of alarm rang out. The rope tore like red-hot steel through his fingers. There came a jerk that almost dragged him from his moorings. His hands tightened and the muscles of his arms stood out hard as iron bands. The strain was tremendous, but it could not have lasted more than a few seconds before it eased.

"You all right, Tom?" called Hallack anxiously.

"No bones broken. Shaken up a bit. That's all. Foot slipped while I was trying for a grip. I'm wedged in safe enough here. Better come on down now. Look out for the last twenty feet."

Bob Hallack knew it had been a near thing. A few pounds more weight would have dragged him from the boulder and they would both have gone plunging into space. He drew a deep breath of relief.

After he had lowered the packs he eased himself into the crevice made by the angling strata of the faults. A few yards brought him to a surface worn smooth except for small loose rubble that gave no foot hold.

"You'll have to let go and slide down. I'll catch you as you come," Hill said.

His partner in the adventure looked down over his shoulder. "How firm is that rock you're standing on?"

"Don't know. A bit wobbly. But it stopped me."

"It might not hold my weight too if I came with a rush." Like most men of initiative Hallack made quick decisions. "Let's have your end of the rope, Tom."

He fastened the loop to a crag just above him and went down carefully hand over hand. An upward fling of the line released the upper end.

A sheer wall fell away from their feet. Hallack had made a map of their route on the back of an envelope and committed it to memory. At this point a rock traverse of sixty or seventy feet was indicated.

They strapped the packs on their backs and began to work across it. Stunted shrubs, crevices, and rough contours helped them. In the uncertain light they could not see far in front of them and came to an impasse.

"Have to back track," announced Bob, who was in the lead again.

Hill worked back for half-a-dozen yards, followed by his companion. An ascending crack in the wall zigzagged to the right.

"Looks possible," Bob said, and went at it.

A thin drizzle of sleety rain had begun to fall. It coated the rocks with a veneer of ice smooth as glass. Every hand grip, every foot hold had to be tested carefully, for each jutting inch of quartz was glazed with danger. Loaded with packs as they were, the climbing was very difficult. It called for muscle and nerve, for a steady head and a sure foot.

They had to take chances. A rounded slab

protruded and cut them off. Peering around this convex barrier, Hallack could see that the crevice continued. It was scarcely four feet from him, but quite out of reach. The tantalizing feature was that it led straight to an incline of broken rock by which an easy descent might be made for some distance.

Bob threw the loop of the rope over the smooth surface of the promontory. It slid down when he put weight on it. He tried again. It held. But would it hold at the crucial moment with one hundred and fifty-five pounds dependent on it? There was only one way to tell.

The moment while he summoned courage to let his feet swing off from solid ground over the abyss was a dreadful one. He filled his lungs as a diver does and an instant later hung above a five-hundred-foot chasm. The impetus of the plunge carried his body to the right. The loop slipped, caught again and held fast. One of his toes found a bit of moss on the edge of the crevice. He pulled himself gingerly to the ledge.

Once there, it was possible to adjust the rope securely to the granite slab so that Hill swung round in comparative safety.

Five minutes later they were jubilantly descending the rock slide. They were clambering toward more danger, but at least they had met without disaster some very ugly bits of climbing.

"Talk about the Andes," boomed Hill. "I'll say

your little old Rockies have got 'em flattened out on the map. Next time I want to play I'm a fly crawling along a window pane I'll do it in the daytime."

"Can't say I fancy this night work myself—not for scaling cliffs. But it was rather up to us, wasn't it?"

"Trouble is I'm not up to it," Tom pretended to grumble. "Too old, too fleshy, too timid. I'll have heart failure if I bump into many more hair-raising stunts like that business up there on the crack. It's all right for you, because you're such a devil-may-care go-getter. But I'll tell you straight, I wanted to quit a dozen times."

"You're here, aren't you?" Hallack asked cheerfully.

"Some of me—all but about ten pounds I've sweated off. What I want to know is, where do I go from here?"

"Heaven knows."

They came, by way of another precipitous wall, to the ledge Hallack had seen through his glasses from the rim. Along this they moved cautiously, looking for a chance to get down. From their feet the precipice fell sheer. They could hear the sound of Arapahoe Creek as the water tumbled over rocks in its eagerness to reach the plain, and they guessed that they were now not more than about three hundred feet from the bottom.

The ledge pinched out. They moved back along it.

"Might make it from here," Hill said. "Trouble is, even if we got down we'd have to leave the rope."

There was no alternative. The end of the rope reached an escarpment from which it might be possible to descend.

"I'll go down and have a look at it," Hallack decided.

They fastened the rope to a rock. Hallack went down, bumping against the wall and whirling like a dancing dervish. After reaching the platform he took in swiftly the cliff leading to the bottom.

"It's easy, Tom," he called up.

"Glad something's easy, Cap. Look out. Here come the packs."

He lowered them, swung off the ledge himself, and came down jerkily.

After he had landed on terra firma Tom looked up the wall down which he had just come. One thing was sure. They would not go back that way.

"Souvenirs of the exploits of two bally goats," he said, showing the blisters on his hands. "Well, Cap, we're here. We've burned our bridges behind us. I'd be happy if I wasn't worrying for fear we may have to spend the rest of our lives in this large-sized vault."

"I know two ways out. One at each end of the cañon. When we're ready to go, we'll go."

"I wonder," murmured Tom mournfully. He was enjoying himself immensely. Who was it that had said engineering had become a profession without any romance?

They shouldered their packs and lowered themselves to the bottom of the cañon by means of scrub trees and the broken surfaces of the sloping cliff.

Hill shivered. "Someone's walking on my grave," he said.

"This sleet is cold. We'll build a fire," Hallack replied.

"To tell our friends the enemy that we're here?"

"Oh, we'll put it out before morning."

A quarter of an hour later they lay on their blankets before a roaring camp fire.

CHAPTER XVII

JOYCE TAKES COMMAND

FROM the city Smithers came to Coalville with several knotty problems he wanted to submit to his employer. "Secretary to the President" was printed on his card and would remain on it because he had no initiative and obeyed orders meticulously. Without Elliott to tell him what to do he was lost when he passed beyond routine matters.

A slim golden girl met him on the porch. She listened to his tale of perplexity and shook her head decisively. "You can't see Dad, Mr. Smithers. The doctors don't want him troubled by business. If he got to worrying—well, it wouldn't be good for him."

"He's getting better?"

"Yes, we think so—very slowly. It was a great shock to his system. He isn't wholly out of danger yet, but he does seem a lot better. The fever's down, though he's weak."

Smithers hung in the wind. "I suppose I ought to consult with Mr. Brokaw, but there are some things—well, that Maclure map of Arapahoe Cañon for instance!"

"What about it?"

The secretary told her.

Joyce considered, made an instant decision. "I'll come in to-morrow if Dad's all right. Get Mr. Brokaw to go with us to the vault. The manager will let us look over the papers in Dad's box. If he objects to me taking away the survey map you'll have to copy it as well as you can."

She drove to town next day in her roadster and found Brokaw and Smithers waiting for her at the bank in the vault of which her father kept a private safety-deposit box. The manager of the vault department made no objection to the removal of the map after Joyce and Brokaw had signed a paper prepared by the latter absolving the bank from responsibility.

The three adjourned to the office of Brokaw and examined the map and report.

"We ought to let Mr. Hallack know about this at once, oughtn't we?" Joyce suggested.

"Yes. I'll get word to him," the lawyer promised.

His stenographer walked into the room. She was a pert competent young person of the latest season model, with a graceful streamlike body and fully equipped as to accessories. Just now she was very much ruffled.

"There's a guy—a person—who says he's got to see you right away, Mr. Brokaw. I told him you were busy and he said he didn't care how busy you were. Name's Anderson, he claims."

"What's he want?"

"Wouldn't say. He doesn't look like anybody particular to me. Shall I tell him you won't see him?" The young woman patted an ear pad to make sure that no part of the external organ of hearing immodestly showed. "He was very rude—quite impudent, in fact."

"There's a man named Anderson working on the survey with Hallack," Smithers suggested.

"Let's hear what he has to say," Joyce proposed in her swift impetuous way.

"Show him in, Miss Pierce," the lawyer said.

Miss Pierce sniffed, eloquently. That sniff expressed entire disapproval of the decision. If any roughneck could bolt into the office and demand to see a member of the firm at once without any appointment—well, things were coming to a pretty pass. She went out of the room abruptly. Technically speaking, she flounced out.

Anderson appeared at once. He was of the Nordic race, high-coloured and fair. At a glance it was apparent he was an outdoor engineer.

"Can I see you alone, Mr. Brokaw?" he asked.

"If it's about the Gateway Pass project you may speak before us all. This is Miss Elliott."

"We're in trouble at Arapahoe Cañon," the man blurted. "Hallack and Hill went down and haven't come back. They're firing at them."

"What do you mean? Who's firing at who?"

"Ordway's men are firing at Hallack and Hill.

163

They must have them trapped down there. We can see some of the men from the rim—and the jets of smoke when they fire."

Joyce broke in. "Do you mean that Mr. Ordway's men are shooting at Mr. Hallack and Mr. Hill?"

"Yes. That's just what I mean. They must be in the rocks somewhere near the wall—our men, I mean. We can't see them but they're firing back."

"Just a moment. Let's get this straight," Brokaw broke in quickly. "How did this clash come about? Tell your story from the beginning."

"Hallack sent us with Hill to make a survey of the cañon. He was coming himself in a day or two. We found both entrances guarded by gangs of plug-uglies. They claimed to be working on a power plant site—doing the preliminary blasting. They wouldn't let us in. Hallack's no quitter. He decided to get in anyhow. We lowered him and Hill Monday night from the rim."

"From the rim? Why, it must be a thousand feet high!" exclaimed Joyce, thrilling to this vicarious adventure.

Anderson looked at the girl. Soft eyes, quick with life, flashed at him from a vivid personality.

"Nearer fifteen hundred. We lowered them only a little way. They had to work down. Looked like a crazy thing to me, but Hallack had spent a day on the rim looking the ground over with field glasses. He'd figured it could be done, and

164

I guess he was right. They must have got down."

"Monday night. And this is Friday. When did the firing begin?"

"Last night—farther up the cañon—near the mouth. This morning it had moved down. Looks like Hallack and Hill slipped away in the night and got into the big rocks at the upper end. We'd begun to worry about 'em before. The plan was that they'd be down there two days and climb back up Wednesday night or Thursday morning."

"But, good Lord!" cried Smithers, aghast. "They daren't kill them. It would be murder."

"Have you ever read the history of any of these fights to get possession of cañon right of ways, Mr. Smithers?" asked Brokaw dryly. "The side that wins is always justified. Uncle Sam's a pretty big figure, isn't he? But when he served notice on the M. & P. not to go through Crooked Creek Gorge it did not make a bit of difference. The road went right through and fought the legal question out afterward. It's doing business through that cañon to-day."

"But, Mr. Ordway—he wouldn't let his men shoot Mr. Hallack," Joyce broke out.

Brokaw smiled grimly. "They're doing it, aren't they? At least they're trying to. Probably Mr. Ordway doesn't know anything about it. Through some agency he has hired a gang of toughs to hold the cañon. He is not looking for trouble. He doesn't expect it. His idea is to forestall trouble by showing that he is prepared to meet it. But the unexpected happens. Someone touches a match to the gunpowder, and it explodes."

"I'll call up Mr. Ordway, right away, and stop it," the girl cried, tense with excitement.

"The best thing you can do," agreed the lawyer. He was a member of the Rocky Mountain Club and knew that Joyce and Ordway were close friends.

Instantly Joyce was at the telephone. "Main 4433 . . . Mr. Ordway, please . . . It's very important. I must talk with him. Miss Elliott on the line . . . Can you tell me where he is . . . ?"

She hung up and turned to Brokaw. "He's gone to Arapahoe Cañon—just left. I'm going too, if Father's all right."

"Is that necessary?" Brokaw asked. "Mr. Smithers and I will go at once. We'll see Mr. Ordway and arrange the matter."

"No. I'm going," she said decisively. "Will you have your stenographer call Coalville, please? I want to talk with Doctor Albert. Ask for a quick connection, Mr. Brokaw." The girl's wistful smile apologized for the abruptness of her speech.

From Doctor Albert she learned that her father was doing very well indeed and that just now he was asleep.

"Will you tell him that I'm detained on business and can't get back till evening? When he wakes,

I mean. And please give him oodles and oodles of love from me," she entreated.

It was the first time since the accident to her father that she had been so long away from him. To wait upon him, to heap upon him the full devotion of her penitence, had been a poignant joy. In these days, while he had lain in the Valley of the Shadow, so weak and stricken, father and daughter had come very close to each other. The stark reality of life had broken down the barrier between them. She was no longer a willful young thing, eager for experiments in sensation. The essential woman in her, the brooding mother that had always lain below the surface, had lapped him in tenderness. She had found it possible to break through the crust of habit and croon over him with bubbling little words of endearment.

He understood. Joyce knew that he appreciated and rejoiced in the concord that had driven away their differences, though he told her with smiles and little pressures of the hand rather than in words.

But as she drove the roadster toward the hills, Brokaw by her side, her thoughts were not of her father but of Ordway. She was wondering when he had decided to occupy the cañon with a force to prevent Hallack from entering it. The recollection came to her that she had spoken of Arapahoe to Ordway the day after the accident to her father. It had been while she and Winthrop had been walking up the crooked little street of Coalville. She had told him that the subject seemed to be on her father's mind, since he had spoken of it in his delirium two or three times. And immediately—the very next day—he had moved his men up there.

Had he taken advantage of what she said, of the unwary words of a fear-filled girl he claimed to love, and used the information they gave him to beat her crushed and broken father? It was not possible. The thing was too base to believe.

The thought carried the girl back a step farther. During the past week she had done more thinking than ever before in her nineteen years. She was trying to find the right answer to the problem of her relation to Ordway. More than once, while she had sat beside the bed of her sleeping father, she had gone over that half hour at the dance when he had asked her to marry him. Did he even claim to love her? At the time it had not struck her at all; there had been no significance to her in the omission of it. But it was a curious and disturbing fact that he had not once mentioned love as a motive for his declaration.

The omission filled her now with a sense of deep humiliation. Asking her to marry him, he had left out what should have been the most important reason for him—and she had not even noticed it. A sentence or two flung out by Jarvis Elliott renewed themselves in her mind.

"You've been living for yourself alone—for excitement and sensation and pleasure. Nobody can find happiness in that." At the time she had resented them, but she knew now that they were profoundly true. That was why she had built up false and tawdry standards of judgment.

She had gone her willful feverish way because she had never disciplined herself to service. There had been in her no social consciousness, no sense of obligation to others. She began to see that the self-indulgent lose touch with the saner impulses of our common humanity, that they are a discord instead of a harmony in that unity of life for which all constructive forces are working.

Joyce saw this only dimly, vaguely. It came to her by individual observation rather than philosophic reasoning. She felt, without being able to give expression to it, that her father was building up the continuity and solidarity of life that made for social order and it was being borne in on her that Winthrop Ordway was a destructive element because he played his own hand with no regard to the community interest.

She was beginning to find a social consciousness.

CHAPTER XVIII

BIG ROCKS POINT

BEFORE the light of dawn had fully banished the lingering grey of night the engineers stamped out their fire and scattered the ashes in the creek. They hid their packs and moved down the cañon to the falls where the gulch swung to the left.

Hill glanced up the painted wall down which they had come in the darkness. The precipice was so sheer that the thought of having climbed down it took his breath.

"I don't believe it, Bob. We didn't do that fool thing. It's a dream," he said.

"Just as well we didn't try it in the daytime. We might have lost our nerve," Hallack replied.

"Hmp! I lost mine a dozen times. I've had all the adventure I want for a year. Hope none of Ordway's crowd find us. I'd hate to be massacred to make an M. & P. holiday," he grumbled in high spirits.

They fell to work on their survey. Some of the old stakes set by Manders and Truesdale were still in place. From these as a basis they ran lines to the falls with the transit. The walls at this point were perpendicular and came so close together that there was only room for the bed of the stream. All day they worked, taking and jotting down measurements, covering as thoroughly as they could every inch of the approach below and above. Night found them with their task still unfinished. They returned to their camp of the previous night.

Two or three times during the day men had strolled through the gorge, evidently passing from one camp to the other. But the surveyors had seen them in time to conceal themselves before they were observed.

It was cold, but Hallack did not dare to light a fire until close to midnight. Somebody might be stumbling down in the darkness from the camp at the upper entrance to the one at the lower. They were pretty well chilled before Hill put a match to the resinous fir limbs they had gathered.

Before daybreak they had again broken camp and were ready for work. They were continually interrupted by men passing back and forth, so that they got very little done. The distance below the falls to the mouth of the cañon was short, and at any time somebody might come upon them while they were running their lines.

They had brought with them food for only two days, but neither of them had any thought of leaving till they had solved conclusively the problem before them. Without breakfast or lunch they stayed on the job Thursday and had the satisfaction of finishing it late in the afternoon.

Hallack was folding the tripod when he looked up to see a pair of amazed eyes staring at him stupidly. They belonged to a squat heavy-set man who suggested the savage cave man of prehistoric days. He had the long arms, the broad rounded stooping shoulders, the hairy hands of the *homo neanderthal.* He was, unless his cunning big-jowled face libelled him, a specimen to be classed sub-civilized.

From his throat came a rumble like the growl of a bear. "Thousand devils! What you doin' here?" he demanded hoarsely.

The fellow was puzzled. It had not yet penetrated his slow brain that the enemy had stolen a march on his employers. His small piggy eyes wandered to the approaching figure of Hill. They lit with recognition. He had seen him when the surveyor had brought his outfit to the mouth of the gorge and been refused admission.

"We're camping. Any objections?" asked Hallack, smiling. He had the information he had come to get and he did not care how soon the fireworks began.

"Where you come from? How'd you get in?"

"From Ohio, originally. My friend's from Pennsylvania. Not working on the census, are you?"

"You laugh at me, hey—at Brad Reed? You don't know who you mock maybe, the best two-fisted he-man that ever came from Powder River. I make you grin on the other side of your mouth, Mr. Funny Man, if you don't look out."

Hallack's trained eye took in the man's huge bulk, his bulging muscles, the flat-footed gorilla-like crouch. There was immense strength here, he saw. To anger the fellow uselessly would be folly.

"We came down the wall," he explained.

"That's a lie," the other said flatly.

"Have it your own way, then," the engineer answered. "Why ask, if you know better than we do?"

Reed's slow brain was functioning. "I take you to the boss. See?"

"Delighted to meet him. Let's go."

The cave man made a mistake. He reached out, caught the engineer by the collar, and dragged him to him. "Sure. Right now."

Hallack tried to wrench free, but the grip on the coat was vice-like.

"Hands off," he warned quietly.

The other showed a row of broken tobacco-stained teeth in a malicious grin. "Oh, I guess not."

The engineer's doubled fist went up in a swift short-arm jolt to the prominent chin. The hand fell away from the coat and its owner staggered back a step or two.

Reed stood with his mouth open, stunned less by the blow than by the audacity of this slender

173

stranger who had challenged him so roughly. Why, he weighed eighty fighting pounds more than this young cockerel. He could make a mouthful of him—chew him up and spit him out.

The fighting man from Powder River let out a bellow compounded of exultant laughter and rage. He loved to fight, and he did not get many chances.

"Thousand devils!" he roared, shook his head to clear it from a slight dizziness, and let it sink between the gnarled shoulders.

"Look out, Bob," shouted Hill.

The huge ruffian rushed him, head down, like a mad bull, his great arms flailing wildly with the drive of a mule kick behind them. If any one of these blows had landed full and fair Hallack would have gone down and out.

But they did not find their mark. Hallack stepped back, side-stepped, ducked, danced out of range. His body and mind were in perfect coordination. Steely muscles, hard and elastic, responded instantly to the command of the brain. Action synchronized with the impulsive thought. Every sense was wary and alert, every nerve under perfect control. The focussed eyes never shifted from the red bristly face of this throwback from civilized man.

It would be impossible to check directly the avalanche of furious energy. Hallack evaded it.

He let the sledge-hammer swings pass over his shoulders or deflected them by adroit arm work. It seemed impossible for him to stand up against that mass of brute force.

But he did, and when for a moment the Powder River champion had spent himself Bob flung at him the counter-attack of one hundred and fifty-five pounds of trained bone and muscle. Hallack's arm lashed out like a battering-ram. Blows swift as light-flashes crashed against the face of the dazed bully. Reed staggered back awkwardly, trying to cover up from the stinging punishment. To do this his arms were drawn up and stomach exposed. Straight for the solar plexus shot Bob's left, the whole force of his plunging body back of it.

The big fellow grunted, swayed for an instant on the balls of his feet, then crashed down like a forest oak.

So short had been the fight that Hill, running to the rescue, reached the spot only when his friend started the victory drive.

"Bully for you, Bob," he boomed.

Hallack had not been champion middleweight boxer of his college for nothing. He knew his foe was out. Reed half turned, writhing with pain, then rolled over and lay still.

"He would have it," explained Bob, breathing fast.

"Prettiest finish I ever saw. He dropped like

175

a steer that's been pole-axed," Hill cried with enthusiasm.

Hallack did not answer. His gaze was fixed on a group of approaching men. They were running. Two or three of them carried stout sticks.

"More company," the chief engineer said.

"Kill 'em," one of the runners shouted hoarsely. He had seen the finish of the fight.

"Friendly, ain't they?" Hill's hand slipped into the pocket where he had his revolver.

"I don't half like this." Hallack's jaw set. He waited till the foremost was a dozen yards from him. "You're near enough," he said curtly. A blue-nosed .38 had jumped to the light in his hand.

The man stopped, abruptly. His mouth fell open. This was an unpleasant and unexpected contingency. Those behind him also came to a stop. Their firearms were at the camp, a few hundred yards away. As far as the present emergency went they might as well have been in China.

"What's eatin' you fellows?" the man in the lead demanded sulkily. "What you doin' here? How'd you get in anyhow?"

"An' what you been doin' to Brad?" another asked, a threat in his voice.

"One question at a time please." Hallack's tone was low and cool, but it had the sting of a whip lash. "We're here because that's where we choose to be. We came down that wall. Your friend attacked me, and I defended myself."

"Two of you to one."

"No. One to one. A fair fight," Hill cut in.

"Like blazes. You can't tell me any little chap like him could put out Brad. Who are you fellows anyhow?"

"My name's Hallack. My compliments to Mr. Ordway and tell him I know now all I want to about Arapahoe Cañon."

In the distance other men were hovering. One was scudding back to the gateway for reinforcements. It occurred to Hill that it was time to be going. Soon the whole hornet's nest would be stinging at them.

He said as much to his chief in a low voice.

"My opinion, too," nodded Hallack, speaking for his friend's ear alone. "We can't get out the lower entrance now. They'll be ready for us."

"Yes. Have to try the upper mouth."

Hallack spoke to those whom his revolver covered. "I'll not detain you longer, gentlemen. The party's over. On your way, and take Mr. Reed of Powder River with you."

The hired thugs looked at each other uncertainly. The leader of the party had gone to the city a few hours earlier. They did not know what to do, but the weapon in Hallack's hand was a mighty persuader. They fell back, grumbling. With them they dragged the prostrate champion, who was beginning to show signs of life.

The engineers packed hurriedly, and took the trail that led up the cañon. For an hour they followed it. Dusk was falling when they reached the upper entrance.

"We might slip by without being noticed," Hill suggested.

"Hardly. The gate's pretty narrow. But we'll have a try at it. If we're seen we'll put a bold face on it. Maybe they won't stop us. If they do, we'll cover them with our guns and make a bolt."

This plan was not a workable one. As they moved forward a gun barked and a bullet struck the sand in front of them.

Out of the gathering gloom a voice called. "Throw up your hands, Hallack."

Before the engineer had time to answer a second gun sounded, this one from a point farther to the left.

The surveyors lost no time. They turned and ran as fast as their legs could carry them, now and then stumbling as their feet struck obstructions on the rough trail. The gathering darkness favoured them. The scattered shots that followed went wild.

The pursuit was hard on their heels. To discourage this they fired into the air several times. For a time excited shouts and the echoes of stray shots reached them. With the coming of night these ceased.

"Fine business!" Hill complained to his chief. "You'd think we were train robbers."

They were for the time safely hidden behind three large boulders.

"Somebody blundered," Hallack answered. "That first shot was to stop us. The second was not planned, probably, but that's the trouble with bringing in gunmen. They're always too ready to kill. Ordway will have a few words to say to the fellow in charge. It's no part of his campaign to get in wrong by killing someone to start with. Of course he'd always have a valid alibi that I drew a revolver and started things."

"Valid, huh? If you call that valid—"

"When it reached the courts Ordway's case would be buttressed by lots of evidence. 'Very regrettable, of course, but Mr. Hallack got buck fever and drew a gun.'"

"How did they know we were coming? Nobody passed us in the gulch as we came up."

Hallack tapped on a telephone pole beside him. "The Magruder ranch is at the lower entrance to the cañon. There's another ranch house not a quarter of a mile from this end. Someone 'phoned up, of course."

"That must be it. Well, what are we going to do now, Cap?"

"Stay in the gorge till morning, then surrender if they'll let us."

"And if they won't?"

Hill could not see the grim lines around the mouth of his friend, but he recognized a note in the voice familiar in old football days. "Stand 'em off."

A boyish faith in his leader still persisted in Tom Hill's mind, but he ventured a suggestion. "With revolvers, against rifles."

"We'll find a place in the rocks where they can't get at us. Of course we'll offer to capitulate if we get a chance. Another point: when Anderson hears the firing he'll get in touch with Brokaw and something will be doing at once."

They followed the trail down in the darkness to a place known to picnickers from the city as Big Rocks Point. During the centuries great masses of rock had crashed down from the precipice above. They filled one side of the gulch, which here was wider than at any other spot, rising to a height of forty or fifty feet.

The trapped men clambered over the large and jagged bits of painted sandstone to a summit where two twisted and stunted pines grew. From dead branches they made a small fire in a crevice big enough to hold them.

"I could do with a large porterhouse steak and some French fried potatoes," Hill admitted ruefully. "What was it Napoleon said about his soldiers marching on their stomachs?"

"You'll have to take a reef in your belt, Tom, and become a follower of the theory in dietetics that it's a good thing for a fellow to miss a meal once in a while."

"Does it say anything about missing three meals in a row, and more to follow?" Hill wanted to know.

They slept, brokenly, waking when the chill of the hard rocks and the pressure of their bodies interfered too greatly with the circulation of the blood. The fire died down. Morning found them cold and hungry. There was nothing to do but wait for the campaign of the enemy to develop. Time, Hallack was persuaded, worked in their favour. Anderson had very likely heard the shots last night. In any event it could not be long until he went to Brokaw, who would at once get into communication with Ordway.

From their place of concealment the engineers watched men moving up and down the bed of the creek. They were searching for skulkers hidden in the shrubbery. A stream of sunlight flooded the upper part of the opposite wall before the search reached Big Rocks Point.

Three men, armed with rifles, began exploring the boulder bed. The one in advance was the Neanderthal throwback.

Hallack stood out on a flat rock and waved a white handkerchief tied to a stick. The rifle of Reed jumped to his shoulder. He fired, just as Hill dragged his friend down to cover.

"No prisoners wanted, eh!" the big engineer

growled. "All right, you treacherous devil, come and dig us out."

His friend began to unlace one of his boots. "He got me in the leg—just below the knee." So matter-of-fact was his voice that Hill for an instant thought he was joking.

It was a flesh wound. The bullet had ploughed through so nearly that the pressure of two fingers forced it out.

Hill tore up the white flag. "We're not going to use this, I reckon," he said grimly.

With the strips he bandaged the wound to stop the bleeding.

At Hallack's suggestion he stopped once to reconnoitre. "They're spreading out. Let's see. There are four, five—there are six of 'em now. Looks like they're going to take a whirl at rushing us."

"They'll change their minds when they get closer," Hallack prophesied, tying the ends of the bandage into a knot.

The plan was evidently to stalk the two hidden among the rocks. Those below were climbing Big Rocks Point, taking advantage of all the cover they could while they advanced. Occasionally a rifle shot echoed from cliff to cliff, but the defenders judged that this was for moral effect.

Not till the attackers were fairly close did Hallack decide to answer the fire. He was peering through a narrow loop-hole formed by two great boulders flung together.

The effect of his first shot was obvious. Two men turned and began to scurry back toward the creek. Another dropped into a hollow and became henceforth a non-active member of the offence. Brad Reed leaped to his feet and plunged forward.

Hill and Hallack concentrated their fire on him. He stopped with a howl of anguish, then turned and ran limping away.

"I guess he'll let us alone," Hill growled savagely.

"It'll be long-range warfare now," Hallack answered.

"How's the leg?"

"Mine or Powder River's?" asked Bob.

"I judge it's not so awful bad or you'd know whose, old chap," his companion grinned.

Hallack's prediction was a true one. The gunmen drew back out of range. They kept up an intermittent fire, but the engineers did not take it seriously. They were well protected. It would presently occur to some of Ordway's thugs to leave the gorge and climb to the rim, from which point they could shoot down at their prey. But this would take hours. Odds were even that before that time orders from headquarters would put an end to the affray.

The thing to do was to sit tight and stick it out.

CHAPTER XIX

JOYCE AT THE WHEEL

BROKAW'S eye involuntarily reverted to the speedometer. He was not alarmed, but he did not see that any good end was served by hurling the car forward at such a pace. A fine rain, almost a mist, was falling. It filmed the wind shield so that Joyce could not see quite clearly and it made the surface of the asphalt slippery.

The girl attended strictly to business. Her whole being was keyed to concentration. She saw nothing but the road, a shining strip of ribbon weaving in front of her. The slight figure was braced to meet an emergency of skidding wheels in case of need. If she drove with the headstrong confidence of America in its teens, she had back of it the almost uncanny skill of efficiency that comes from experience to the young.

The rear wheels slid as she took a curve.

"I've a wife and three children," Brokaw said, smiling at her.

"Yes, I know Mrs. Brokaw. If there's any message you want sent—"

"I was thinking I'd rather carry it myself if you don't mind."

Joyce throttled down a notch or two. Presently she swung off to a dirt road and headed straight for the west. The brown cow-backed hills rose close. Into them the road wound, rising steadily as it followed the line of least resistance. After half an hour of climbing they looked down upon the plains, a checkerboard of irrigated fields and dry pasture, with the dwarfed city showing in the distance.

In the mountain park just beyond they rolled over a smooth roadbed of disintegrated granite. Joyce speeded up. They flashed past a motorist having engine trouble.

"Ordway," the lawyer said.

It was in the driver's mind to stop and pick him up, but the car was already so far away that she kept going. If her father's engineers were being attacked in Arapahoe Cañon she ought to lose no time in getting there. She had no doubt whatever that she could stop the battle if she were not too late. That was in keeping with the unconscious arrogance of her confident youth. Men always did what she asked them to do.

A group of tents had been set up across the entrance to the cañon. A man came forward to meet the runabout. He was a hard-faced citizen with a close-clamped mouth.

"Where are Mr. Hallack and Mr. Hill?" Joyce demanded instantly.

He stared coolly at her while he took his time to answer. "I don't know as I'm their keeper, miss," he said when at last he spoke.

"They're in this cañon somewhere. You've been fighting with them."

"Have I?" His insolent eyes appraised the girl. "You seem to know all about it."

Brokaw spoke. "This won't do, you know. It's this sort of thing that lands men in the penitentiary."

The faint far sound of a shot reached them.

"I'm going in," Joyce said quickly.

"Oh, no, you're not. That's dynamiting. We're building a power site—excavating for the plant. It wouldn't be safe for you." The fellow grinned impudently.

He and two camp stools occupied the only space left for a car to enter.

Joyce touched the starter and threw in the clutch. The runabout leaped forward. With ludicrous haste the man in the road scrambled out of the way.

Brokaw looked back at the wreckage of two stools and at an amazed guard dragging a revolver from his belt.

"Look out!" the lawyer cautioned.

A bullet whistled past and struck the sand ahead. Involuntarily Joyce ducked her head. She speeded up, intent on getting out of range.

"He fired in the air," Brokaw explained.

"Oh, don't spoil my adventure," she begged. The eyes she flashed for an instant upon her companion were very bright and shining. "I want to tell all the girls I've been under fire— like a Red Cross nurse I know who was in France."

"You may have a chance yet, if you're not careful. Stop at once, in case you get an order from someone posted on the road."

"Yes," the girl promised.

Brokaw took in, not without admiration, this young woman's flushed excitement. The danger into which she was flying did not appear to frighten her. It interested him to find in this slip of a girl some of Jarvis Elliott's bold instinct for solving a difficulty by slashing through it. She had high courage. That was clear.

Even as a child she had been a wild lawless little creature. The reputation still clung to her. She had once on a bet ridden her horse up the stone steps of the State House and called on the governor, who happened to be her uncle. There was a story going the rounds now—his wife had told it to him only that morning—of some escapade at night in the hills with Ordway. Disgraceful, Mrs. Brokaw had called it, not mincing words; if she went on as she had been doing she would not have a shred of respectability left. But Brokaw, looking at her in profile as she drove, found it hard to credit ugly rumour. The clean courage of her seemed spirit-born. A line from *Paradise Lost* jumped to his mind:

"Godlike erect, with native honour clad."

Wild she surely was, but not one who would give her memory dark chambers of defilement into which to peer.

Joyce took in low speed the very stiff grade that led to the hanging bridge over the falls, but as soon as she was on an easier incline her foot pressed the accelerator.

The road crossed the creek half-a-dozen times, running now close to one wall and now along the base of the other. They heard no more shots, but that might be because the noise of the automobile swallowed up the echoes of the explosions. In Joyce's imagination the battle was waging constantly.

To come upon the small valley below Big Rocks Point and to find it apparently peaceful as old age was a surprise to her. For she knew at once this was the scene of action. The sun lit the bowl of the flower-sprinkled meadow with the mellow warmth of spring. A meadow-lark on a telephone wire flung out a joyous full-throated chant of love.

A man with a rifle rose from behind a rock and came toward the car.

"You can't go any farther. The road's blocked," he said.

"Who blocked it?" Brokaw asked.

"You got no business here at all. Why didn't Rouse turn you back at the entrance?"

"Where are Mr. Hallack and Mr. Hill?" Joyce demanded. Then, with mounting vehemence: "What have you done with them? Have you hurt them?"

The answer to her question came instantly, more dramatic than words. The sound of a rifle shot, echoing from wall to wall, boomed like a cannon. From somewhere up in the crater of Big Rocks Point a lesser explosion threw back defiance.

Spellbound, Joyce stood looking up at the pyramid of rocks from which her father's engineers had flung their war cry. A sense of unreality stirred in her. It was the sort of thing she had seen in moving pictures. These men could not actually be firing at each other with intent to kill. That would be absurd, ridiculous. This wasn't a war zone, nor were these frontier days. The little smoke puffs could not possibly have back of them potentialities of destruction.

From the rim far above another shot sounded. The man with the rifle who had come to meet them looked up quickly to the top of the great wall.

"Now we'll smoke 'em out," he cried jubilantly. "The boys'll pepper 'em from the cliff."

The girl's eyes followed his. No sign of the

marksman could be seen, but she knew at once that the position of the besieged had become untenable. They were exposed to a fire from which they could find no cover.

"Are you in charge here?" she flashed.

The man took his time to drawl an answer. "Well, Miss, I am an' I ain't, as you might say. The boss went to town an' ain't got back yet."

"Stop it. Stop it right away," she cried.

"You'd better," Brokaw said. "I'm a lawyer. If either of the engineers are killed it will be murder—and you'll be responsible."

"I reckon not. They attackted us."

"Two of them attacked a dozen of you? That would never stick in court."

"Are we going to stand here and *argue* about it while they murder our friends?" Joyce broke in sharply.

"All they got to do's surrender," the gunman said doggedly. "It's up to them, not us."

Again from the rock rim a thousand feet above came the menacing crack of a rifle.

The girl stood a moment, rigid, tense, the colour ebbing from her face. What could she do? How could she prevent the impending tragedy?

Across her brain the answer flashed. "I'll get them to surrender," she said.

"Suit us fine," the rifleman replied with obvious sarcasm. "We been tryin' that same quite a spell, an' I'll say they're stubborn guys. But if you've

190

got a way, miss, why, go to it. We ain't set on collectin' no scalps to-day."

"How?" Brokaw asked Joyce. He was a practical man, one whose mind naturally moved to methods of procedure. "They can't hear you from here."

"I'll go to them and explain," she eagerly urged.

"No," he vetoed promptly. "Some idiot might take a shot at you."

"With a white flag—your handkerchief."

"That's not a bad idea—if you can call your men off a while," the lawyer said to the other man. "Except of course that I'll go."

He drew his handkerchief out by way of getting things going.

With a little jerk Joyce plucked it from his hand. She turned and ran, straight for Big Rocks Point.

To Brokaw her action was wholly unexpected. The ways of impatient and imperious youth were not his. He trod a safe and sane path hedged by precedent and convention. It took an instant to adjust his mind to her purpose. Then he started in pursuit.

"Come back," he shouted.

She paid not the least attention.

The feelings of the lawyer exploded in a burst of exasperated annoyance. "Damned tommyrot!"

None the less, he followed in the footsteps of her feather-footed madness.

191

CHAPTER XX

HALLACK GUESSES,
BUT NOT OUT LOUD

JOYCE took the hill with swift lightness, the white handkerchief streaming in the air. A queer commotion of excitement that was not fear churned in her bosom. It was a kind of exaltation. She had known the lift of it before when caught in the tide of adventure; once when on a dare she had dived from a twenty-five-foot platform into a swimming pool, and again when she had ridden down the main corridor at the State House, three or four protesting attendants at her heels, and knocked with the crop of her whip on the door of the governor's office.

The eyes of a dozen men focussed on her, a young flame of vivid life moving across the battle-field with the ardour of a modern Joan of Arc. Instinctively she had done the wisest thing. There was no more firing. By a common impulse the combatants suspended operations to watch her. What did she mean to do? Where had she come from? Who was she? And what rash folly was carrying her straight to the titanic rock pile where the two trapped men were making their stand?

If Joyce was slender, she was silken-strong. She took the rough rocks lithely, sure-footed as a mountain goat. Well behind her puffed Brokaw. Usually he did his climbing in an automobile.

From the hollow at the summit of the boulder bed two men emerged. They descended toward her. One of them limped. At difficult places he used his companion as a crutch.

A voice clear as a silver bell called up to him. "Are you hurt?"

With a gesture of sharp command he motioned her back. "Not safe here. Don't you know they're firing at us?"

"I'm here to stop that foolishness." She swung across a little crevasse from one rock to another, still moving upward.

"Don't come any nearer. Some crazy fool might fire."

"Not if I'm with you. Did you fall? Or did they hit you?"

"They hit me, and they might hit you. Keep back, I tell you."

"Oh, I've a flag of truce." Joyce waved the handkerchief toward the sharpshooters, and somehow the gesture implied that an armistice had been declared.

From the rim of the cañon far above a flutter of white signalled back to her.

"See," she went on confidently. "It's all over now. Why didn't you put up a white flag and then talk it over? I never heard of anything so silly as lying there and letting them shoot at you."

Hill ventured a suggestion. "That's how Bob was hit. He stood up and waved his flag."

"He did? And they shot at him?" Her voice held the rising inflection.

"One of them did. We'd had trouble with him before."

Joyce clambered up a rough stairway of rocks and joined them. Hallack, to favour his leg, had sat down.

"Is it pretty bad?" the girl asked.

"No. A flesh wound."

"We'd better go on down, then," she said in a matter-of-fact manner, quite as though men wounded in battle were an everyday occurrence with her. "That is, if it doesn't hurt too much. I can send some men up to carry you down."

"Afraid they'd drop me accidentally in a crevasse," Hallack replied. "I'll peg on down somehow."

"We'll help you." The girl turned to the assistant engineer. "I'm Mr. Elliott's daughter."

Hill lifted his hat and mentioned his name. "You know Mr. Hallack, I think."

Joyce barely glanced at the wounded man. "Yes, I know Mr. Hallack. He was very kind to me once. Let's go."

At the touch of careless scorn in her words the engineer flushed beneath the tan. He said nothing

194

till she stepped forward to lend a hand when he hesitated at a long step across from one boulder to another.

"I can make out nicely, Miss Elliott. Thanks, just the same."

"Oh, very well." She moved springily across the small gulf. If he did not want her help she was not going to insist on it.

"You had no business coming up here," Hallack said stiffly, when they had reached an easier place where conversation was more feasible. "It was a crazy thing to do."

"I'm in the habit of doing what I please, Mr. Hallack," Joyce answered, her chin up.

"So I notice," he answered. "And of course that makes it right if you do it." His leg was paining a good deal and he resented her manner. Yet he was irritated at himself. The thing she had done held his admiration. It had taken courage to climb the rocks under the menace of a possible fire; and she had accepted the chance to save their lives. Why couldn't he show his gratitude instead of acting like a sore bear?

They moved slowly down the rock incline, accommodating their speed to that of Hallack. Hill supported him once or twice.

Below them, halfway up, Brokaw waited. He mopped a perspiring face. When they were close enough he voiced reproaches. "You shouldn't have done that, Miss Elliott. It turned out all right, but it wasn't safe. If those fellows up there hadn't noticed right away that you were a woman—if they had shot at you—"

"Are you going to scold me too, Mr. Brokaw?" she interrupted. "Don't mind me. Go right on. Mr. Hallack has had his say. He thinks I ought to have let them shoot him. It wasn't nice of me to interfere. I don't know what Mr. Hill thinks. It'll be his turn presently."

The big engineer smiled at her acidity. "I'm strong for what you did, Miss Elliott. It was bully of you. Thanks, awf'ly. I don't know whether those fellows were trying to hit us or not, but I wouldn't put it past some of 'em. They're hired killers, and it's hard for that kind of cattle to resist when there's a chance. Anyhow, it wasn't any fun lying there while they plugged at us."

"Of course, I'm grateful, too," Hallack added awkwardly. "It was rather splendid of you to—to—"

Joyce gave a little lift to her shoulders. "All right. Enough said. I'll let you off the rest, Mr. Hallack. Hello, there's Mr. Ordway."

She waved gaily at him the flag of truce. The excitement of the adventure was still quickening the blood in her veins. For the moment she had forgotten that she intended to give him a piece of her indignant mind.

"Seems to be giving his thugs Hail Columbia," Hill grinned.

This reminded Joyce of something. She turned swiftly to Hallack. "Did you lower yourselves into the cañon to find out if a railroad can be run over or round the falls?"

"Yes."

"Well, we've seen the Maclure survey. It can't be done."

"I don't have to depend on the Maclure survey now. I've been over the ground myself," he said.

To Joyce there seemed something significant in his grim smile, some hidden meaning the words failed to express.

"Well? You can't run a railroad through." She modified her flat statement by the added anticlimax of a question. "Can you?"

He answered Yankee fashion. "If Mr. Elliott thinks that, why is he fighting for the cañon? Why did Mr. Brokaw go to Washington to see the Secretary of the Interior personally?"

"I don't know why. Do you?"

His smile still suggested some source of amusement from which she was excluded. "I don't know, but I can guess."

"Yes?" Her manner implied that his guessing was not of much importance one way or another. "And what's your guess?"

"I'm not at liberty to say. Sorry."

"Why not?"

"It's Mr. Elliott's privilege to tell it when he wants it told, not mine."

"But Dad's ill—unable to attend to business. You know that. Mr. Brokaw is in charge, and I want to help him. It's not necessary to keep secrets from us." She faced him with the direct bluntness of which her father's daughter was capable.

"No, but I think I'll wait a while. It's a thing that does not have to be decided to-day."

"Aren't you rather exceeding your authority, Mr. Hallack?" she asked with a flash of anger.

"Not at all. This isn't a matter of authority. It's merely a personal opinion of my own—a guess at something that Mr. Elliott has chosen not to confide to anybody. Possibly I'm wrong. Anyhow, I'll keep it to myself." He spoke coolly and with decision—insolently, Joyce chose to think.

"Very well."

The girl turned disdainfully away and started down to meet Ordway, who had reached the foot of Big Rocks Point.

CHAPTER XXI

ELLIOTT WHISPERS
A SECRET

ORDWAY breasted the slope to meet her, strong and masterful in every line of his well-set body.

"Bubbles, you oughtn't to have done that," he said. "If you'd been hurt—"

"Oh, sing another song," she cried impatiently. "I've heard that one twice in the last five minutes. What would you expect me to do—sit still and let your men kill Dad's engineers?"

He waved that aside. "Not as bad as that, Bubbles. It was comic-opera stuff."

"Was it?" Joyce asked tartly. She nodded toward the limping man. "What about that?"

"Oh, Hallack's a stormy petrel. He's always starting trouble. It seems he beat up one of my men and then shot him. He brought it on himself. That's not the point. I don't want any hard feelings between my men and your father's. I'm greatly annoyed. When I've run this down some of my fellows are going to get a wigging. My orders were to start blasting for a power plant site, not to pull off a Wild West moving picture."

The girl flashed stormy challenging eyes at

him. "Do you usually have them do their blasting with rifles?"

He laughed, but the gambler's eyes that met hers were cold and vigilant. "Not usually, but you see I know that man Hallack."

"When was it you gave orders to occupy the cañon?"

"About a week or ten days ago. Why?"

"Nothing. Only you didn't mention it when I told you Father was worrying about Arapahoe in his delirium. Your gang came up next morning, I'm told."

"Not sporting of you, Bubbles. You know I didn't use any information you gave me. We had already made arrangements to move a camp up here and begin work."

"Mr. Brokaw says you haven't any right to hold the cañon. He says the Government hasn't passed on the application yet," she charged.

"True, technically. But in business we anticipate the future. I notice Mr. Hallack didn't wait for the Government to give your father a right-of-way before he began his survey. If Mr. Elliott had been well, of course we would have come to a gentleman's agreement, but with Hallack in charge—" He shrugged his broad shoulders.

The three descending the hill reached them. It was to Brokaw that Ordway spoke.

"Sorry my men had to wound one of your surveyors. From what they say I gather that he was hell-bent on trouble—wouldn't have it any other way."

"If they told you that they lied," Hill denied flatly. "We came down that wall at night to avoid trouble. One of your hired thugs attacked us and Mr. Hallack had to thrash him."

"Drew a gun on unarmed men, didn't he?"

"Afterward. When they started to rush us with axes and pick handles. But he only held them off. We tried to get out of the cañon and they fired at us. That was last night. They attacked again this morning and wounded Mr. Hallack when he waved a white flag. The thing's a high-handed outrage, Mr. Ordway. It's a pretty dirty business, no matter how they camouflage it." The big engineer spoke with heat. He did not intend that Ordway should get away with any such explanation of the affair.

"You put your heart in it," the M. & P. field general said, a little contemptuously. "Of course you would. Your methods will stand some explaining. My men refused you permission to enter the gorge on my orders. I didn't want anybody hurt by the blasting. Why didn't you come to me for a permit to make your survey?"

"Are you issuing permits for American citizens to enter on the public domain, Mr. Ordway?" asked Hallack.

The two measured each other with steady eyes in a long silence.

"I'm protecting them from getting hurt by falling rocks," answered the other coldly.

"Pure altruism," jeered the engineer. "You're not trying to prevent us from running a railroad through here, I suppose?"

"Nature has taken care of that, Mr. Hallack."

"Has she? That's what we came here to find out."

"And you've found out?"

"We have."

"That you can't get down?"

Their words snapped like the crack of whip lashes.

"I didn't say what we had found out." Hallack turned to Joyce. "Will you arrange an interview for me with your father as soon as the doctors feel it will be safe, Miss Elliott? I've something important to talk over with him."

Joyce nodded assent. "I'll let you know when," she said.

Her personal feelings toward Hallack had no bearing on this. She might not like him. In point of fact she did not. But he was her father's representative, and she wanted Ordway to understand that in this fight she was on the side of Jarvis Elliott from start to finish.

As the party walked down toward the cars Ordway paired with the girl.

"I want you to know that all Hallack had to do was to ask me to get into the gorge for a survey and I would have ordered my men to give him all the help he needed. If he hasn't finished I want him to go on and satisfy himself. I don't intend to be put in a false position, Bubbles. Your father and I are on opposite sides, but I mean to be sporting about it. You know that, don't you?"

"Oh, yes," she admitted. "I suppose you do, Win."

But she carried back to the bedside of her father something less than conviction on that point.

Elliott's tired eyes lit at sight of her. He had missed her, but he did not say so. It was only right that she should have days of relief from the tedium of a sick bed.

"Did you have a good time? Where were you?" he asked, stroking the soft hand that lay in his.

"You'd never guess," she answered, smiling warmly.

He was better than he had been at any time since the accident. The doctor had told her it would be safe to talk over with him matters of business if she took care not to tire or worry him.

"Golfing? Playing bridge?" he hazarded.

"No. Up Arapahoe Cañon saving the lives of two of your railroad builders."

He saw that she meant it. "Tell me, Joy."

"If you'll remember that it's all past and won't get excited or anything."

"I'll promise," he smiled.

"Time for your medicine, sir." She gave it to

him, straightened the bed covers, and drew a chair close.

He listened to her story, eyes gleaming. All of it interested him, but he made no comment till she came to Hallack's refusal to tell what he had guessed.

"You urged him to tell?"

"Yes, Dad."

"And he wouldn't?"

"No. I don't like him a bit. He acts as though he had a poker down his back."

"Good boy. Thought I was picking the right man for the job." He smiled a little. "Know it now."

"But why, Dad? What harm would it have done to tell us?"

"He gave you a reason. It's my secret, not his. He was right and you were wrong."

"Umph!" She nodded. "I see now he was. If I learn this great secret it'll have to be from you, then, won't it?"

"Do you want to know it, Joy?"

"If you want me to know," she cried softly, and her eyes were eager.

He did not speak at once, but lay there watching her, a new content in his heart. His little girl had been lost and was found. The barrier between them was down. No matter what life did to either of them it could not separate the kinship of their souls. Deep spoke to deep now. She had been reading to him yesterday Le Gallienne's "Soul of the World." Smiling at her, he quoted some verses.

> " 'With you beside me in the desert sand,
>   Your smile upon me, and on mine your
>   hand,
>   Oases green arise, and camel-bells.' "

"I believe you're making love to me, Daddy," the girl whispered, laughing dimples in her cheeks. "You're on the very edge of it, anyhow. The next two verses are breach-of-promise stuff." She declaimed them, with mock derision.

> " 'For in the long adventure of your eyes
>   Are all the wandering ways to paradise.' "

"That's what I used to think when I looked at your mother, my dear. 'All the wandering ways to paradise.' The words weren't written then, of course, but I suppose emotions don't need words."

"Was it like that between you and Mother, Dad? Oh, I'm so glad." After a moment she went on, tremulously: "I never knew, but—I always hoped so."

"The one woman in the world for me—and I lost her so soon. I was much older than she." He was looking at her, but she knew it was another woman his mind visioned, the slender gentle mother her memory could just bring back out of the mists of the past.

"If Mother had lived maybe I would have been different."

Jarvis Elliott came back to the present. "But I don't want you different—not just now at least." The flash of humour in his eyes mitigated the sentimentality. "Now for the secret. Ordway is right. We can't get down through Arapahoe."

"Then what's the use of fighting for it if you can't use it—sending Mr. Brokaw to Washington and everything?"

"Ordway wants a fight. He's bound to have one. I'd rather fight him for what I don't want than for what I do."

Joyce was puzzled. "But—I don't quite see the point yet, Dad."

"No? His plan is to bottle us in the hills—drive a cork into the neck so that we can't get out. I don't want him to hammer that cork into the cañon we're really coming down."

The little mischief devils kicked up their heels in her eyes. "You mean you're keeping his mind fixed on Arapahoe so that he won't get to thinking about the right way out of the hills?"

"Exactly. Time enough for him to find out that when he sees me spiking my rails down through Box Elder Cañon."

She clapped her hands softly. "Oh, Dad, isn't

that scrumptious? And all his hired thugs sitting there at Arapahoe with guns in their hands waiting for you?"

"I get a smile out of it myself sometimes," he admitted. "You see now why I haven't told anybody. If a breath of suspicion reached him before I was ready to move I'd have my hands full of trouble."

"And that's what Mr. Hallack guessed?"

"Part of it. He couldn't guess what way we are coming down. Maclure made the survey for me quietly while he was working on an irrigation project."

"I rather owe Mr. Hallack an apology, don't I?" she mused aloud.

"An explanation at least. He did right. I picked well when I chose him. He's one out of ten thousand. You should have seen him in that underground furnace of hell. Pluck clear through. What other engineer would have gone down the wall at Arapahoe to find out what he felt he had to know? How many would have had sense enough to keep their mouths shut about what he found out, not only to Ordway but to you and Brokaw? He's the man for the job."

"Well, I don't like him a bit," Joyce announced flatly.

Elliott laughed at the hop, skip, and jump of her mind. "I do."

"That's more important," she admitted.

"Yes, I'm not picking a son-in-law, but a man to build the Gateway Pass project. I believe he can do it."

"Maybe he can. He's got that kind of a jaw."

"Yes."

Mirth bubbled up into her face. "It's not the kind I want your son-in-law to have if he's to be a friend of mine, but it'll do very well to build a railroad with. Now, Dad, you've talked enough. It's time you took a nap."

He obediently did as he was told.

CHAPTER XXII

PUNISHMENT

A S soon as it was safe to move him Jarvis Elliott was taken to his home in town. His improvement was steady but slow. He had skirted death by a hairbreadth. Only a strong constitution and an inflexible will to live had pulled him through.

The time came when Smithers could bring to him from the office questions of policy to decide. Frail and weak he still was, but he announced that his motto was "Business as usual."

With Joyce he talked over plans for the cut-off. Together they studied the maps and read the brief but frequent letters of Hallack. These told details of progress, but they were carefully guarded as to information that might be of value to the enemy. Intercepted letters have been the means of deciding more than one big business campaign.

But though Joyce was interested in the Gateway Pass project it did not wholly absorb her mind. Now that her father was out of danger the youth in her began to seek expression. Elliott saw to it that she renewed interrupted social activities. He did not want an old head on young shoulders.

"I won't have you cooped up here all day, Joy.

Get out and meet your young people. Ride, golf, play tennis, dance. Anyhow, I have to dictate letters to my stenographer and can't have you around all the time." His smile robbed this last of its brusqueness. It told her that his concern was for her and not for his business.

Joyce was eager to go out again. She wanted to sit in the stand and watch a polo game, to see Winthrop Ordway striding toward her across the lawn after his playing had brought victory to the team he captained. She longed to dance, to feel the music of it quickening her blood. It had been a long time since she had drunk tea at the Rocky Mountain Club and gossiped with friends.

She found an impalpable difference in the atmosphere, one difficult to put into words. In the manner of the older women, the more important matrons, was a shade of reserve toward her. They were the mothers of the girls of her set, and their attitude found a reflection in the young people. There was no change in the boys. They hailed her reappearance cheerfully and warmly. But their sisters were a little less exuberant. She had been a leader by virtue of personality and position. It seemed to Joyce that they held back now from acknowledgment of this.

Perhaps it was her fancy. She was not sure. The change might be in herself rather than in them. After having been brought face to face with a near-tragedy it might be that the marks of her anguish remained with her so that she could not quite enter wholly into their carefree fun. And it was this these young people used as a standard of judgment. A thing was fun, or else there was no fun in it. They embraced or condemned it entirely by this criterion.

Joyce was dressing in a sport suit to go out to the Country Club one afternoon when the telephone in her room buzzed. Louise was on the line, bubbling exclamatory slang and chortles of young incoherence. Her friend sat down, for Miss Durand was of that legion of women who use the 'phone as a medium of lengthy entertainment. She could talk for twenty minutes and protest indignantly that she had not had the line more than a few moments.

" 'Lo, Bubbles," the cheerful young voice came over the wire, "how is you is this morning? I'm down at D. & K's—just bought the dearest love of an old-rose sweater. Honeybug, it's a *dream*. I'm daffy over it. 'N I got a pair of those scrumptious sport shoes—like yours, you know . . . Yes . . . Yes . . . 'N say, kid, who d'you think I met at the glove counter a minute ago? That *marve* man of yours, W.O. Know who I mean? He was so busy at first he didn't see me. He was talking to that Miss Fellows, the one that nursed your father when he was so bad. She isn't a bit pretty either, so I 'spect he was just asking how Mr. Elliott had got along."

The girl's voice, with its hopping notes of emphasis, breezed on gaily. She talked of what she had been doing since she had seen her friend, which included attendance at a dinner at the Rocky Mountain Club given by the young wife of the head of a bond house to a selected group of intimates. Louise told in detail what *he* had said and what *she* said, the antecedents of the personal pronouns being her latest devotee, Bert Randolph, and Miss Durand herself.

"I'm *crazy* to tell you all about it, Bubbles. Why weren't you there? We missed you awf'ly, all of us. You oughtn't to poke off in a sick-room *all the time* now Mr. Elliott's better," Louise remonstrated.

"Did Geraldine miss me?" Joyce asked dryly, naming the hostess.

There was an instant of surprised silence at the other end of the wire. "I s'posed you couldn't come 'count of your father. Didn't Jerry *ask* you?"

"Not unless her invitation was lost on the way."

"That's funny. Have you and she—?"

"No, we haven't."

"It's so *queer*. Do you think—?"

Joyce did not care to say what she thought, not over the telephone at least. It was the first time in her young and active life that she had ever been snubbed socially and she was furiously angry. Geraldine Westover was a climber. It had been a long step up when she had married Ralph Westover, whose mother was social dictator of the city's most exclusive set. Into this circle Joyce had been born. She considered it hers by right of inheritance, though she poked fun at it and stepped outside of its beaten track whenever she pleased.

Mrs. Westover, Senior, was punishing her, of course, because she had been independent enough to ignore the fences that lady had set up. Geraldine was what Louise called a 'fraid-cat. Of her own volition she would never have dared to cut out from her dinner one of the small group of young people who played together as intimates and called each other by their first names. Her mother-in-law was back of this. She was whipping Joyce into line. The excuse probably was the Box Elder Cañon ride with Ordway, but the real reason was that the girl had been playing her own hand without deference to the grim but smiling lady who expected her word to be law.

Her clear brain guessed shrewdly at the motives hidden in the mind of Mrs. Clay B. Westover. To be the social arbiter of the city was the very breath of her being. For twenty-seven years she had held this position. Often she had used her power ruthlessly and a good many were restive under it. They were waiting for a leader. If Joyce were to marry Winthrop Ordway the disaffected would naturally turn to her. In case of a clash of forces she would be a very potent factor. Hence the need to discredit Joyce, to clip her wings, to humble her, and to receive her back repentant into the fold.

The girl had come of fighting stock. The intimation that her position was in jeopardy did not frighten her at all. She did not believe it. The pride and strength of youth in her were far too strong for such an admission. All the Westovers in the world could not keep her from being Jarvis Elliott's daughter, the heritor of his name and place and power. Every instinct in her moved toward rebellion.

There was one way in which she could spike her foe's guns instantly. The news that she was engaged to Winthrop Ordway would send a flutter over the Country Club district. They would be deluged with invitations, she and her fiancé. Nobody would dare hang back, for it would be apparent at once what an irresistible combination they made.

Joyce toyed with the thought, neither accepting nor rejecting it. Nevertheless she dressed with particular care, for Ordway was going to play over the course with her. She had not been alone with him since the morning when she had seen him in Arapahoe Cañon. Would she still be so greatly interested in him and that future he had asked her to share? That was one of the things she had to find out. Her pulses beat fast with pleasurable anticipation. There was a throb of triumphant malice in her expectation. She would not marry Winthrop unless she was sure. But if she did—well, Mrs. Clay B. Westover would find her power challenged very promptly and would discover that the tyranny of her rule was broken.

At the Country Club Joyce's resentment received a fillip. She and Louise were in a small dressing room arranging their wind-blown hair when they heard voices outside and almost at once the name of Joyce.

"Funny she wasn't there. Thought she and Jerry were such friends," one said.

"Joyce isn't going out much nowadays."

The answer came from Esther Dare. Both of the girls recognized the lisp she affected. The significance of the thing said was less in the words than in the manner. Without seeing her they could visualize the lifted eyebrows and the satiric smile.

"Do you mean—on account of her father?" the first speaker asked.

Esther laughed softly, with malice. "Of course—on account of her father."

The sound of the footsteps outside died away.

"Aren't she a spite-cat?" Louise said to her friend. "To hear her you'd think she'd been at the dinner instead of frettin' her heart out because she didn't get an' never could get a bid there.

All the samey, somebody ought to *smack* Jerry Westover for leaving you out, Bubbles."

"It wasn't Jerry left me out."

"Who then?"

"Mrs. Clay B. Westover."

Louise pursed her crimson lips to a whistle. "Think so?"

"That's just what I think, Wese. I'm to be left out of things for a while—till I learn to eat humble pie."

"*Good* night! She can't leave *you* out, can she?"

"We'll see if she can." The eyes of the girl were hard and shining. In them was the gleam of battle.

Joyce was filled with scorn and anger. Esther Dare's implication was that she was in disgrace and had taken advantage of the accident to her father to go into retirement until the scandal about her and Winthrop Ordway blew over. It was absurd, of course. Ridiculous. There was no scandal. There could be none about the name of Joyce Elliott. To hint at what she was afraid to say openly was like Esther. The worst of it was that if Mrs. Westover had decided to punish her a lot of people would believe whatever they were told—unless she refused to accept that august lady's verdict and fought back successfully.

There was no question of ostracism. A lot of her friends would stick by her. Plenty of good houses would be open to her. But there would be some unpleasant experiences to endure, some omitted invitations she could construe as snubs; and even those who stood her friends would think there was a certain measure of justice in the discipline she was undergoing.

In a fight of this kind an unmarried woman would be at a great disadvantage. Joyce recognized this instantly. But if she accepted Ordway they could have a big house and entertain lavishly. She had a social flair. Mrs. Westover was stiff and formal. *Her* line would be informality, lightness of touch. Real men and women would come to her affairs and they would be themselves. She saw a salon growing beneath her skilful promotion.

Decidedly Mrs. Clay B. Westover would regret her ill-advised attempt at suppression.

CHAPTER XXIII

WITH A STIPULATION

HALFWAY down the fairway leading to the ninth green Ordway asked Joyce if her father was worse. His was not the most finely attuned soul in the world to shades of atmosphere, but it occurred to him that she was rather silent and distrait.

"No. He's getting along fine. Why?"

"You're worried about something, aren't you?"

"No-o. Not worried." She smiled, ruefully. "I'm being stood up in the corner."

"By Mr. Elliott?"

"By Madam Grundy."

He gave that a moment's reflection before asking, "What for?"

"Oh, for being alive without Mrs. Westover's permission," she answered sharply.

"What have you been doing now, Miss Madcap?" he wanted to know, with an indulgent smile.

"Nothing *now*. I s'pose it's that fool Box Elder Cañon ride."

"Oh, if that's all!"

"Enough, isn't it?" She spoke impatiently. "It's a good peg to hang her disapproval of me on. I ought never to have given her the chance. Dad was right about that."

"She can't do you any harm—not permanently."

"If you think it's fun to have people whispering lies about you."

They had deflected from the fairway to the shade of a large maple. "You can stop that whispering any day you like," he told her.

"Yes?"

"Let me give it out that I have the honour to be engaged to you."

The thought had been in her own mind scarcely an hour before, but she did not at all like its being in his. Her dauntless soul was not beaten, and she had no intention of flying to him as a refuge in distress. So far as she understood her own feeling it had been that if she were going to marry him anyhow she might as well get what fighting advantage there was in the publicity of the fact, But Win Ordway need not think that she would come to him with wings clipped. She could hold her own well enough without him.

"You are suggesting that I get engaged to you to—to reëstablish myself socially. Is that it, Win?" she asked with dangerous sweetness.

The flash of her eyes warned him. "Nothing of the kind. Miss Joyce Elliott does not need any social rehabilitation. You know that well as I do. But if it will save you any unpleasantness—since we're going to be engaged anyhow—"

"Are we? When did you decide that?"

"I've been hoping it for months, Bubbles."

His capitulation took the edge from her challenge. The smile she met was disarming, not so much because of what it said as because of what it left unsaid. He stood there strong and dominant to the last well-groomed inch. By the sheer power of him he was shaking success from a world that would have liked to trample him down. But with her the strength of his position was in its acknowledged weakness. He could not take her by the throat, cave-man fashion, and drag her into his life. Her courage had the temper of a Toledo blade. Back of it was a pride and a dignity that would not permit her to be won by sovereignty. Lie must come as a suitor, not as a conqueror. And it was so that he came to-day.

He could afford to come in seeming humility. For he brought with him advantages the blind could see. Joyce wished the light of them might not have been quite so dazzling. It was not necessary for her father's daughter to marry a prince of the realm.

The thought of her father stabbed her. It would be a blow to him if she married the man who led the attack on his railroad. But of course that could be adjusted. Win would not continue to oppose the father of his wife. She did not realize that big business, like war, is a matter of policies and not personalities. If Ordway and her father patched up a peace the campaign of the M. & P. against the Gateway Pass cut-off would continue as before. The transcontinental line could not afford to have a road slashed across the Rockies that would tap its territory and reduce the running time from coast to coast.

These brain reactions flashed like cinema pictures chaotically across her mind. Mixed with them inextricably was a rising emotional excitement. When Ordway's eyes grew sultry as they looked at her there always rose in her bosom something tumultuous. She was generally a cool young person, mistress of her emotions. But there was a quality in this man's personality very disturbing to her calm, a magnetic masculinity that demanded response. She felt the blood hot in her veins, knew a pulse was fluttering in her throat.

"I don't know," she said, her brows knitted in a frown. "Am I different from other girls? Do they know when—when—?" With a little lift of the shoulders she let the sentence die away.

"It's fate—kismet," he told her. "Why struggle against it?"

"But is it?" She looked at him in the frank fashion of the maiden of to-day. "I don't know what you're really like at all. Marriage is such a—such a deadly intimate thing. Wese counted up once and found she'd have to sit across the table from one man about twenty-five thousand times if she stayed married to him till they grew old. It's rather awful to think about."

"Then don't," he suggested. "Think of all the good times, all the jolly larks we'll have together."

"We do have good times, don't we?"

"The best ever. We'd make a go of it, Bubbles."

Her eyes wandered to the caddies, who had drifted together one hundred and fifty yards away, then came back to Ordway reluctantly.

"You *say* so. But how can I be sure?"

"You can't. You'll have to take a sporting chance. Everybody does."

"Don't you believe in love?" she asked him bluntly.

"Good gracious! Of course I do. Isn't that what I'm trying to tell the dearest girl in the world—that I'm in love with her?"

"Are you? I hadn't heard you mention it before."

"I could tell you glibly enough—if I didn't mean it so much."

"I see. Still waters."

"Exactly. Joyce, I'm going to chase those two young devils off the landscape and kiss you."

"You're such an ecstatic, urgent lover, aren't you?" she mocked, with a flash of sparkling eyes toward him. "No, let's finish the course, Win. We've got forty years to decide this."

"Forty minutes, say," he demurred, moving

beside her back to the fairway. "You've got to make the plunge some time, Joyce. Make it now—before we've finished the eighteenth hole."

"You're so anxious, aren't you?" she derided softly.

"I don't wear my heart on my sleeve, but I'm a good deal more anxious than I show."

Their eyes met. She felt again that racing of the blood which so disturbed her cool hard young poise. Was it love? Did it mean that she had met her mate?

"If I say 'Yes' I'll take it back if I find I don't— care that way," she told him flatly.

"Content," he cried.

"And you, if you don't want me, you'll let me know, Win. We don't want to make any mistake."

"I'll jilt you without remorse," he promised.

In sight of the caddies they shook hands on their bargain.

The girl's game for the last nine holes was badly off. A sense of unrest penetrated her. What she had to tell her father would be very distressing to him, and on her own account she was far from sure that this strange man striding beside her was the one she ought to marry. She sliced a drive. Her approaches were either topped or poorly judged. On the green her putting was not steady.

Ordway played with the precision of a machine.

If anything, his game improved. It took on the confidence of the victor.

Did he have to win always? Was it written in his horoscope that he must succeed in everything he attempted? Joyce accused herself of ungenerosity at the slight flare of irritation that stirred in her. Why should she want him to foozle shots because he had just become engaged to her? Would it prove him a more devoted lover to lose his nerve and act like a moonstruck dolt?

CHAPTER XXIV

ON SPECIAL SERVICE

JARVIS ELLIOTT listened to his daughter's story silently. Not for some moments after she had finished did he speak.

"When do you expect to get married?" he asked.

"Not for a long time, Dad. I want to be sure first."

"Aren't you sure?"

"I like him awf'ly well."

"Don't let him hurry you, Joy. Take your time. You're right about that. Be very sure before you go further."

"Yes, I told him it'd be a sort of trial engagement." She leaned forward and put her hand with a swift impulsive pressure in that of her father. "Do you mind, Dad—so terribly much?"

He chose his words. "I want you to be happy, dear."

"I know that."

"And not to get hard and selfish and worldly."

She tried to visualize Winthrop Ordway as a companion in idealism and for an instant her heart grew empty. It would be so easy to waste herself on second bests. All she would need to do was to follow the line of least resistance. Her flash of clairvoyance passed. It left her defending herself and the man she had chosen. To get anywhere in this world—to be potent for good or evil—one must have power. This was what Ordway offered her. They would work together to use it well.

"I wish you knew Winthrop better, Dad. You haven't seen the best side of him. I'm going to make him drop this fight on your railroad."

He smiled, grimly. "Even if he wanted to he couldn't stop it. You needn't have any illusions about that, child. All he can do is to drop out of it himself—and he won't do that."

"How do you know he won't?" she asked quickly.

"He's not that kind of a man."

"That's just it, Dad. Are you sure you know what kind of a man he is?"

"Are you sure *you* do?" He added, a moment later: "It wouldn't be a fair test, anyhow. Why should he give up a legitimate enterprise to please you, to satisfy your whim or to salve your feelings? The thing cuts deeper. What he's doing in fighting the Gateway Pass project is either right or wrong. If our railroad is in the interest of the people, if it will develop the state and help solve its transportation problem, then the M. & P. controlling crowd are wreckers and buccaneers, moved by wholly selfish motives to stand in the way of the common good. If I am an unscrupulous adventurer, playing a confidence game to get the money of investors with no chance of building the road I promise, then Ordway is doing a public service. There's no middle ground. One or the other must be true."

"You're so—uncompromising, Dad."

"I face the facts, if that's what you mean."

"Maybe he sees the facts differently from you."

"Probably he does. You'll have to think it out for yourself, Joy, and decide who is right."

"Oh, I know who's right. My Dad is." She nodded a smiling allegiance at her father. "But I'm hoping there are two rights. There must be if I'm going to have any peace of mind."

She carried away with her from the talk a conviction that it was not going to be easy to reconcile Jarvis Elliott to the thought of the son-in-law she proposed for him. He would not oppose her actively. But he could not change his opinion that Ordway was an unscrupulous vandal preying upon the welfare of the community.

In the morning neither of them referred to the subject of their talk. They would come back to it, of course, both in allusion and discussion, but neither wanted to wear out the other's patience with argument that could not convince.

Smithers, colourless and deferential as usual, was at the house before breakfast to see his chief on important business. Elliott talked with him for a few minutes and the secretary left for the office.

As soon as they had finished eating the railroad builder called his daughter into the room he used as a library and study.

"How about your engagements, Joy? Anything important on?" he asked at once.

"No-o. Nothing much. Do anything for you?"

"I've got to get a message to Hallack. It's very important. I can't trust the telephone. Can you take it up for me?"

"I'd love to, Dad. Where is he?"

"Camped this side of the divide—above Crown Hill—on the French Gulch road."

"I'll have to stay all night."

"Two or three nights. I want you to keep me in touch by 'phone."

"Shall I stop at the camp?"

"Or at a ranch near—the X C V. I'd have Hallack come down, but this is a hurry-up job. Smithers has just got word, through a spy in the camp of the enemy, that Ordway is equipping a large gang to send into the hills. Why? What for?"

The shaggy brows above the keen deep-set eyes of the man met in a frown of concentration. Joyce, watching him, felt a throb of pride in her kinship to this big man with the leonine head. For all Ordway's driving power he would never be such a force as her father. He might beat him. The money interests back of him had fifty times the financial resources of Elliott. But man to man she knew which one was the greater of the two.

"You think—" she said incompletely, eyes gleaming.

"I think it's a move to block me. But where? At what point? Ordway is uncannily shrewd. He strikes at his foe's weakness. I've studied his history. It's full of bold dramatic climaxes that led to victory. No chain is stronger than its weakest link, you know. Does he know the weak link in our chain?"

She looked down upon the dreamer at the desk who was giving his life to make a great dream come true. She caught again, as often of late, a gleam of the vision that animated him. The fire of its reflection began to glow in her heart. Surely this was what life was for—to do great things greatly without counting the cost.

"What do you mean—our weak link?" she asked.

"He knows we can't go through Arapahoe Cañon. It must have dawned on him that I have other plans. Of course he's had scouts out looking the ground over. He may know more about my intentions than I've given him credit for."

"That we're going through Box Elder?" she said, startled.

"There's a bare chance he's guessed that, but it's not likely. All the talk has been of coming down the south fork of the Rio Blanco. We can't run our line down the north fork without tunnelling Thunder Mountain. It would be an impossible grade. And if we take the south fork Box Elder Cañon is fifty miles out of our way. No, I don't see how he can figure on Box Elder as even a possibility for us. But I've learned not to underestimate my opponent. We can't run a risk of losing the cañon. You've been all over these maps with me. You understand them. Take them to Hallack. Trace the route we're going to follow. Tell him from me to throw a gang into Box Elder and begin work at once, following the creek bed. I want him to rush the grading—to put into the cañon every man he can find room for. He's to play Ordway's own game—hold the gulch by force till we get our right-of-way permit. Brokaw left for Washington yesterday to push our case before the department. Meanwhile it's up to Hallack to run his line, build his track, and spike down his rails. Understand?"

She nodded, eyes gleaming. "I'll tell him, Dad."

"Another thing. I'll have guns and ammunition waiting for him at the mouth of Box Elder—in a truck, with an X painted on it."

"Will he need guns?" Joyce asked, startled.

"I hope not—to use. But if he didn't have them he couldn't hold the ground."

"I wish we didn't have to do that, Dad."

"So do I," he answered, his lips a straight grim line. "But that's the way Ordway has chosen to play the game. He's not the kind of a man you can hit over the head with the Decalogue and get results. My men are not armed to attack, but to hold the just rights of the public against a pack of wolves trying to destroy. Hallack is cool-headed. He won't start any promiscuous fighting any more than I would. Chances are that when Ordway finds we're prepared for him he'll accept the fact that we beat him to the cañon."

"If we do beat him."

"Hallack must see we do. I'll keep an eye on this outfit Ordway is getting ready. If they start to move I'll throw a dozen gunmen into Box Elder with orders to hold it till Hallack comes. Will you tell him that?"

"Yes, Dad."

"I have to send you, Joy, because I can't trust anybody else. If Ordway got word of this—if he forestalled me—we'd be pretty nearly smashed. Be careful what you say when you talk to me over the 'phone. Better speak as though you're on a fishing trip."

"Yes," she said, and then impulsively: "I'm glad you're sending me, Dad. I want to help—'deed I do. We'll show Winthrop Ordway whether he can stop us from building the cut-off."

Her father smiled. "You're for me, then, not for him?"

"I'm for you all the time, Dad. I'm for him when he's not against you."

"That ought to satisfy me, for it means that you're on my side all the time and not at all on his," Elliott said.

"I see I'm not going to be able to convince you that he's not your enemy. I've brought you up awf'ly obstinate, Dad."

"He's not my enemy, but he's the enemy of the cut-off," he corrected. "Well, good luck, Joy. Who'll you take with you on your trip?"

"Nobody. Then I won't be afraid of someone telling Winthrop that there's a deep dark secret. And don't you forget to take those white powders, Dad."

He promised to be a good nurse to himself.

CHAPTER XXV

INTO THE HILLS

JOYCE found snow in the hills, more of it than she had expected. For the winter was young and the heavy falls usually come late. As she wound farther into the mountains it grew deeper. She could see that it lay heavy in the draws that ran into the gulches. In places the road was covered with it almost to the hub, but traffic had kept the ruts well packed.

She made good time in the roadster till she deflected from the main highway and followed tracks that led over the hilltops toward French Gulch. Here the snow was looser and her chains had to bite deep to get a grip.

Heavy clouds hung close to the peaks. There was, she judged, a lot more snow in the sky. If it began to fall and blocked the roads, moving camp would not be a very pleasant task, but Hallack would have to get his wagons through somehow. Jarvis Elliott was the kind of leader who asks for results and not for explanations.

The engine of the car boiled as it bucked its way up Crown Hill. A good deal of drift snow had gathered on the shoulder of the hill and she found it necessary to back and plunge forward at the packed banks. There was a time when she thought she was not going to make it to the top, but after an hour of steady work she reached the summit.

Two trails joined here, and from that point the going was easier. There were signs that many wagons and trucks had passed back and forth. She began to meet them and at one of the cutouts asked a driver how far it was to Hallack's camp.

"About three miles," he answered, watching her with furtive curiosity. He wondered what a young woman of her type was doing alone in these mountain-tops far from any habitation except the X C V ranch. Manifestly she did not belong at the ranch or she would have known where the camp was.

Dusk was falling when she drove into the small valley where scores of tents dotted the level ground close to the creek.

She asked a teamster where Hallack was to be found. He pointed out the engineer's tent and she stopped in front of it.

The flap was flung back and a man emerged. He was a big young fellow in laced boots, corduroy trousers, mackinaw, and a broad-rimmed grey pinched-in hat.

"Great guns, Miss Elliott! Where did you come from?" he asked.

"From Denver, Colorado," she answered, her

face crinkling to laughter. "Did you think I flew down from heaven, Mr. Hill?"

"You didn't come alone?"

"Alone, unchaperoned."

The engineer strode forward and shook hands. "I was thinking about the roads. They bad?"

"Only up Crown Hill. A good deal of drifted snow there. Think I must have taken the wrong turn below."

The tent flap lifted again. Hallack stood in the opening, too surprised for words.

Joyce descended from the car and beat together her gauntleted hands. It had been getting cold and her fingers were stiff and numb from lack of circulation. In her high-laced boots and sport skirt, her sweater of hunter's green with knitted cap to match, she looked very young and boyish. A nipping wind had whipped the colour into her cheeks. In this two-mile-high altitude she glowed like a Cherokee rose.

"Father sent me with a message," she explained.

Perhaps she read incredulity in Hallack's face. The telephone wires were not down and mail still reached the camp. Even if Elliott should send a confidential message surely he would not choose this wildling daughter to carry it.

"It's an important one," she added, with just a flash of proud challenge in the dark eyes. No doubt this Hallack thought she was fit for nothing but frivolity. He was probably one of those archaic men who believe that a girl's place is in the home. She would show him about that before she was through.

"Won't you come in?" The engineer held back the flap to let her pass.

A small stove warmed the tent, in which were two cots, two camp stools, and a table. There was no disarray of clothing or equipment. Everything was in apple-pie order. The girl discovered that in the first sweeping glance. Of course it would be, she reflected; he was just that old-maid kind of a man. Since she did not like him, Joyce was quite ready to disparage him in her mind.

"My suitcase is in the car. There are maps in it that we'll need," she said.

Hill brought in the suitcase and put it on one of the cots. Joyce opened it and found the papers she wanted.

A warm smile, apologetic, flashed upon the assistant engineer. "I'm sorry, Mr. Hill, but Dad's instructions were definite. I'm to give his message privately to Mr. Hallack."

Her look conveyed to him a comforting wireless. It said that if she were following her own choice it would be he and not his chief with whom she would confer.

"I've got to go anyhow and check up Simmons's report," Hill answered, his vanity not in the least disturbed.

Joyce unrolled a map and pinned down the corners with a paper weight, a pair of scissors, a magazine, and a pocket knife. There was a certain businesslike directness in her movements. She wasted no energy in futile fussiness, Hallack observed.

With cool level eyes she looked at him, as one man might at another. "Of course you found out when you were down there that we can't run through Arapahoe Cañon," she began.

She waited, expecting an answer. He said nothing.

His silence annoyed her. "Father says you did right not to tell me what you found out down there. It doesn't matter. Whether you know it or not the fact is that we can't use the cañon. Father never intended to use it."

"I've guessed that since we made our survey."

"Perhaps you've guessed where he does intend to go."

"Yes, but it's only a guess." He emended this. "Well, a little more than that perhaps. After eliminating impossibilities there was not much of a choice left."

Looking at him, the girl weighed this in the back of her mind. "That's important—if you've guessed right. Because if *you* could Mr. Ordway could too."

"That doesn't follow. I've lived up here for a year, though not at a stretch. From an engineering

237

point of view I ought to know the lay of the land better than he does."

"Yes, but—" She broke off to start again. "That's why I'm here. Mr. Ordway is sending a big outfit of men and supplies into the mountains. Father's afraid he means to seize the cañon we need. He's shrewd and far-sighted—Mr. Ordway, I mean. If there is any way for him to find out our route—"

Hallack considered this, eyes narrowed to concentrated thought. "Possible, but not at all likely—unless someone has betrayed the secret."

"Nobody knew it," she said quickly. "Nobody but Father and me."

"Mr. Elliott's whole plan of compaign has been worked out very skilfully. The newspaper discussions, the surveys, the fight for Arapahoe Cañon all presuppose that the cut-off is to follow the south fork of the Rio Blanco. That would be the natural way to go and it is the only route that has been mentioned. To go down the north fork a railroad would have to climb a second mountain range and wind down through earth rifts that seem impossible. Perhaps they *are* impossible. I don't know. But the cut-off is going down that way or it isn't going down at all."

"We're going to tunnel through Thunder Mountain," she explained.

"By Jove!" He caught at once the advantage of this. The road would miss both the heavy grades

238

and the deep snow that would be met if the track climbed across. "Splendid, if the grades on the other side are feasible. It will cost like sixty, but in the long run will be cheaper. Is it Box Elder Cañon the roadbed goes through?"

She nodded, eyes a-sparkle. She forgot her personal dislike of Hallack. They were partners for the hour in a great enterprise, one in which it was plain he was as much absorbed as she.

"Yes. We get to the cañon from Thunder Mountain this way. See?" With a pencil she traced on the map the line of the proposed railroad.

He asked questions, one after another, with crisp brusqueness. To his surprise she was able to answer them. Jarvis Elliott had gone over the subject with her in detail more than once and the attention she had given had not been perfunctory.

"I'll have to get my trucks and wagons loaded after supper," he told her. "Looks to me like snow and lots of it. If we wait till morning we may have a hard time breaking through. Besides, if Ordway's headed for Box Elder we've got to beat him to it."

"Yes," she agreed. She stood for a moment, fixed in thought. A memory had come back to her and was taking on significance. Louise had told her that she had seen Winthrop Ordway talking to Miss Fellows, who had been her father's nurse. Was it possible that—? But no. She pushed it from her as a discreditable suspicion. Win would never do that. It would be a dastardly thing to bribe a nurse to tell what her patient had said in his delirium. Especially under the circumstances. It had been Joyce herself who had given him the suggestion, that morning when her father lay stricken after the mine disaster and she had told Ordway he was babbling about Arapahoe Cañon. But he wouldn't—he couldn't take advantage of a chance word dropped by the woman he claimed to love, use it to destroy her father when he was sheared of all defence.

But wouldn't he. Even Jarvis Elliott kept paid spies in the camp of the enemy, just as they did in his. That was different, she told herself, though there was something about it that outraged her frank clean pride of fair play. It was an understood part of the game they were playing, entirely within the rules as both sides understood them. Yes, it would be quite another thing for Ordway to pay a hired watcher for a report of the delirious mutterings of his business enemy. If Winthrop had done that, claiming all the time that he loved her, she would know how to give him his answer without doubt.

She had taken his word in the case of Arapahoe Cañon. From her thoughts she had dismissed the suspicion that he had used what she had let fall to forestall her father. But they recurred now, the flashes of distrust she had thrust from her. Some deep instinct told her that if Ordway was rushing men to Box Elder now his action was dictated by information picked up from the lips of Jarvis Elliott during his illness. She did not think there was any other way he could know that Box Elder was the only outlet for the railroad from the hills.

Joyce refused to believe this of him. Yet, somehow, she did.

CHAPTER XXVI

JOYCE SETS HER TEETH AND CARRIES ON

IT was already snowing hard when Joyce stepped out from the big dining tent after supper. Usually the men would have been in their quarters playing cards, writing letters, or making ready for bed. But now everyone was busy hitching teams, packing supplies, and loading trucks.

"You can have our tent to-night, Miss Elliott," Hallack told her. "Tom and I are going ahead to the cañon. There may be trouble keeping the road open till I get my outfit through."

Joyce looked up quickly. "I'm going too."

"You can't do that," he protested. "We'll be up all night."

"Why can't I? It won't be the first time I've been up."

"There's a storm gathering. We may not get through."

"Of course we shall. If you think I'm going to stay here—in a camp full of men with no other woman—you can have one more guess, Mr. Hallack."

"I could take you to the X C V ranch."

"It's five miles out of your way. Why should you? Besides, Dad sent me up here to keep him informed about how we get along. A lot I could tell him from the X C V."

"I can 'phone him to-morrow."

"He told *me* to 'phone him. You may as well make up your mind to it. I'm going along."

Hallack shrugged. "All right. Don't blame me if you're not comfortable."

They strapped a small tent to the running board of her car. Hill went with her. Hallack led the way with his old rattletrap, the tonneau of which was packed with food, blankets, and another tent. As they started Joyce could hear the trucks moving into line, but their lights were soon lost in the rear.

In the darkness, over the mountain grades, it took careful driving to hold the road. The wind shield packed with snow so fast that Hill had to use the rubber cleaner almost continuously. Fortunately there was no wind to fill the ruts with drift snow.

Twice Hallack stalled and Hill went forward to help him buck his way through. It was easier for the runabout, since the wheels could follow in the tracks already made.

Hours passed, and the speedometer marked off the miles. The flashlight of the engineer showed that they had travelled twenty since they had left camp.

"Want me to drive awhile?" he asked.

Joyce shook her head. She was in a heavy fur coat that wrapped her to the mouth, but the fingers inside the gauntlets were almost frozen.

Hill smiled understandingly. "Know how you feel exactly," he said. "But we ought to start fifty-fifty on this thing. Let me get at the wheel for a while."

They changed seats and while she was not cleaning the wind shield she massaged her fingers and shook them to restore circulation.

"Some cold, I'll tell the world," her companion said cheerfully. "This bucking blizzards isn't what it's cracked up to be."

"No," she admitted gaily. "I never did care for Arctic explorations myself."

They ran down into a gulch through timber which protected them from the snow. After three miles of this they climbed to the flat tops slowly. Snow was filling the tracks in the road, so that it was difficult to keep the centre of it.

Both of the engineers were apprehensive. If the storm continued it would not be possible to break a way very much longer. Ranches were few and far in these uplands. They might be caught a long distance from shelter. It was important, in case they were held up, to find some wooded draw where they could make a reasonably comfortable camp. The flat tops would not do at all.

"How far to the next gulch?" Hill asked his

chief, shouting to make himself heard above the running engine.

"Two miles, I should say. We run into a real road there."

"Seems to me the storm isn't as thick."

"Not so bad as it was ten minutes ago. We'll hit it up to the gulch anyhow."

Half-a-dozen times they stuck in the drifts before they got off the flat tops. Somehow they missed the road and had to search for it. The storm had worn itself out and only scattered flakes were now falling. But the sky was still heavy with clouds and the night was dark. It was some time before Hallack found what seemed to be the road.

"I'll have a try at it," he said. "Wait till I get down before you start, Tom."

The descent into the gulch was a chancy one, but Hallack took it slowly on the brake. For choice he would not have picked a snow-packed mountain edge, in the darkness of night, upon which to experiment. At any turn of the wheel a tire might plunge through the soft snow into space and land him with a broken neck at the bed of the creek. Inch by inch he crunched down, clinging close to the rock wall on the inside of the slope.

From the bottom he shouted back. "All right, Tom. Look out you don't skid at the turn."

But Tom was not driving. The girl had taken

the place at the wheel while Hill had been out looking for the road with Hallack.

The engineer made no protest. Nor did he give her any advice as they crept forward. The bright lights were on, and they flung a stream of illumination on the white path ahead. She followed the tracks made by the other car except at the turn where it had almost slid into the gulf to the left. The method she chose to negotiate this bad place was characteristic of her. She might cling close to the wall, in which case the rear wheels would certainly slip as had those of the touring car. Or she might keep farther out, break a new track, and cut at an angle the track already made. There was danger in this, for if she could not hold the wheels to their place very little skidding would bring them to the edge. But Joyce had learned from her outdoor life that the apparently hazardous course is often the safest. She cut a new trail, gave the engine gas, and almost leaped across the slippery snow to the comparatively secure ground beyond.

From there to the creek it was easy to follow the track already cut.

"Good work," Hill said heartily in his booming voice.

Hallack made no comment on her achievement. What he had to say referred strictly to the business in hand. "The snow's not so deep here. We'll keep going."

Evidently the storm had not been so heavy here. For when the engines snorted explosively and took up again the chant of the road the travellers moved into tracks not entirely obliterated by the recent snow. They ran faster. The sky was still very lowering and heavy, and Hallack was anxious to find a place for a camp before it began to storm again.

By Hill's watch it was past two o'clock when they entered the upper gateway of Box Elder Cañon. Joyce had not been here since the night of her escapade with Ordway and the memory of it was vivid as the lights swept the white gulf at the edge of the road.

Her companion had taken the wheel again and she was snuggled down in her great fur coat, hands thrust deep into the pockets of it for what warmth they could find there. She was cold and tired and very weary about the shoulders, but she would not admit it to the big engineer beside her.

Halfway down the cañon a valley opened into it. Hallack swung from the road into a draw that offered a level place for camping.

"We're here," Hill announced, descending stiffly from his seat. "And I'm certainly glad to arrive, for I'm frozen to the eyebrows. About 'steen times I figured we'd quit in a snowdrift. We would have too, if Bob wasn't such a go-getter he eats up blizzards for breakfast."

He helped the girl down. She too was so stiff

that she could hardly stand. Hallack joined them and gave crisp orders.

"Bob, you'd better clear a place for a fire and a tent, then find some firewood. Miss Elliott, you can help Bob."

Joyce took this without protest in words. Inwardly she rather resented it. She had been intending to help anyhow. He might have given her a chance to offer before he ordered her like a navvy.

From the running board Hallack unpacked a small explorer's tent of balloon silk. He brought dry wood from his own car and started a small blaze which soon grew larger. While Hill was chopping a dead-and-down pine he set up the tent and furnished it with a folding cot and bedding dug out from the mass of stuff packed in the tonneau.

Presently he joined Joyce at the fire, where she was gratefully absorbing heat from the resinous pine knots Hill had piled upon the kindling.

"Your bed is ready, Miss Elliott. I expect you're pretty well done up, aren't you?"

"Oh, I'm all right," she said, stifling a yawn. "I'd rather cook myself awhile first before turning in. Aren't you going to put the other tent up?"

"Not now. Bob and I will have to run back to see how the trucks are getting along. You won't mind staying alone for a few hours?"

"No-o. But I'm sorry you have to do it all over again. The trucks can't be very far back unless they've stuck."

"A few miles. I've left a small revolver beside your bed. You won't need it, but you may feel safer. If you hear a mountain lion howl, don't worry about it. The fire will keep him off."

She nodded, drowsily. "Good of you to put up the tent for me. I am just a little tired. Do you know where my suitcase is?"

"I put it in the tent. Would you like it here?"

"If you please, where I can see to get the things I want."

Hallack brought it and undid the straps. "Anything else?"

"Nothing more, thank you."

He disappeared in the darkness and presently Joyce heard the sound of an automobile engine. She saw the lights sweep round as the car moved to the road on the return journey. The sound of it died away.

Joyce made her preparations for the night, moved to the tent, partially undressed, and slipped inside the blankets. She snuggled down closer for warmth, and almost instantly fell asleep.

CHAPTER XXVII

THE BATTLE FRONT

JOYCE woke to the sound of heavy voices, of snorting engines, of creaking wheels. She lay for a few moments, wondering where she was, then dressed swiftly to meet the new day.

When she opened the flap of the tent it was to look out upon a man's world. Loaded wagons were coming into the draw, which was already packed with tents, trucks, stoves, bedding, boxes of supplies, and tools. Men were at work, under the direction of Hill, bringing order out of the chaotic jumble of confusion.

"Good morning," she called to him. "I see the trucks got through."

"Yes," he told her after answering the greeting. "Bob got 'em through. We found the first stalled on the flat tops. Timer out of commission. Everybody standing around not knowing what to do. Couldn't move the darn thing. Inside of an hour Bob had a road built round it and the other trucks on their way."

"Where is Mr. Hallack now?"

"At the mouth of the cañon. He took twenty of the men with him."

"Was he in time?" she asked eagerly.

"Haven't heard yet. Don't you think you'd better have some breakfast?"

"Yes, I do. Won't you lead me to it?"

The eyes of the men followed the progress of this green and golden girl as she walked to the dining tent beside Hill. She moved with perfect ease and grace, lightfooted as one of the mountain deer that inhabited these wilds. Her fine-textured skin was soft as satin. The clothes she wore would have cost six months' pay for one of them. Her vibrant valiance belonged to a world many generations removed from some of these floaters.

She was a member of the new aristocracy emerging out of our casual and haphazard social system. All its prejudices and preoccupations were presumably hers. For and by the sex to which she belonged an elaborate caste system is being built. The engineer knew that, just as he knew that she was of the ultra-moderns who plunge at life for the thrills it gives them, or rather at the small and shallow segment of it represented by their set.

To see her eating flapjacks from a tin plate and drinking coffee from a tin cup, seated on a long bench at a grimy table, with a greasy and soot-smeared cook's flunky waiting upon her, should have been incongruous—and yet was not. She so manifestly enjoyed herself. The eager little boy in her that craved adventure danced joyously in her eyes while she listened to his tale of the night.

"Isn't it bully?" she exclaimed after he had finished.

That night trek through the storm, not yet ended for all engaged in it, had been an achievement. From Hill's story it was plain that the dynamic force back of it had been Bob Hallack. He had coaxed, bullied, literally lifted, his small army over a mountain range hardly passable.

"I don't know another man could have done it," the engineer said.

"My father could—before he was hurt," Joyce answered instantly.

"Perhaps so, but my statement is still true, for I don't know him."

"He's a wonder." The girl's face bubbled to laughter. "I don't like your Bob Hallack at all. He's too—sour. But I'll tell you a secret, Mr. Hill. I have to keep remembering I don't like him. The way he gets things done is kinda fascinating, isn't it?"

"I'll say so," her companion agreed promptly.

"Did he really swallow a poker? Or is it an exaggerated rumour?" she asked with an impudent and insouciant tilt of the chin.

"You don't understand Bob. He's the best fellow alive. He'll go farther for you—do more. You can bank on him and know he'll carry through. And he's lots of fun when you come to know him—not a bit stiff or formal, though he does sometimes seem that way."

"Just a little," she agreed sweetly. "Does he think *all* women should be swept into the Gulf of Mexico? Or is he featuring me?"

"There's a story back of that." He hesitated, read encouragement in her eye, and plunged on. "Bob didn't use to be that way—stand-offish with women, I mean. He's one of these quiet fellows that women like. While we were at college girls fell for him hard. You can see why, can't you?"

"Because he's so rude," she suggested.

"But he isn't rude. He's naturally a most courteous chap."

"Then he must be a product of art and not nature."

"Honest Injun, don't you like him?" he asked confidentially.

"Honest Injun, I think he's the limit," she said with her most boyish grin.

"I heard about it in Denver. He fell in love with a lady there, and she took it as hard as he did. She chucked him for another fellow—or because he didn't look like a million dollars to her. Maybe you know her. She's a Mrs. Barnes."

"Tessie Barnes?" the girl asked quickly, interest sparkling in her eyes.

"Yes. You do know her, then?"

"In a way. She's rather well known."

"Good-looking, I've heard."

"The loveliest thing you ever saw."

"A good sort?"

There was a momentary pause before Joyce said, "I don't know her at all well—just by sight."

Hill knew he had been answered. "Well, she chucked him, and it's left him rather bitter. There was another fellow, as I said before."

The girl opposite him felt a quickening of the blood, for a sure instinct told her who the other man was. "Just when was this—this romantic episode in Mr. Hallack's life?" she asked lightly.

"In the winter and early spring."

Joyce did some mental arithmetic. It was about this time that Winthrop Ordway had begun his rather notorious affair with Tessie Barnes. She knew now why Hallack had refused to take him to the city in his car the night of the Box Elder escapade. It was for him that Mrs. Barnes had jilted the engineer.

"Think of any sane woman passing up Bob Hallack when she had a chance at him," his friend said.

"Impossible," she said dryly.

He laughed. "Well, of course I don't mean that. We always have to exaggerate to express ourselves at all."

"You're sold on your Mr. Hallack all right, aren't you? I think he's got you hypnotized."

She rose, walked to the other end of the big tent, and thanked the cook for her breakfast, with a smile that won him instantly. Henceforth he was sealed of the tribe of her friends. That warm and friendly smile was an asset Miss Joyce knew the full value of. Yet it would not be fair to say that it was based on calculation. She gave it spontaneously to a world that interested and entertained her.

"I'd like to go down to the mouth of the cañon now," she told Hill. "I want to 'phone my father this morning and tell him how things are."

She ran down in the roadster over a road already packed by the broad wheels of trucks. In a small draw, near the gateway, was a group of men. Some were busy putting up tents and unpacking supplies. The girl caught sight of Hallack, standing on the floor of a truck and superintending the distribution of rifles to some of his men. After they had gone he came across to where Joyce sat in her car.

"You were in time then?" she said.

"Just. Ordway's outfit has started. I've just had word. Your father sent a car filled with armed men. They're at the entrance now."

"You don't think there'll be—trouble?"

His eyes met hers coolly. "Not of our making—so long as they don't try to come into the gorge."

"But—will they try?"

"Not if they know what's good for them."

"You wouldn't—?"

"I'm going to hold Box Elder," he said quietly.

"Do you know whether Mr. Ordway is with his men?"

"No. They're not here yet. Mr. Elliott rushed his men through to get to the mouth of the cañon first. We ought to hear from the enemy any minute now."

They heard, before the words had died out of his mouth. A rifle sounded from below.

Joyce looked quickly at him, startled. "They're not—?"

"No. It's only a warning for them to keep back."

"Let's hurry down," she urged.

"No need for you to go. There's an off chance they may be foolish enough to try to force a way in."

"Of course I'll go. I represent my father. There will be no attack if I'm there."

"I'd much rather you didn't go. There may be danger."

"Well, I'm going. It's all nonsense about the danger."

Hallack hesitated. He had half a mind to forbid this slender positive young woman any part in the parley and to enforce the prohibition. The impulse to a clash of wills with her was strong. That imperious manner of hers set his back up. Did she think she could disturb important issues at her whim? That her father had sent her up here to supersede his superintendent? He would show her that this was no affair for a woman to mix in.

But wasn't it? If Ordway was with his men her appearance would spike his guns at once. Even if he was not, the man in charge would hesitate to go far in her presence. The very fact that he knew she was here might prevent bloodshed. This was important. The effect of a battle would be bad. If the public and the Government sided with Ordway it might have a disastrous result on the fortunes of the Gateway Pass project. Reluctantly Hallack gave way.

"Will you be careful and do exactly as I tell you? I mean about not exposing yourself."

"Careful? Certainly." She spoke with crisp decision, already feeling for the starter. "Jump in."

"No spectacular rescues to-day, Miss Elliott, if you please."

"Oh, don't preach," she flung out impatiently. "Are you going with me, or aren't you?"

He took the seat beside her. It irritated him that his mind could not put her in her place once for all. She was as irrepressible as a Jack-in-the-box, he told himself. Apparently she had never been taught how unimportant she really was in the scheme of things. Yet, though he silently scolded her, there stirred in him a grudging admiration. If the rising generation of her sex was like Joyce Elliott, there was one fundamental virtue in them that might save them from themselves. Beneath her hard finish she had courage. She would go through to a gruelling finish. He had seen her last night, at the end of an exhausting drive, fagged and frozen but still indomitably smiling.

They swept down toward the plains. At the point where the road made its last bend before running into the open two guards rose from behind boulders.

Joyce stopped the car. Other men could be seen on the hillside above and in the wooded slope that ran down to the creek at the bottom of the gulch. The sight of them sent a thrill through her. She felt as though she were on a battle-front. At any moment the roar and flash of guns might fill the gorge. Her imagination saw the pine-clad descent as a bit of the Argonne forest.

The engineer asked questions and the men answered. Half-a-dozen trucks loaded with men and camping equipment had come up the stiff grade leading to the entrance of Box Elder. Anderson had fired into the air as a warning to them and had gone out to tell the enemy that the cañon was occupied.

"Let's go out," Joyce said quickly to the man beside her.

He had been about to propose the same thing. "All right, Miss Elliott. We'll see what they've got to say for themselves."

A knot of men were gathered round a car at the head of the line of trucks strung along the road.

Joyce recognized instantly the man at the driver's seat. As soon as she was near enough she called to him.

"Morning, Win. Nice day for a picnic."

Ordway descended from the car, shouldered through those about it, and came across to Joyce.

" 'Lo, Bubbles. Didn't expect to find you here."

"But you're glad to see me of course," she rapped at him quickly.

He laughed, harshly, with no amusement. "Well, I am and I aren't."

"That's just your modesty. You don't like your good deeds to shine in a naughty world. When you take a lot of honest working men on a nice picnic like this—"

"Is it a picnic?" he asked.

"Isn't it? You can't be going to build a power site in Box Elder too."

She was both amused and triumphant at his discomfiture—and he knew it. Beneath a cool aplomb he covered acute annoyance. It was the first time she had seen him in the role of the defeated. Used to success, he was not temperamentally fitted to endure the frustration of his plans. A cheerful and ruthless winner, he chafed under the ridicule that accompanied failure.

"Not at all. I'm on my way up to the headwaters of the South Fork."

"A roundabout way, isn't it?"

259

"It's not the first time I've been through Box Elder on a roundabout way," he told her.

Joyce flushed angrily. "Thanks for reminding me, Win. It's tactful of you—and so decent under the circumstances. But since we're on reminiscences you'll recall that you rather made a mess of trying to go through then. Maybe you're expecting better luck this time."

Hallack spoke, for the first time, coldly. "If so, Mr. Ordway's expectations will outrun performance."

Ordway turned cold hard eyes on the railroad builder. "Meaning that you'll keep us from going through?"

"Not at all. We'll give you a special escort and see you through."

The eyes of the men clinched and held fast. Each read in the other's gaze implacable hate, a mutual antagonism that might easily flame into murderous action; each struggled with his rage and trod it down.

"That's what we want—to go through," Ordway snapped. He had to save his face and carry out the program he had on the spur of the moment announced. "We'll not trouble you for an escort. We know the way."

Joyce caught in an instant Hallack's plan. He intended to see the enemy through the cañon and let Ordway's trucks get bogged down in the deep drifts of the hills. Ordway did not know how heavy the snowfall had been, though he could guess from the low hanging clouds that more would soon follow. He was expecting to cross Ramshorn Pass and get back to the city by way of Red Cañon. But he would not make it through the deep drifts. The party would have to camp in some gulch and probably would be held there a week or more till it could dig out.

Joyce was savagely glad over the prospect that faced her fiancé. Deep within her was a conviction that he had done a dishonourable thing, that he had been traitor to the love he professed for her. The persuasion of it hurt. She wanted to punish him for his unworthiness.

"It's a guard of honour, Win," she mocked, smiling at him. "A very special attention we reserve for you. If you like you can ride in my car at the head of the procession."

Ordway did not like her smile. It carried no message of friendly banter or genial comradeship. He looked at her, a little sulkily. She thought she could make a fool of him, did she?

"So glad you came," she assured him with cheerful malevolence. "I want to have a little talk with you—on an important subject—if you don't mind."

The man to whom she was engaged grunted what an optimist might have taken for an assent, a pessimist for a smothered "Damn!"

Joyce opened the door of the car to let him in.

He hesitated. "No need for you to go. I have my own car."

"I'd rather you went with me. I've something to say to you."

With ill-concealed annoyance he took the seat beside her.

CHAPTER XXVIII

ORDWAY EXPLAINS HIS BUSINESS CODE

SITTING beside Joyce in her car, Ordway had a feeling as though he were being exhibited in a Roman triumph. He could hardly refuse to ride with her, but he resented very much the circumstances of the ride. In his relations with her he had always carried the day with a high hand. She had known him always masterful and dominant. Now he was playing a poor second best.

For once the fortunate star under which he moved had failed him. The prestige of success was worth a lot. He had expected to add another famous coup to his record. Instead, he must slip back to town defeated and face the covert amusement of men who would not dare openly laugh at him. His failure stung, like a barbed arrow, no less because he considered it wholly temporary. The position he found himself in was ridiculous and humiliating. He had walked straight into a trap, laid for him by the man who hated him for shattering his romance with Tessie Barnes. It did not increase his self-satisfaction to know that he had made the mistake of underestimating his opponent and was paying for it now.

"This important business you want to discuss— what is it?" he asked Joyce heavily.

"Important to me," she amended. "I want to know the real reason you came with your men and your trucks to Box Elder."

"Thought I told you. I'm on my way—"

"Tell that to the newspapers, Win," she interrupted tartly. "You came to intrench yourself in the cañon. I know that. I'm not a child."

"Very well. If you know it, what's the use of my telling you?"

She had been swinging round a curve and guiding the car up a bit of narrow road that needed her full attention. Now she came to a stretch well rutted. Her challenging eyes swept to his face.

"I want to know the truth. What makes you think we mean to use Box Elder?"

"You mean to use it, do you?"

"Is that what Miss Fellows told you?"

The swift stabbing look he flashed at her was a betrayal. It asked, in blank amazement, how she had found out. His eyes might, and did, take on instantly the cold wary film of inscrutability. But it was too late. She knew her question had struck home like the point of a rapier. He was convicted.

"Who is Miss Fellows?"

"A lady you met at the glove counter of

D. & K.'s day before yesterday, just before you came out to the club to play golf with me and incidentally to ask me to marry you."

"Oh, your father's nurse."

She stopped the car, without killing the engine, to face him more directly. "Yes, my father's nurse—from whom you gathered what you thought was information about his plans." Her scornful voice was like the lash of a whip.

He laughed hardily. "That's twice you've accused me of being a short sport, Joyce. About time to show evidence, isn't it?"

"You haven't denied it."

"That's only half of it. I'm not going to." He set his square jaw obstinately. "If you want to believe that of me you can."

"I don't want to believe it. You know I don't. But—"

"But you do."

She did not flinch from her guns. "Yes, I do." She added, a suppressed sob in her throat: "We're miles apart, Win, in the way we look at things. I begin to see now. It wouldn't do at all—what we were thinking of."

"Not if you mean to accuse me of some new crime every week. The trouble is you have too much imagination. I stop your father's nurse to ask her whether he's been getting along all right and you make it an offence. You're not a very good sport, Joyce."

"Maybe I'm not, but that needn't trouble you now because we can't go on."

"Why not?" he demanded. "What do you know about me that you didn't know two days ago? Has this fellow—what's his name, Hallack?—been talking to you of me?"

"No, he hasn't. Mr. Hallack and I discuss only business."

"What is it, then? Why do you jump to conclusions that I can't meet your standards of honour? I don't pretend to be over-scrupulous when I'm in a financial fight. If I did I'd lose every time. I'm as fair to the other fellow as I can afford to be. The law of the game is that you have to use the weapons you've got, and you can't be too particular about whether it's a court decision or a big stick you're whacking the enemy with."

"Yet there are rules of the game to be observed, aren't there? You don't hit a man when he's down, for instance."

"You hit him when he's up or down, going or coming," he said bluntly. "Big business fights are war. Somebody is bound to get hurt. I'm looking out for the interests I represent every minute of the time. If I'm strong enough I'll win: I lose if I don't hit hard and often. That's the law of success. I didn't make the rules, and I'm not responsible for them. I have to take 'em the way they are."

"Do you mean that there's one creed of morality for individuals and another for business?"

"Exactly. You've said it. Camouflage it all you please, in business might makes right. The battle is to the strong. We play to win. It does not matter how."

He set forth his tenets of faith dogmatically. She could take take them or leave them as she pleased. He made no apology for the fact that they frankly disregarded ethical considerations. She knew of course that he would not have been so candid, so brusquely scornful of morality, if he had not been annoyed. Probably he was saying more than he meant, more at least than he would later be willing to defend. But even so she saw clearly the colour of his mind.

Contrasted with him she saw her father and Robert Hallack, men who were builders and not gamblers, dedicated to a great purpose, yet forced by the moral callousness of Ordway and his kind to use weapons they despised in opposing him. She made her choice swiftly.

"I think it does matter," she said quietly. "It makes all the difference between—"

She gave up, in despair of making him understand. How could she make him see that if one didn't believe in those abstractions we call honour and right and justice there could be no joy or gladness in the world?

"—between Mr. Hallack and me," he finished for her.

She ignored his sneer. But there flashed to her mind a sentence her father had once used. *No man is great unless he's good.* That was the trouble with Winthrop Ordway. He refused to believe that the principle upon which actions should be based is good will. Over the walnuts and raisins Joyce had once heard Jarvis Elliott talk of a new world that was to emerge out of the present one—a world in which the application of scientific principles directed by good will would eliminate largely the waste and cruelty perpetuated by inertia and habit and selfishness. His vision had stirred her imagination, but she knew instinctively that Ordway would smile ironically at such a hope. He had no faith in the essential goodness of human nature, or in the value of life in the mass.

The honking of the trucks behind them brought Joyce back to the immediate. The runabout moved forward.

"Is it all off between us? Is that what you're trying to tell me?" he asked.

She nodded. "Yes, Win. It wouldn't do at all. I ought to have known all along."

He laughed, harshly. "Pleasant for me. I announce my engagement to you. Next day I have to say that you have changed your mind."

"I didn't do right," she said with conviction.

"No doubt, but that doesn't help *me* any," he replied tartly.

"You can say that you've changed *your* mind," she suggested, with a touch of malice.

"I'd be justified."

"I dare say." She tacked a rider to her admission. "Anyhow, you'd get plenty of people to believe it. I'm a member of the 'In Bad' Club just now."

They fell into silence which lasted till they reached the upper end of the gorge. From a heavy sky the first flakes of snow were beginning to fall. They were large and feathery.

Joyce drew in close to the wall to let the trucks pass. With a curt "Good-bye" Ordway joined his chauffeur, took the wheel, and followed the trucks.

Hallack came forward from the truck filled with armed men which had brought up the rear. "We can turn just above the point here, Miss Elliott," he explained.

"Yes," she agreed.

A page of her life had just closed, not very satisfactorily. She was heavy of heart. The process of disillusionment is never pleasant.

CHAPTER XXIX

ACROSS THE SNOWFIELDS

OUT of a water-logged sky snow had come down for twenty-four hours. It was as though the ceiling of the world were sagging. During a short cessation of the storm Joyce looked out of her tent upon peaks truncated by low-hung clouds. The draw was shrouded in damp mist.

That had been yesterday. To-day the dazzling sun was reflected from ten thousand crystals of snow. It was a new world, awakened to joy, touched by the wand of a fairy godmother to white beauty.

Immediately after Ordway's forces disappeared into the mountains Joyce had sent a cryptic message to her father by the driver of the automobile in which the guards had come. She had written:

Dear Dad:
We are camped in Box Elder and having a lovely time. No other parties in the cañon. Win Ordway and some friends came, but they decided not to stay and went farther up in to the hills.

Don't forget to take that medicine, Daddikins. Everything splendiferous here. See you soon. Will call you up to-morrow on the phone. Bushels of love.

Joyce.

She knew he would read between the lines and understand, but she knew, too, that he would be waiting eagerly for details. Now that the storm had passed she must get word to him that all was well.

Joyce walked to the road at the lower end of the draw. Except the cook and his helpers everybody was away on the job. For Hallack had begun work the moment the weather permitted.

A man ploughed up through the snow from the creek to the road, making slow progress in the drifts of the steep incline.

"Mr. Hallack! Mr. Hallack!" Joyce cried, waving a handkerchief at him.

He deflected and came toward the girl.

"I want to talk with my father," she said. "Do you know where the nearest telephone is?"

"At Tex Kilso's place—six or seven miles away—up the draw and over the saddle-back here. I was just going to eat a bite and start there. Think I ought to let Mr. Elliott know how things are moving."

"How *are* they moving?"

"All right. Hill is doing the preliminary survey work. We've decided from the lay of the land where the roadbed must be at the upper part of the cañon. There's no choice. It must follow the creek. Anderson has a gang busy with ploughs, scrapers, axes, and shovels."

"When are you going to open the road out of the cañon?"

"No hurry." He took her into his confidence with a smile. "So long as it is closed nobody will be around asking inconvenient questions. The less travel there is through Box Elder until I get the grading well under way the better pleased I'll be. Every day establishes the fact of possession more definitely. We have supplies enough. What more do we want?"

"I'm content, except that I want to talk with Dad," she said.

"I'll give him your message," the engineer suggested.

"No. He wants to hear from me direct. And I want to know how he is. I'd rather talk to him myself. How can we get to this Kilso's?"

He looked doubtfully at the slender glowing girl. The untamed joyous freedom of her movements told of strength. So Ada Rehan walked in the golden days of her prime. With such a poise of light erectness Joan of Arc must have stepped resiliently to her mission when the glory of it was first strong in her, he thought.

"On skis. It'll be a long hard pull. Can you use runners?"

"I've been down Genesee Mountain on them fifty times," she answered. "Last winter we girls all did it."

"I'm not talking about going down mountains but up them," he told her.

"You have to go up Genesee before you can go down it," she countered, with the slight tilt of the chin that would have expressed debonair impudence if the friendly eyes had not explained that she reserved this for those in her good graces.

"You're slender. How about your strength? I don't want to overtax it. Are you sure you can make it to Kilso's and back?"

"Don't worry about my strength," she answered promptly. "If you're not pretty fit, Mr. Hallack, you'd better not go with me."

Her smile robbed this of any semblance of boasting. She rather wished someone were here to tell him that she had won the woman's tennis championship of the city in straight sets, that she was an expert swimmer, that she was known as a fearless rider. Since there was nobody, she had to leave this important evidence undivulged.

"All right. We'll start at once," he said.

In truth he wanted to take her along. Misogynist he might think himself in his more bitter moments, but there was in this girl a boyish valiance that penetrated the cynicism in which he had incased his feelings. She was an arresting, an exciting personality. The swift and eager flashes of her spirit, the glint of mocking humour in the eyes, had a disturbing effect upon his detachment, upon his settled determination to have no more to do with women. He remembered Masefield's line,

"The music of her dear delicious ways."

His heart hardened. There had been another woman in his life who had an enticing manner, one whose lovely eyes grew warm and cloudy for him, whose passionate kisses had been his. She had wooed him with all the warm seduction of her feminine appeal—and she had betrayed him for the fleshpots her soft nature craved.

He did Joyce Elliott the justice to admit that she was different. She was of the modern type, hard as nails in some ways, frank as Tom Hill himself. As far as was possible she had discarded sex in her relations with him. Her father's representative, she demanded nothing but fair play. She was a young woman in her manner only because nature had stamped her sex upon her in a score of charming ways.

"I'll have a pair of skis fitted for you," he said.

They presently started up the draw for the saddle-back, Hallack leading the way. He was dressed in laced boots of the Canadian pack type, heavy knit socks, trousers of whipcord, an o.d. flannel shirt, and a leather vest with corduroy sleeves. The sun was shining brightly, so that the glare of its reflection smote their eyes, over which they wore smoked glasses as a protection.

Hallack moved with a slow swinging stride, taking the slope at an angle and not straight up. It was a pleasure to watch the undulations of his figure as he pushed forward. He was a brown, cleanly built man and his muscles, in perfect coordination, fell naturally into easy and graceful sinuosities.

They reached the saddle-back and stopped a moment to look back upon the white field dotted with canvas tents, wagons, tools, and teams.

"If I were a man I'd be a field engineer," Joyce said impulsively.

The brave life of the open was having its way with her. She glowed, both from the exertion of the climb and the joy of the adventure. Down in the city, where little people went so seriously at the business of amusing themselves with little pleasures, Wese and a lot of her friends were at that precise moment playing auction, having just finished luncheon at the club.

Joyce had counted on being there, the most important guest present, with Winthrop Ordway's ring on her finger. It was to have been an occasion, a demonstration to Mrs. Clay B. Westover of the futility of any ban she might attempt to lay upon her. The girl could see herself there, gay, excited, triumphant. Instead, she was mushing across snowy wastes, dressed in old riding togs and a flannel shirt.

What took her by surprise was the consciousness that she would rather be here than there. Her friends would not understand her absence, and her un-friends would think unkind things about it. Mrs. Westover would score heavily, and now that she had broken with Winthrop it would be difficult to recover lost ground. But she did not care. It all seemed to her now of no importance, a trivial matter that had power to hurt only if she gave it that power. In this clean white world that stretched endlessly to the horizon only realities mattered. What she was and not what people thought of her: that was what counted.

They were in a world of winter, a white undulating stretch empty of life. This was the country of the deep snows, where was stored the moisture which in summer irrigated thousands of acres of fertile land stretching toward the Mississippi Valley. In its gulches and ravines the drift snow would gather, deeper and deeper as the winter drew out, till a stone flung with sufficient force would sink into the pack to a depth of fifteen or twenty feet.

Hallack turned. "All right?" he asked.

"Fine and dandy," she answered cheerfully. "I like this."

"Better than a fox-trot?"

"Heaps better, just now. I s'pose you never do anything so frivolous as dance, Mr. Hallack?"

"I'm out of the way of it, but I used to like dancing before I became a senescent."

"Good gracious! Are you all that?"

She thought but did not say that he certainly did not look it. The vigour of him, so lean-flanked and muscular, held the confident strength of youth. His face had taken on the lines that come from responsibility and from introspective living, but to see him on the job, a man out of ten thousand, reliable as tested steel, using his tremendous driving power to achieve an end, was to know that the fires of early manhood still ran turbulently through his veins.

Joyce did athletics well. She combined in consistent and harmonious action a unity of brain and eye and muscle. But she had spent hours on snowshoes where Hallack had spent weeks.

"I'm going too fast," he said.

"It isn't for me to say so, after all my bragging," she laughed breathlessly.

"Skiing calls into use a different set of muscles from motoring," he commented with a smile. "You'll be stiff and sore to-morrow and for a week. But we're not doing a Marathon on runners. We'll slow up."

Alone on the snowfields, their spirits came together for companionship. In the background of their minds there had always been a half-unconscious clash of will between them. Each had built up as the other a figure of straw and resented the qualities it was supposed to possess. They made explorations now into each other's minds, sent out tentacles of approach that met response.

The hours flew, unnoticed. As they descended the slope toward Kilso's place Joyce observed with surprise that the shadows were growing longer.

"We'll not get back to camp to-night," she said, a little disturbed.

" 'Fraid not," he said. "I didn't realize the snow was so bad for travelling. Have to put up here till morning."

He was more disturbed than she, for he had observed that no smoke was coming out of the chimney of the ranch house. Had the Kilsos gone to town and left the place deserted? It looked like it.

CHAPTER XXX

FALLING BARRIERS

THE door was locked, but Hallack found a key hanging on a nail driven into one of the porch posts. From the hall they passed into the living room. There was a hot-blast stove, but the fire in it had gone out. Fuel and kindling were piled in a box beside it.

"Probably went to Circle before the storm and couldn't get back," Hallack surmised aloud.

In the kitchen there was food, plenty of it. The bread box held a loaf, probably three or four days old. Hanging from a rafter was a knuckle bone of a ham. Canned goods were piled on an upper shelf, including rows of preserves that had been put up by Mrs. Kilso. Coffee and tea were in canisters.

"We'll not starve anyhow," Joyce said. "Good of Mrs. Kilso to leave a pantry so well stocked, but I wish she'd been here to welcome us herself."

"Yes," her companion agreed.

The situation was embarrassing. Womanlike, she put a better face on it than he did. For one thing he blamed himself for letting her come. If he had realized that it was likely to take so long, that the going was so heavy—And he should have known it before he let her start. They were confronted now with the necessity of spending the night together alone at a ranch far from the nearest neighbour.

Joyce felt an unwonted sense of shyness, but she had none of the mental distress that had filled her at the time of her escapade with Ordway. She was here in the line of duty, sent by her father because he had been unable to come himself. That night had caught her at the ranch alone with Robert Hallack was unfortunate, but she could not blame herself for any indiscretion. They had no way of knowing that the Kilsos had gone to town.

She took charge, briskly, to cover the awkwardness. "You'd better light a fire. We'll have to make ourselves at home."

He set one in the kitchen stove and put a match to it. Within a few minutes the room was warm. Joyce took off her sweater and hung it on a hook.

She asked for a connection with her father on the wire. In a surprisingly short time she heard his voice.

"That you, Joyce? Where are you?"

She told him, and added details. "It's a little awkward, Dad. We came on skis, but it took us longer than we expected. It's too dark to go back to-night, and the Kilsos have gone away somewhere. We're alone here, Mr. Hallack and I."

"Are you comfortable?" he asked. "Food and fuel and that sort of thing?"

"Yes, plenty. That's not what I mean—exactly."

"I understand. Don't worry, Joy. Stay where you are till morning. How deep is the snow up there?" And after she had told him, he plunged into business. "How is the fishing going? Is it successful?"

The girl followed his lead. "Very much so, Dad. We've caught all the fish we want, but I don't think Mr. Ordway's party has caught any. They didn't stay in the cañon—went right up through it into the hills. I suppose he was afraid we'd got the best fishing. We're doing fine. Mr. Hill is fishing the upper end of the cañon to-day. He and his party took their lunch with them as they thought they would be busy and they could save time."

She answered a question or two, then turned the receiver over to Hallack. His talk with Elliott was brief and pointed. It covered a great deal of ground in three minutes.

Darkness flowed into the valley. They found lamps and lit them. While Joyce decided on toast, bacon and eggs, coffee, and canned plums for dinner Hallack built a fire in the living-room heater. Presently it was roaring in a red-hot drum.

They were hungry from their long trip across the mountain and they ate with zest. The supply

281

of toast ran out and Hallack made more. He would not let Joyce do it.

"You're worn out—must be. Stay there and let me."

"I'm not either," she protested with mock indignation. "What's a little walk across a mountain?"

"Through snow a foot and a half deep," he added.

Afterward they did the dishes together, the sleeves of her flannel shirt rolled to the elbows of the firm rounded arms. The intimate closeness of the relation that had been thrust upon them stirred in both their hearts. The storm had isolated them from a world which now seemed a thousand miles away. They were alone, a man and a maid, as Adam and Eve were in the primeval days of the Garden. Solitude engulfed them, miles of white snow waste in which no sound would stir but the possible howling of a wolf or the scream of a mountain lion.

He drew up the lounge before the fire in the living room and she nestled into it. They talked— of her father, of the railroad, of her life in town, of his far up on the roof of the continent, and at last of Ordway.

"Why do you hate him?" she asked. "What has he done to you?"

The muscles stood out on his cheeks like whipcords above the clenched jaws. She could see the steel harden his eyes, and she reproached herself for having let herself hurt him.

His answer was a Yankee one. "Are you going to marry him?"

The brusque directness of it took her breath. "You're nearly as impudent as I am," she said, smiling at him.

"If we're going to talk about Mr. Ordway I want the ground cleared first," he said bluntly. "I can't discuss him with a young woman to whom he's engaged."

"I'm not engaged to him," Joyce said on swift impulse, wondering why.

The look in his eyes startled her. She knew, without any need of words, that he was glad.

"But you're his friend."

"I'm not even his friend." There was the shadow of sorrow in her low voice.

"I thought—I had heard rumours—"

"Go on," she told him.

"That he wanted to marry you." He did not look at her. The stove occupied his attention. He was throwing some coal into the glowing mass of heat.

"Do you believe all you hear, Mr. Hallack?" she asked lightly.

"No, but I believe that. Of course he would want to."

"Why of course?"

He looked at her then, a golden girl to dream

about, buoyant with the rhythm of life, vivid as the crimson bloom of a hollyhock. He knew why, but he could not tell her.

"I thought you were great friends," he said lamely.

"We were." Again she felt the lift of an impulse. "Until the last time I saw him."

He asked no question, though she could see by his intentness that he was absorbed in her avowal.

"We—disagreed," she went on. "There was something came up . . . He's too much of a buccaneer for me."

"That's a good word for him—a social and business buccaneer. Captain Kidd in dinner clothes."

"He's very entertaining—awf'ly likable when he wants to be. Then, too, he's such a sixty-horsepower man. If he weren't so—destructive," she said ruefully.

Hallack nodded. He saw this girl with eyes from which the scales had been removed. She had seemed to him an example of a new type of woman that repelled him—hard as iron beneath the soft smiling surface, worldly to the core, self-willed and pampered, out for number one quite ruthlessly. Her thoughts began with dress and dances and joy rides, he had supposed, and ended with men, considered wholly in their relation to her pleasure.

He could have laughed sardonically at his

priggish folly. Her hardness had carried her without a murmur of complaint through a gruelling night of storm, had brought her gaily across mountain snows when she was ready to drop with fatigue. She had shown how worldly she was by giving up a man who could offer her all the material advantages of wealth and position. Self-willed, perhaps, as all eager and impulsive youth must be, but certainly far from pampered. How could he help loving the dear spirit of her that reached out through her flippancy for the joy and beauty of life?

"You're for your father in this fight then?" he said, though he needed no reassurance now.

She looked at him, surprised. "All the way. What do you think I came here for?"

He flushed and made a clean confession of it. "At the time I first met you I was prejudiced against you. I thought you—different. I'm a stubborn fool and an idea sticks with me. But I've known I was wrong ever since you came into my tent at the camp."

She gave him a smiling little nod of approval. "It's very decent of you to say so. And when you say you thought me different you interest me, kind sir. How—different?"

"It would embarrass me to explain," he replied, trying to meet her light touch.

"Like Tessie Barnes, perhaps. That what you mean?"

She was sorry the instant the words were out. For his face froze. Yet she had spoken purposely, even though without deliberation. Her thought had been that talk on that subject would be a relief to him. He had eaten his heart out in silence long enough. What he needed was to bring his trouble to the light, to shun no longer friendly sympathy.

He rose and stood stiffly.

"You're tired, Miss Elliott. I'll give you a chance to retire. If you'll take the bedroom next this room I'll go upstairs."

"Very well," Joyce said in a small subdued voice.

She had been properly punished, she told herself, for intruding into the privacy of a man's heart. She blamed herself, yet blamed him too. Did he think that he was some kind of Hamlet and that this love affair of his had to be held to the high tragic note? It was absurd to consider any flirtation with Tessie Barnes on such a basis. She was too light-minded to be taken seriously.

Why didn't he have a sense of humour instead of acting as though she had struck him a mortal blow?

"Do I have to go to bed? Can't I stand in the corner instead?" she asked flippantly.

He was already moving to the door. "I hope you'll sleep well, Miss Elliott."

"And say my prayers and ask to be made a better little girl," she mocked.

CHAPTER XXXI

TWO—ALONE

JOYCE knew of no place so favourable for thought as bed in the darkness of night. Alone, with all objects obscured, free from any possibility of interruption, her brain could function clearly and work out troublesome problems.

That was what she meant to do to-night. While she undressed in the living room before the warm stove she deliberately pushed into the background of her mind the developments of the day. She did not want to face them until she was free from even the trifling preoccupations of preparing for bed.

She closed the draughts of the stove and carried the lamp and her clothes into the other room. When she had blown out the light she shivered down into the blankets, drew them close to her form, and cuddled up. Before she began to review what had taken place it was necessary to get warm, so that she would not be disturbed by any awareness of discomfort.

First, Winthrop Ordway! She knew that she had definitely and finally broken with him. For that she did not blame herself. He had done something she felt to be dishonourable and he had hardly taken the trouble to deny it even formally. But she had whips of scorn for herself because she had ever let herself become engaged to him. It was all very well to flirt with him, to let herself go a bit emotionally, to let him make love to her if she felt so disposed. That did not trouble her at all. What filled her with disgust was the fact that she had, even for a moment, been willing to use him in her fight to hold her own against Mrs. Westover. That was the sort of thing she despised in other women—the willingness to use all sorts of means to further their social campaigns.

She told herself that hadn't been the reason why she had become engaged to him. But hadn't it? It had had some weight with her. How much? Had it been a determining factor? If she was honest—and that was just what she meant to be, so far as she herself was concerned—she must admit that it had given a triumphant exultation to the announcement of the engagement. She had accepted him at the very hour when she was casting about for weapons with which to hold her own.

Joyce found herself too sleepy to think clearly. Her eyes were heavy, her mind wandered. She had treated Winthrop shabbily. He had a right to resent it, and he probably would very effectually. It would not be necessary for him to say a word to convince their world that he had broken with her for reasons which he was too generous to mention. One look, with the proper implications of silence behind it, would be enough for Esther Dare, say.

Well, she would have to hold her chin up and whistle. Somehow it did not seem so very important what folks said, she felt drowsily. Not up here, in these hills . . . where by some magic you were washed clean of meanness . . . where the great white wastes stretched to the horizon and one saw naked aspens shivering and firs with their lower branches drooping heavily to the ground . . . and alders half buried in drifts . . .

It was broad daylight when she awoke. Vaguely, as she still groped with the mists of semi-sleep, she knew that someone was rattling the damper of a stove. She yawned and stretched her legs. Instantly the muscles below the calves reminded her painfully that she had yesterday been on skis.

The movements in the other room ceased. She must have slept again for a few minutes, for when she opened her eyes again the door of the room was closed. Near it were a pitcher of water, a wash basin, soap, and a towel.

Joyce rose. She put the tip of her finger into the water and found it hot. After she had bathed and dressed she passed through the living room into the kitchen. The delicious odour of bacon and hot biscuits was in the air.

"Good morning," she said.

Hallack looked up from the coffee pot he was filling. It would have been impossible for him not to meet in kind the smile of this golden girl.

"Morning. Did you sleep well?" he asked.

"All round the clock."

Joyce did not ask him how she could help. Without instructions she began to set the table.

He was in his shirt sleeves, a fine figure of efficient muscular development. Even as a cook, he made few waste motions. There was a certain strong economy in the way he obtained results. The girl approved the rich brown colour of his firm flesh. He was an outdoor man, a product of wind and sun and the mountains. But it was civilization that had given him the close-gripped jaw and salient chin. Human contacts had helped to make him what he was, a leader by grace of the force within him.

They ignored the clash of last night until they had finished eating, though both felt it as a barrier between them.

He apologized, chin in hand, looking straight at her across the table. "My fault—last night. I'm too sensitive."

"No. I oughtn't to have said it. I'm like that. Always rushing in. I thought—Oh, well, it doesn't matter what I thought."

He would not let it go that way. For two minutes both talked at once, each trying to take the blame. Neither would listen to the other.

Joyce broke off, laughing. "We're not very polite, are we?"

He laughed with her. After that no explanations were necessary. The slate had been washed clean of any disagreement between them.

CHAPTER XXXII

SNOW BLIND

THE last word of Jarvis Elliott over the telephone had been an admonition to ring up again in the morning. After breakfast Joyce put in a call for her father but found it hard to get him on the wire. The operator mentioned trouble on the line as an excuse and promised that it would soon be cleared up.

"I'm going to look around and see if there is any stock on the place," Hallack said. "If there is I'll have to feed. Kilso will probably get back to-day. He'll likely snowshoe over."

"All right," Joyce agreed. "I'll stay and try to get Dad. Soon as I do we can start back to camp."

The operator presently notified Joyce that Mr. Elliott was on the wire. They talked for a few minutes, the father and daughter. He was mainly concerned to know that all was well with her. She was hanging up the receiver when Hallack came into the house.

"A man's coming down out of the hills," he told Joyce. "Probably Kilso, but if so he hasn't been to Circle, for he's coming from the opposite direction."

"Did you find any cattle or horses?" Joyce asked.

"Yes. Half-a-dozen cattle and two horses. I've given them hay enough for their needs."

"I'm glad Mr. Kilso's coming back. I don't like to think of cattle suffering."

They walked out to the porch and watched the black figure of the man coming down the slope.

"What's the matter with him?" Hallack said. "He acts as though he's drunk."

"Yes. See how he weaves about. He gets off the trail and staggers about till he finds it again."

In spite of the sunshine the day was a little hazy. The diffused light was too strong for the eyes. Joyce went into the house and brought her smoked glasses.

The approaching man was well down in the valley now. He followed, in a vacillating and erratic way, the trail they had made yesterday in coming to the ranch.

"I believe he's sick," the girl said. "Let's go help him."

They put on their skis and shuffled across the field. From the throat of Joyce came a small cry of surprise.

"It's Winthrop Ordway."

She was right. As she hurried forward she called to him.

"You sick, Win?"

Without answering, he plunged full length into the snow.

He was trying to recover his feet when they reached him.

"What is it, Win? Tell me," she cried, filled with apprehension.

Hallack helped him up. He swayed, and steadied himself, looking in the direction of the girl.

"Is it—Joyce?" he asked.

"Of course. Don't you know me? Can't you see me?" She caught his arm and looked anxiously up at him.

"I've gone blind—snow blind," he told her. "Where am I?"

"At Kilso's ranch." Her mind hurried back to the disaster that had befallen him. "Do you mean—quite blind?"

"I can just see you—as if you were a tree. It's been hell." His fingers tightened on Hallack's arm. "Get me a doctor, Kilso. Or do something for me. I've got red hot cinders in my eyes."

Between Joyce and Hallack wireless messages flashed. It was better not to tell the stricken man just yet that it was to his enemy he had appealed. He had enough to bear without that added humiliation.

"We'll get you to the house and look after you," the engineer said. "When did it begin to trouble you?"

"Yesterday afternoon. I started over the snow—

to do some telephoning. Lost my way—and night came on."

"You've been out all night?" Joyce was tremulous with sympathy.

"Yes."

"Oh, Win!" she wailed.

He was exhausted, as well as in great pain. Evidently he had discarded his snowshoes because he could not guide them without sight. For hours he had wallowed in deep drifts and ploughed through heavy masses of snow. He staggered as he moved, clinging helplessly to Hallack's arm while he lurched toward the house.

Joyce gulped, to keep down a sob. In her bosom she was a river of tears for him. Her imagination pictured that night of horror—the cold, the pain, the deadly weariness, the horrible uncertainty as to where he was going. He had probably stumbled and fallen dozens of times, as he had done just before they reached him. Only the indomitable will to live had kept him going—and if it had not been for the chance that had held them here overnight he would have succumbed at last.

They got him into the house, to the lounge in the living room.

"Soak your handkerchief in salt water," Hallack suggested, and while Joyce flew to do this he wrested the frozen boots from the feet of Ordway.

By mutual consent it was Joyce who nursed the tortured man, Hallack who supplied her with what she needed. There was a hot-water bag in the house. The girl gave this to Ordway to warm his hands and body. Hot bricks she put at his feet. The bandage over his eyes she changed whenever it grew hot and dry.

Ordway had never been ill in his life for more than a day or two at a time. Like many men of robust health he did not endure with patience pain or sickness. They were too foreign to his habit of thought. He tossed and groaned restlessly, resentful of the fate that had laid him low. The fear gnawed at him that he had become permanently blind, though Hallack assured him that the chance of this was slight.

"Easy for you to say that, Kilso—if that's your name—but it would be different if it was you," he complained.

Joyce was struck by the contrast with her father in his illness. The old railroad builder had been a stoic, full of gentleness and consideration for those who waited on him. His daughter traced the difference between him and Ordway to the philosophy that animated them. Ordway was an anti-social animal. He was out to play his own hand. A blow at his own well-being was fatal to his scheme of life, since the foundation of it was frankly selfish.

Hallack prepared other simple remedies known to the mountaineers who lived in the country where blindness of this sort was common. He grated raw potatoes and Joyce applied them gently. He steeped tea leaves. He gathered soot, with which she painted the hollows under the eyes.

The blind man ate a breakfast prepared for him by Hallack, after which he was in better physical trim. The heat was restored to his body and his blood was circulating again normally. Toward noon, from complete exhaustion, he fell into troubled sleep.

"I'd better call Dad again," Joyce told Hallack. "We'll have to stay all night now, won't we?"

"Unless I go to the camp for help," he replied. "And I don't know what good that would do. He's better off here than there. We're doing everything for him that can be done."

"Besides, he wouldn't want to go to our camp. He'd hate to be taken there. While he's at the ranch he's on neutral ground."

Her companion nodded appreciation of this. In Ordway's place it would hurt his pride very much to be carried helpless to the camp of his enemy and there nursed.

"I *could* go to the camp and send Tom over in my place," he suggested. "Ordway doesn't hate him as he does me. He wouldn't mind so much being under an obligation to him, although as far as that goes he's not in my debt at all. I did what it was up to me to do. That's all."

She shook her head emphatically. "To-morrow,

maybe, not now. I don't want you to leave while he's in such pain. You know better than I do what to give him. But I think you're right about sending Mr. Hill. To-morrow will be soon enough, though. He won't see to-day, will he?"

"No. Perhaps not for two or three days."

She looked up at him, eyes shining. "You don't hate him any more, or you wouldn't be scheming to save his feelings."

His smile was a little grim. "You can't hate any one who has gone blind, can you? I'm saving it up for him. I'll hate him plenty when he's himself again."

"You won't," she prophesied. "You can't do things for a man—decent kindly things to help him—and keep on hating. That isn't the way we are made. Besides—"

She stopped, a little breathless.

"Besides—?" he prompted.

"I'll tell you the rest some other time." Her eyes fell away from his. She was flushed beneath the tan.

"I'll remind you of that promise—soon."

She moved to the telephone. "I'll get Dad if I can."

Unaccountably, she felt within her an emotional heating of the blood. Excitement throbbed in her pulses.

There was no sense in being silly, she told herself severely.

CHAPTER XXXIII

A MOUNTAIN LION HOWLS

DUSK was falling over the valley.
Joyce had stepped out to get some deep
breaths of fresh air. She was facing a western sky
of deep purple in a saddle between two peaks, out
of which a radiant afterglow of sunset was slowly
fading. The crisp crunch of feet on the snow crust
brought her gaze swiftly back. A short heavy-set
man had come round the corner of the house.

It is difficult to say which of the two was the
more startled, but certainly the young woman
recovered first. She could give a fair guess as
to who this was. Kilso could not leave his cattle
to starve. In a way she had been expecting him.
But the man was not looking for her at all.
What under heaven would a girl like this be
doing at his snowbound ranch in the heart of the
hills?

"Mr. Kilso, isn't it?" she said.

"Yep, Tex Kilso." Only his eyes asked who she
was.

"I'm Joyce Elliott. We came over from Box
Elder yesterday to telephone and had to stay all
night."

"You're a daughter of Jarvis Elliott, the man

who is building the cut-off?" His words were a question rather than a statement.

"Yes. Mr. Hallack came over the hills with me. We've rather made free with your house and provisions."

He waved a hand in the large Western way. "What they're for. Sorry Mrs. Kilso wasn't to home. We got caught in town."

"That's what we thought."

"Had to break through to feed my stock. Make yoreselves to home."

She laughed. "We've certainly done that. Mrs. Kilso is a good provider. Mr. Ordway is here too. He's snow blind."

"By Godfrey, you don't say. I've noticed it's more apt to hit them fellows with light blue eyes."

"You know Mr. Ordway then?"

"Met him a coupla times. He high-toned me."

"Did what?" asked Joyce.

"High-toned me, if you know what I mean. Looked through me like I hardly wasn't there."

Joyce understood. Winthrop Ordway could be very entertaining and extremely winning when he took the trouble, but he had a way of ignoring blankly those whom he did not consider worthwhile. This did not make for widespread popularity.

"That's just his way," she apologized for him.

"Well, his way ain't pleasin' to me. Course he's

welcome here while he's sick, but soon as he's able he can go right down the road any time he's a mind to. That don't apply to you and yore other friends." The rancher looked at her with the level fearless gaze of the outdoor hillman. He was used to saying exactly what he thought.

"We found him staggering around in the snow. He'd been travelling all night, without being able to see where he was going. Then he had crossed our trail and followed it. He was in a bad way. We had to bring him here."

"Sure you had. That's all right. I'm not kickin' any. All I'm sayin' is that I don't like the colour of his hair or the way he walks or a thing about him. Up here we're all for the Gateway Pass cutoff. Ordway and his gang are a bunch of financial cutthroats, by our way of thinking. An' we ain't concealin' our opinion any."

"Mr. Hallack fed the stock," Miss Elliott mentioned, after a moment's pause.

"Good. I expect they et that hay right ravenous."

"Yes." She mentioned aloud what was in her mind. "It's a little awkward, Mr. Kilso. This railroad fight is pretty bitter, you know, and Mr. Hallack and Mr. Ordway aren't friends. Mr. Hallack is leaving for camp in the morning, and since Mr. Ordway can't see we thought it better not to tell him that Mr. Hallack is with me. You see, he jumped to the conclusion that you were the man that helped him to the house. So we let him think so."

"Suits me. Let 'er ride the way she is."

They passed into the house, where Hallack was lighting the kitchen fire for supper. Joyce was not an expert cook, but she had taken lessons and knew something of the art. She baked potatoes, boiled rice, and made biscuits. When they had eaten, Tex appointed himself dishwasher.

Joyce brought to the kitchen the dishes of the patient. Ordway was improving. The burning in his eyes was less painful. Within a day or two he would be able to see. As a convalescent he was disposed to claim all the time his nurse would allow him. He felt dependent upon her, and his helplessness made him feel the need of her companionship. In his anger he had accepted her decision as to their relations without much demur, but he was disposed now to fight for his place in the sunshine of her favour. All day she had been kind and tender to him. He did not want to let her go out of his life. Why should he, merely because she had flown out at him? He had always known that she was high-spirited and temperamental. It was one of the things he had liked about her.

"Come back and read to me," he said as she had left.

"After a little. I want to go out and exercise a bit."

"Don't be long, then," he pleaded.

"No," she promised.

He was like a child in his demands, she thought, impatient with anything that stood in the way of his comfort or pleasure. She did not resent this. The mother love that is in all women, active or dormant, went out to his need. His exacting claims, the unconscious arrogance of them, amused and touched her.

"I've got something to say to you, Joyce," he said, reaching for her hand and finding it.

She let her hand lie in his a moment. "Tomorrow," she suggested. There was a gentleness in her voice he had not heard before.

Like most young girls he knew she had been avid for pleasure. The ego in her had demanded deference, attention, admiration. He found in her now a deeper and less clamorous charm. She had become a woman, had begun to learn the age-old lesson that her sex must give more than it takes.

Joyce bundled up and went outside. She had made no appointment to meet Hallack, but he was waiting for her as she knew he would be. In the still night their feet crunched as they walked over a beaten path to the top of a hillock not far distant.

It was a night of ten thousand stars and a moon that drenched the valley with soft light. The white world was touched with enchantment.

He waited till they had reached the summit before he spoke. "Was there ever a more perfect hour?" he said, and there was reverence in his voice.

"Never—not since the world began." She took a deep breath of delight that was almost poignant in its intensity. "I don't wonder that you love your hills—if they're often like this."

"Their beauty gets into the blood—becomes a part of one," he replied. "The mountains have a thousand moods in every season. Even in winter they are not always clean and cold and austere. Sunrise, sunset, dawn, and dusk—always new and wonderful pictures that almost hurt in their loveliness."

They were silent for a long time.

He turned to her, smilingly. "Besides—?", he reminded her.

"I didn't say *when* I'd finish that sentence," she defended.

"But since I'm going away in the morning and I may not see you again alone you'll tell me now, won't you?"

The day had brought them much closer, though they had been with Ordway most of it. Intuitively she knew that he would not repulse her if she attacked his reserve now, but she was not sure that she wanted barriers to fall between them.

She tried for a light note. "You might send me to bed again for not behaving like a nice little girl."

"You told me you had forgiven that," he reproached.

"No, I told you I was to blame—and I was. But—"

"But and besides—"

Joyce met him eye to eye. A mounting tide of excitement was racing in her blood. "Besides, since you want to know, you ought not to hate Mr. Ordway for saving you from doing something that would have ruined your life."

She could have counted her heart-beats before he answered. "No, I should be grateful to him. I've known that ever since I was in Denver last time."

"But it still hurts," she said, softly.

"Only my vanity, I suppose."

"You cared—a great deal?"

"Yes," he said simply. "I didn't understand that we were playing a game, that we were to experiment with emotion and let it take us where it would. I'm not expert at—such things. I suppose I've lived too far from the female of my species. So I don't understand her very well."

She laughed a little. "Who does?" Then, "Haven't you any sisters?"

"No. Perhaps that's why I was always a little afraid of girls. I put them on pedestals. That's why I made a fool of myself about this. I was entirely serious. She wasn't. I see now she had no intention of marrying a nobody."

Joyce volunteered information out of the deep intuition of the feminine mind. "She meant to marry Winthrop Ordway if she could. Probably she still means it. She's very clever—and very lovely. It wouldn't surprise me one bit if she pulls it off."

Hallack looked at her in surprise. She spoke with detachment, as if it were no concern of hers. What she had said was in itself rather amazing to him. Would Ordway marry a woman after a torrid flirtation in which she had compromised her reputation?

Joyce read his mind and flushed. She was recalling a joy ride with Ordway in which he had made *her* talked about.

"Win's vain," she explained. "If she flatters him in just the right way—if she makes just the right appeal to him—I believe she could land him. He's very much attracted by good looks, and heaven knows she has enough of them. I've always known that he admires her a great deal."

Presently he asked her diffidently, "Don't you care at all?"

She shook her head. "It's queer, but I don't. They'll say it was Winthrop that jilted me."

"That will hurt, won't it?"

She laughed, ruefully. "I suppose it will, but that's the funny thing about it—I can't seem to think that it's of any importance what folks say. I've been studying my father. He does what he thinks right. People can say what they like. If it isn't true it will fall to the ground, he believes. When you come to think of it, society—I mean country club sets and that sort of thing—is a piffling little business, isn't it? We run around in circles and get nowhere. We ought to want freedom for expression—and that's the very thing society deprives you of. All the women I know are for the world and against the spirit," she said reflectively.

"All of them?"

"Oh, no, not all. But most of them—and they're dear good kind women, too."

"It's true of men, too, isn't it?"

"Not so much so of men. I'm not putting it well. What I mean is that we women let the real things that count get crowded out by non-essentials. We're like sheep. We all troop through a gap in a fence because our leader does. We don't know why. It's the thing to do, so we follow."

"*You* don't," he denied.

Her tender mocking smile derided his dense masculine perception. "Now you're putting *me* on a pedestal, and I'll never in the world be able to stay there."

"You don't need to be on a pedestal. You're what you are."

"And what am I?" she wanted to know in the most casual of voices.

"You are—Joyce Elliott."

What that had come to mean to him he could not tell her. She was the promise that one day would be the crown of some man's life. For him she was wrapped in the exquisite mystery of a maiden's dreams. All things fine and brave and generous found expression in the flow and rhythm of her movements. Yet the thought was charged with comfort for him that she was intensely, faultily human—a creature born for dear companionship.

Joyce looked at him—and looked away. "I must go in," she said.

"Why must you?" he protested. "It's my last night. I'll go back to the job—and you to town, with all that means. Here I'm your friend, but down there I'm nothing. You're absorbed in a thousand things I can't touch."

"I'll be busy going through that gap in the fence with the other sheep," she said, smiling. And she held out her hand. "Good night. I've got to go now. I promised not to stay long."

His eyes were hungry for her, but he felt dumb and inarticulate. If he could show her his vision and his dreams—the fine fervour with which she was beginning to inspire his life—

But he could not. The tumult of feeling in him would not overflow into words. It was impossible to tell her what she meant to him.

Perhaps she guessed. She said, not very surely, with high spots of colour beneath her eyes, halting words of comfort.

"I'd like you to know something—about me. I've found—up here in the hills, in these three days—what I needed tremendously. I can't tell you just what I mean—not exactly. I'd been drifting into wrong ways of looking at things. Dad knew it. He warned me, and I thought he was just a back number. But he wasn't. He was right. I see clearer now. I'm not going through that gap in the fence—not if I can help it."

From the timbered slope above there came a horrible unearthly scream, as of a woman in deadly fear and pain.

Joyce caught at her friend's hand. She was white to the lips. "What is it?" she whispered.

"Only a mountain lion," he reassured.

The shock of that weird shriek had left her limp. Her body for a moment swayed almost imperceptibly to him.

Then, by some impulse outside the volition of either, she was in his arms murmuring weak protest.

"Not yet—please!" she begged.

And even as she spoke her arm was creeping round his neck and her lips were lifting for the sting of his kisses.

CHAPTER XXXIV

THE ETERNAL TRIANGLE

THERE was a change in Joyce that penetrated the blindness of her patient. He could feel her shining eyes, the tremulous vibration of her low full voice, the warmth and colour of her glowing personality. Used to her moods though he was, this one puzzled him. What had she found, out there in the darkness of the snow, that had so filled her with throbbing life?

She was very impressible. A stretch of blue sky edged by sunset lights, the lifted joy-song of a bird, wind in trees that told of coming winter: any of these might stir her to emotion. But it was in character for him to seek another cause.

"Who's the man that came just before supper?" he asked suspiciously.

"Someone that works here."

"I didn't ask where he works. I said, who is he?"

"His name is Kilso."

"Thought the other man was Kilso."

He had cornered her. She might have known that he would. It had been a mistake not to set him right at once as to who had been with her when they rescued him.

"No, he came with me from our camp."

"You didn't tell me that. You let me think he was Kilso." His voice was sharp, accusing. "What man?" He answered his own question instantly. "Hallack, of course."

"Yes."

"You've been deceiving me, laughing up your sleeve at me, pretending—"

"No, Win," she cried. "That's not true. You were sick and blind. We were afraid you wouldn't want to take help from Mr. Hallack. So when you thought he was Mr. Kilso we just let it go."

"I was so helpless that you pitied me. You were going to do me good and be generous about it," he retorted bitterly. "By God, I ought to be grateful. You went into a conspiracy with a man who hates me, to sugar-coat a bitter pill. Because I'm a down-and-outer, I suppose. Well, I'll show you about that."

"What's the use of talking so—so harshly, Win?" she asked gently. "I want to be friends with you—if you'll let me. Can't you see? There wasn't any conspiracy. It's absurd to say so. We just didn't want you to feel under any sense of obligation to Mr. Hallack, so we didn't correct your mistake."

"We—We," he iterated. "So you're lined up with him, eh? Well, you needn't worry. I don't feel under any obligation. When I get ready I'll crush him like an empty eggshell."

311

"Don't, Win. Don't talk that way," she begged. "You're not a god sitting on Olympus. You have to lean on others just as we all do. Why do you hate him so? He's never injured you. It's been the other way, hasn't it?"

"How do you know? Who told you anything about it?" His mind jumped to a recent humiliation. "No man alive can make a fool of me and get away with it. I'll tell you that. He knew if we got into the hills above Box Elder Cañon our trucks would get bogged down in the snow. Some day he'll settle with me for that trick."

"Why, that was all in the game. Don't you see that? You were trying to get the cañon from us, and we got here first. You pretended you only wanted to pass through. So Mr. Hallack called your bluff. There's nothing personal in that."

"That so?" In a flash of insight he found a reason for the hate she had mentioned. "Do you think I'm a fool? You're jilting me for him."

"I'm not jilting you," she cried in a low voice. "You know I'm not. I told you if I ever found I didn't love you—"

"He's helped you find that out, has he?"

Joyce lifted her head proudly and yet humbly. "Yes," she answered.

"You're—you're going to marry him," he burst out.

"I am."

Ordway was for the moment struck dumb.

He could hardly believe it. Her declaration was an offence to his vanity. Always he had been a victor. From the days when he had passed from buoyant youth to manhood women's eyes had followed his triumphal career. This was the first time he had been told by one whom he favoured that she preferred another. He could not understand it. Not a year ago he had stepped in carelessly, audaciously, and taken from Hallack the woman he loved. Now the tables were turned. This fellow had stolen from him the mate he had chosen. A surge of impotent rage beat in his veins. He longed to get his fingers round the throat of the man who had thwarted him.

But this would not do. He had to carry through in the proper conventional way.

"I wish you joy of your choice, Miss Elliott," he said with obvious irony.

There was nothing more to be said. His attitude precluded further discussion of the subject. But to Hallack, as he was leaving next morning, she gave as well as she could some of the reasons for her choice.

The night had brought him only amazement. He was a modest man, and it was difficult for him to believe that he had won the heart of this golden girl. He said as much to her.

"Why not Ordway instead of me?" he asked. "He has everything that I haven't to make life pleasant for you—wealth, social position, financial standing, success, good looks, strength, confidence. He's one of the seven wonders of the world, and I—I'm only a poor struggling engineer. I've nothing to offer you."

"Nothing—except the things I happen to want." She smiled at him, with the world-old wisdom of her sex. "Winthrop Ordway has too much to offer. I'd like to give a little myself. I want to marry a man who needs me."

"I need you badly enough," he admitted, almost humbly.

"Of course you do. If you didn't I wouldn't look at you. But Win Ordway doesn't really *need* any woman. He's sufficient to himself."

"But you're not marrying me just because I need you."

Her warm dancing eyes carried mock derision. "Do you think I'm going to give myself away to start with, Bob Hallack? Maybe I kinda like the way your hair curls. Or the way you swing those shoulders. I'll have heaps of time to tell you about that. I don't mind telling you one thing, though. You remind me of my dad in some ways."

"You're paying me a big compliment."

"I am," she nodded. "You don't look a bit like him. That's not it. But—Dad's so—so four-square."

"Thank you."

Joyce hurried on to matters less personal.

314

"Now, you go back and build that railroad. If you don't Dad will be kicking to me because you don't give him an eight-hour day. See you in town next week."

"Yes," he agreed.

They shook hands. Kilso was in sight, and this was their formal good-bye. A more demonstrative one had been given in private a little earlier.

Hallack struck across the valley toward the hill opposite. The girl watched him till he reached the summit. He turned and waved a hand to her, then disappeared over the ridge.

She went back into the house to nurse a surly patient.

CHAPTER XXXV

LOUISE SAYS "CHRISTMAS"

LOUISE sat up in the chaise-longue, her brown eyes wide with surprise. A flicker of excitement sparkled in them.

"You're not telling me, Joy Elliott, that you're going to *marry* the grouch with the tin Lizzie," she exploded.

"That's not what I call him *now,*" her friend replied, flashing a boyish grin.

"Christmas! Some more of your speed, Bubbles. Why, you haven't been away from town a *week.* You musta stepped on the gas hard."

"Yes," Joyce admitted demurely.

"I'll tell the world you're a speed." Louise came to another aspect of the situation with a little joyous rush of anticipation. "And Winthrop Ordway! What about him? Lemme see, it was a week ago Thursday we girls were kissing you on *his* account. You were going to marry *him* as big as cuffy."

"We've changed our mind."

"Which of you?"

"Both of us. We talked it over and saw it wouldn't do. So we shook hands on it and quit."

"*Why* wouldn't it do? You were made to order for each other, seems to me. Did you let this garage man who claims he's no gentleman vamp you while you were skiing over the hills with him?"

"He's not a garage man, Wese. He's an engineer and builds railroads. I'm awf'ly lucky to get him," Joyce said, dropping her bomb casually.

"Lucky! Jarvis Elliott's daughter lucky to catch one of his workmen. What's got into you, Bubbles? Are you a *socialist*—or something?"

"That's it, Wese. He's a workman," Miss Elliott explained. "And he's a good one. He gets things done. Building the Gateway Pass cut-off is a man's job. He's going to win—he and Dad together."

"Yes, but—" Louise stopped to light a cigarette and pass the box to her visitor. Also, she wanted to marshal her arguments. "He's not your sort. You and he weren't brought up in the same pasture."

Joyce rejected the proffered cigarettes. "I'm off them."

"Doesn't your gar—your railroad engineer like women who smoke?" Louise asked with friendly malice.

"I don't think he'd like me to smoke."

"So you've quit."

"So I've quit."

A thin trail of blue smoke followed Louise's

gesture of exaggerated amazement. "And this is Bubbles the independent, who rode up the State House steps in spite of indignant protests, who drives around the mountains at all hours of the night and—"

"She doesn't any more. She's tamed," Joyce broke in, smiling gaily.

"H'm! You've gotta *show* me," Louise said incredulously. "Why, this fool notion of yours is only a mental joy ride, kid. When you wake up in the cold grey dawn of the morning after— Oh, boy, what a jolt for your gar—for your engineer."

Joyce shook her head. She was still smiling, but in her face was an expression sure and steadfast. "No, Wese, it's for keeps this time. Poke fun at him if you like. I don't mind. You won't do it after you know him. If he were a garage helper I'd marry him just the same. I'd know he wouldn't stay that. No, dear, I'm not a socialist. I'm just in love."

"But, holy smoke, Bubbles, why didn't you fall in love with someone who talks our language. Betcha a box of chocolates he doesn't know a putter from a mashie."

"You're on. I happen to know he plays a good game of golf. But if he didn't—if he thought in Chinese—I'd start learning it to-day."

Louise threw up her hands. "If you're as far gone as that."

Her friend nodded. "I am. It's not just Bob Hallack, though that's a big part of it. What he stands for—That's the important thing. I've always wanted really to live—to do something worthwhile. Look at me, Wese Durand. What am I good for? To the world, I mean. How do I earn my board and lodging?"

"You don't have to as long as your father is good for a million or two," answered Louise literally.

"I do have to. That's just it. I'm a parasite, but I'm not going to be any longer. I've been working ever since Dad was hurt. I've really done something for the first time in my life. It's fun— lots more fun than trying to amuse myself all the time. That's what I mean when I say I'm lucky to get a man like Bob Hallack. He needs me. I'll make myself useful. There's another reason too of course." Into her eyes came an expression soft and tender, one so rapt that it startled Louise and shook her faith in the wordly wisdom she had been parroting. "It just happens that I love him."

"Oh, well!" Miss Louise did an about-face instantly without waiting to pave the way. "You're not like other girls, Bubbles. If you're honest-to-goodness in love I'll not say a word against your knight of the tin Lizzie. Only if I had to drive it I'd get him to put in a self-starter, honey."

Louise rose from the chaise-longue and swarmed over to her friend. She smothered her with kisses and good wishes expressed in exclamatory slang. In spite of her hard finish she believed implicitly in true romance.

CHAPTER XXXVI

"AND EVER"

DRIVING home from the Durands, Joyce passed a sport car into which a man and a woman were getting. Neither of them saw her. They were absorbed in each other. She smiled. A prediction made by her appeared to be on the way to fulfilment. For the smiling lady being helped to her seat by Winthrop Ordway was Mrs. Barnes.

A maid met Joyce in the hall. "Mr. Hallack on the 'phone to talk with you, Miss Elliott," she said.

Joyce moved to the receiver, a lilt in her heart. Nobody could have guessed it from the few words spoken by her.

"When did you get in? . . . That's good . . . Come to dinner. Better come early. Dad will want to talk with you . . . Good-bye."

That was all, but the sound of his voice had been like a trumpet call to joy. She went straight to the library where her father was working with Smithers and his stenographer.

"You've worked long enough, Dad. 'Member what Dr. Van de Vanter said about taking things easy for a while."

"Just finishing, Joy. Don't forget to have Brokaw look at that contract, Smithers. That will do for to-night."

When they were alone Joyce went swiftly to her father and sat down on the arm of his chair. She put an arm around his shoulder.

"Someone coming to dinner, Dad. Guess who?"

He knew of old that subdued but quivering excitement in the low full voice. "How many guesses do I get?" he asked.

"Three."

"Then I'll guess Robert Hallack first, Bob Hallack second, and R. Hallack third," he said promptly.

"Why do you pick *him,* Dad? He's not the only man I know."

"I pick him because I know your ways, young woman. I've heard nothing for two days but what a wonder this young fellow is. Till you get tired of him—or find someone else to play with—"

She interrupted, very softly. "I'm not going to get tired of him, Dad."

Jarvis Elliott pulled her from the arm of the chair to his knees and swung round the fair head so that he could look into the telltale eyes. A soft warm colour beat into the cheeks of the girl.

Her father had been given to understand that she was off with the old love, but this was the first direct intimation that she was on with the new.

"You'll like him, Dad," she promised.

"Shall I?" he asked, rather grimly.

"I picked him because he's like you, kinda."

"Hmp!" he grunted, by way of notification that he was impervious to flattery.

"He's devoted to you—thinks you're one of the great men of the country."

"I see. Both of you were thinking of me and not of yourselves when you—came to an understanding," he suggested ironically.

"I wouldn't go that far," she admitted; then decided boldly to carry the war into the country of the enemy. "But it's your own fault. You sent me up to the camp to get me away from Winthrop Ordway—to interest me in other things. Oh, yes, you did. I know *your* little ways too. Can you blame me if I did get interested?"

"Did I ask you to fall in love with one of my men?"

"No-o, but—" Her arm tightened round his neck. "Listen, Dad. I want to tell you about it, 'cause it's the real thing this time."

"Go ahead," he told her, nodding his grizzled head.

She opened her heart to him, not sparing herself. Part of the story he already knew or guessed. Ordway's boldness, the glamour of success about him, his dominant personality, had fascinated her and yet repelled. She had admired tremendously the bigness of the man.

The accident to Jarvis Elliott had diverted her interest and stirred in her a latent dissatisfaction with the life she was living, and she had tried to persuade herself that marriage with Winthrop Ordway would open new channels of usefulness.

It was while she was in this state of restlessness that she had become engaged to him, but she made it clear that meaner considerations had entered into her decision. The entirely selfish desire to hold her own against Mrs. Westover's attack on her social position had been a factor, and there had been others no more worthy.

Then she had gone into the hills, and the white cleanness of them had washed her soul of littleness. She had been drawn into and become a part of a great enterprise, one in which men gave their best without counting the cost. From her eyes the scales had fallen. She saw Ordway as he was and contrasted with him Hallack. Before she knew it love had taken her unaware.

"Sure of that?" her father asked. "Sure your happiness lies with this man?"

"As sure as Mother was when she found you."

"He can't give you what Ordway can."

"He can give me what Mr. Ordway can't—what you gave Mother."

"And what was that?"

"Not only love. 'Member that verse you once quoted to me, something about wearing

'. . . with every scar
Honour at eventide.'

Bob Hallack can do that when his evening comes, and if I marry him I can do it too."

"You feel that about him?"

"Don't you?"

"Yes. My judgment is that he is square. But it's not enough that he is a good man. You have to know that he is the one man you want to walk beside all that long journey between now and eventide."

On that point she gave him serious but smiling reassurance.

He carried back to a word she had used earlier in their talk.

"You mentioned my accident. It wasn't an accident. An ignorant foreigner set off a large charge of dynamite in the mine. He had been stirred up by men hired to incite trouble at the Invincible. Ordway was at the back of it, my detectives say. I don't mean of course that he paid to have the mine blown up. That was a consequence he did not foresee. But he is morally responsible for it."

"So am I partly. I gave aid and comfort to the enemy," Joyce said.

"Nonsense. You didn't realize that the man is unscrupulous. How should you, knowing nothing about such people?"

A maid came in to announce Mr. Hallack.

Elliott shook hands with him and looked hard into his eyes.

"What's this I hear about you and Joyce? Have I been paying you wages to make love to my daughter?"

The engineer flushed. "It doesn't look quite right on the face of it, sir, but it's more right than it looks."

"What do you mean by that?"

"I mean that I did not deliberately try to win my employer's daughter. I couldn't help caring for her, but I meant not to say anything about it. Somehow I was carried out of my intention."

"Able to support her, are you, in the way to which she's been accustomed?"

"No, I'm not. That troubles me."

"It would trouble you more if I could show you her bills for the past year," the older man warned. "I've found her a most expensive luxury, Hallack."

"Then you ought to be glad to get rid of me, Dad," Joyce contributed gaily.

"I'm not." Elliott turned to the young man. "Joyce will have to train herself to economy. But she can do it. She can do anything she wants to do. It's up to you to see that she wants to. I suppose you know that she's a girl out of a thousand."

"Yes sir."

"Then be good to her. Protect her from herself. Be patient with her impulses. Whether she will be a good wife or not rests with you as much as it does with her." He took Joyce in his arms and kissed her, smiling a little sadly. "Think I'll go and lie down for an hour before dinner, my dear. I daresay you'll be able to entertain Mr. Hallack without me. Later I'll want to talk with him about the work."

Joyce watched him go, sudden tears in her eyes. She had a vision of life's cruelty toward the old, and with it a feeling of resentment on behalf of her father. She would show him that he had not lost her. More than ever she would love him now.

Her remorse was but for a moment. There was no room in her heart for anything but gladness. Already her lover's arms were round her and was whispering, "My Joy in life."

"We *will* make it up to him, won't we, Bob?" she cried in a low voice. "He's old, and I'm all he has."

"Of course we will. But don't forget that *I'm* young and you're all *I* have."

"That's different. You may get over it, and he never will," she challenged blithely.

"Nor I," he promised, with the valorous optimism of untested love. "It's for ever and ever."

"And ever," she added softly.

Books are
produced in the
United States
using U.S.-based
materials

Books are printed
using a revolutionary
new process called
THINKtech™ that
lowers energy usage
by 70% and increases
overall quality

Books are
durable and
flexible
because of
Smyth-sewing

Paper is
sourced using
environmentally
responsible
foresting methods
and the
paper is acid-free

Center Point Large Print
600 Brooks Road / PO Box 1
Thorndike, ME 04986-0001 USA

(207) 568-3717

US & Canada:
1 800 929-9108
www.centerpointlargeprint.com